"Well-detailed romantic interludes and high suspense around the looming war between bears and lions add spice. A touch of spookiness surrounding the cave sacred to both animals attaches a deeper dimension; highly recommended."
—*Library Journal* on *Waking the Bear*

"The strong alpha, Griff, could make anyone fall for him, me included.... *Waking the Bear* is a quick shifter read that will have you coming back for more from this author, I know I will."
—*Night Owl Reviews*, Top Pick

"Tons of fun...touching and cheeky."
—*All Things Urban Fantasy* on *Waking the Bear*

"I can't wait to read more books in the series!"
—*Alpha Book Club* on *Waking the Bear*

TAMING *THE LION*

AND
SAVING HIS WOLF

KERRY ADRIENNE

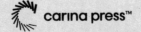 carına press™

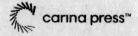

carina press™

ISBN-13: 978-1-335-00492-5

Recycling programs
for this product may
not exist in your area.

Taming the Lion

This edition copyright © 2017 by Harlequin Books S.A.

The publisher acknowledges the copyright holder of the individual works as follows:

Taming the Lion
Copyright © 2017 by Kerry Adrienne

Saving His Wolf
Copyright © 2017 by Kerry Adrienne

This edition published by arrangement with Harlequin Books S.A.

® and TM are trademarks of the publisher. Trademarks indicated with ® are registered in the United States Patent and Trademark Office, the Canadian Intellectual Property Office and in other countries.

www.CarinaPress.com

Printed in U.S.A.

CONTENTS

I'd like to dedicate this story to my friend Vero Aranda, an amazing artist and lovely person.

TAMING THE LION

Chapter One

"Let's do this." Alicia wiped the sweat from her forehead, tugged her medic pack higher on her shoulder, and trudged deeper into the forest, away from the cave.

Every muscle burned and her head throbbed. Surely she'd found all the wounded bears by now.

Can't take a chance I've missed anyone. Too many lost already.

Once she was positive all bears were accounted for, she'd collapse into bed. But until then, she'd search. The air hung heavy with the dank odor of battle, dried blood, and the ghosts of violence. A full day had passed, but Deep Creek was forever scarred from the agony that had ripped shifters apart on its forest floors.

Healing would take more than bandages and incense.

Damn lions. Always looking for a fight. The bears wouldn't forget the day the lions attacked.

"Alicia?" The voice sounded from behind her, a hint of agitation in the tone. "Where are you going?"

She paused, steeling herself, and then turned.

Derek.

Concern clouded his face. Rarely one to show stress,

the battle had shaken him profoundly, and deep hollows had formed under his eyes. Shell-shocked, yet still the strong alpha always concerned about those he cared about. Bria was fortunate to have such a powerful protector as mate.

"I'm checking for wounded." Alicia pushed a lock of red hair behind her ear and cinched her ponytail. The after-battle taste of nausea and heat burned her throat and sat in her stomach like a rock. She didn't need to hear Derek's speech, but she knew it was coming.

"Alone?" He put his hands on his hips.

"I'll be back before dark—there are several hours of daylight left." A tingle of dread traveled up her spine. Though she loved being a medic and healer, battlefield trauma treatment was a bit beyond her training.

"You shouldn't be by yourself. The lions might be prowling around looking for their own wounded. Or a stray bear to ambush." Derek's hair hung loose and limp around his shoulders. His beard was scraggly and he had a dark bruise over his eyebrow.

She'd never seen him look so rough.

Of course he'd try to stop her. He wasn't being bossy. He worried. "I need to check thoroughly. Just in case." He wasn't the only one who worried, but she'd never forgive herself if she missed a wounded bear.

He tromped toward her, his steps heavy with exhaustion. "I'll help. We've lost too many friends and family already. I'm not losing you too."

"There's nothing you can do to help."

He stared into the forest and sniffed the air. "I can shift and we can cover more ground."

"Go back to the cave. I'm sure Bria needs you right

now. She's been exposed to so many new things, some violent, in a short amount of time. I know she's a strong woman, but it's a tremendous amount for a human to process. She's been thrown into the middle of this war, unprepared."

Derek scowled. "I know."

She touched his shoulder and looked into his eyes. "She needs you by her side, not left alone with a bunch of grumpy and wounded bears."

He pulled away. "But she's safe in the cave. You aren't."

"Seriously?" Alicia crossed her arms and formed the sourest face she could fake. "You really think I can't take care of myself? I've been doing it a long time."

"It's not that."

"Then what? The lions have gone home with their tails between their legs."

"I worry about you." His voice softened.

"I know you do, and I appreciate it. I'm going to check the brush on the way to the creek then I'll be back. I won't be gone more than an hour or two."

His scowl deepened, and he chewed his lip hard, annoyance flashing in his features. "You're so stubborn."

"Your mate needs you. Go."

She almost smiled, but held back. It was easy to see why Bria was attracted to Derek. He'd always been a good friend, looking out for Alicia as they grew up together in the clan. Sometimes he was overprotective, but she understood why most women swooned over him.

Who didn't want a giant bear hug from a good-looking *and* sweet man?

He sighed and kicked at the ground.

She knew she'd won. "I want to get this over with. I'm tired." If she hadn't been tending the wounded at the cave all morning, she'd have started her search sooner.

"Fine."

She met his gaze. "I'm not a pigtailed schoolgirl anymore. I've grown up and I have my own job. Let me go do it."

"I know." Derek's shoulders sagged and he pivoted to scan the forest around them, cocking his head to the side to listen. When he seemed satisfied, he relaxed. "I realize you can take care of yourself."

"I'll be extra careful." She nodded. "Always. Grandmother Tawodi has taught me well."

"Yes, she has." He sniffed the air again, turning in all directions. "Don't smell any lions but they're out there."

"I know."

She hugged him and he kissed her on the top of the head.

"I'll come looking for you if you aren't back within a reasonable amount of time. I mean it."

"Go." She shooed him away.

He walked toward the cave, kicking up dust and dirt in his wake.

Alicia watched him for a few moments, then yanked her kit higher on her back. Derek was the older brother she'd never had. Including the annoying parts. Thank goodness he'd not been killed in the battle.

She moved deeper into the woods, all senses on high alert to pick up anything out of the ordinary.

The forest, quiet in the aftermath of the battle, was as familiar to her as her own hands. Yet an unease wended its way through the trees and settled around her. If the lions could attack unprovoked, what might they be planning now?

Lions had always been the enemy. The bane of the bears. Even the annoying wolves didn't come close to being as dangerous.

Derek had saved her from lions before, and had since made it his duty to watch over her. The memory still stung. She and her best friend Ria had wandered away from the other cubs on an outing to the grassy meadow where a beautiful waterfall splashed into a pool with droplets and spray as bright as cut crystal.

The lions had been there too. Ria hadn't survived the attack. The cold crush of guilt and grief washed over Alicia, as fresh as that spring day so long ago. She hated the lions for taking away her best friend. If she never saw one of the mangy creatures again, it would suit her fine.

She closed her eyes to calm her nerves. Grandmother Tawodi had always told her not to let her emotions take over when danger lurked. She blew out a long breath, calling on her muscles to relax. Deep Creek might be bear territory, but the lions had proven they could encroach right up to the Cave of Whispers.

Solstice would be forever remembered not as the day of longest light when summer broke through the veil of seasons, but as one of the darkest days in Deep Creek's history.

Sneaky bastards.

The wind picked up, carrying the acrid odor of death, tingeing her nostrils with an unforgettable tang.

She veered right, toward the creek. Though she usually thought of herself as an optimist, she couldn't see many positives from the battle that had sent too many souls to the starry ether.

Sweat trickled down her back as the summer sun painted its glory on her damp skin. She trudged the narrow path between large oaks, an abandoned game trail to the creek. Once a favorite spot, now the branches seemed to bow under the forest's grief.

Her temples throbbed and she paused to take a gulp from her water bottle. She listened for any sound, however faint, that might be a sign of life in the underbrush or off the trail.

Grandmother Tawodi had shown her the ways of empathy and herbal healing, and even though some of the bears teased her, she knew better than to cross her adopted grandmother. With a name meaning "hawk," her grandmother's tenacity was only surpassed by her compassion for other living creatures. Tawodi had taken Alicia under her wing at a young age, when Alicia's parents had disappeared.

Tawodi was the closest thing she had to family. True family.

Alicia stepped over a limb, crunching a smaller one underfoot, and the snap jolted her senses. Looking behind her to check to see if she was being followed, she relaxed when she confirmed she was alone.

Her uncanny perception was part of what made her rise above the other bears who'd trained in first aid and traditional medicine.

They didn't have Tawodi's guidance.

She closed her water bottle, slipped it into her pack, and moved more quickly as the path widened. The rush of the creek was faint to her human ears and she followed the sound.

So far, so good. No wounded bears.

Tawodi had told her that her gift of empathy was not to be squandered and Alicia tried to always be aware. She experienced other creatures' pain deep in her spirit, just as her grandmother did. The first time she'd felt another's pain, she'd almost passed out. *Ria*. Alicia had felt everything. The pain. The fear. She blinked back the sting of tears. Gift or curse, she would not leave an injured animal to suffer.

She stuck her water bottle back in her pack.

The hill to the left rose tall, the deep-green grass flattened from the hand-to-hand combat between the lions and bears. A rusty bloodstain near the path had almost turned brown in the heat, but she knew.

A lion had fallen in that spot, his neck snapped by a stronger bear.

She wrinkled her nose and reached for her own neck. The image burned in her mind, as clear as a color photograph. Pain and death would linger in the summer grass for weeks, and in her mind forever.

Chin up, she held back the threatening tears but they surged anyway and a single drop traced her cheek, followed by the trails of a few more. She wiped them away. The final death toll hadn't been tallied, but the bears would be burying a lot of friends and enemies in the Cave of Whispers over the next few days. Many tears would fall in Deep Creek over the coming weeks.

Shoshannah was already preparing the final resting places for the physical bodies as the dead's souls marched through on their way to the river of stars.

Right now, saving others was a way to honor Ria's death.

I couldn't save her but I can make sure no one else dies in the forest today.

The damp heat of the day slithered through the arched curtain of trees that wilted in the humidity. Summer in Deep Creek had always been one of her favorite seasons, but today, it was the basis for a terrible memory.

Maybe it was lack of sleep, but right now, she longed for snowy winter's long naps and warm dens. The mewling of cubs wouldn't even bother her. Though the bears of Deep Creek didn't truly hibernate, they slept a lot during the cold months. And sleeping meant forgetting painful memories. She glanced up at the spots of blue sky visible through the branches.

Plenty of daylight left.

A fly buzzed near her face, and she swatted it away, stopping to check the dense brush at the side of the trail more thoroughly. She sniffed the air and stilled her mind, reaching out and feeling. Listening. If anyone was close enough, she should sense them.

No one.

Derek was right. Shifting would help her cover more ground in a shorter amount of time, and her senses would be heightened. She'd have trouble carrying her pack of medical supplies, but she could leave them and come back for them if she found anyone. Shifting also made her more vulnerable to being spotted. It was a tradeoff she couldn't risk.

A chipmunk scurried across her path, flicking its stubby tail and pulling her from her memories. She pushed on, nearly to the copse of trees at the edge of the deeper forest.

She shaded her eyes and zeroed in on the low bushes that lined the perimeter of her vision. No sign of movement. She almost wished she'd taken Derek up on his offer to help her search.

The endless forest sprawled in front of her in a maze of trails and trees. Another third of a mile to check before reaching the creek. She yawned. *Got to keep going.* A few hours could mean life or death to a wounded bear that dragged itself out into the woods to hide. Not much of a chance any injured animal would've crossed the creek, since it would know it would be hard to track, so that was her search boundary.

What would she do if she ran into a lion? Though she was confident in her abilities, running into a vicious lion was more danger than she'd faced alone. After what happened to Ria... She jerked her head around at the slight sound to her left, her heartbeat surging.

A small animal rustling in the leaves, nothing more. *I can do this.*

Heading east toward the creek, the sun would be at her back as it began to set in a few hours, keeping the glare out of her eyes. She'd be long finished searching by dark.

The rain overnight had cooled the air and filled it with moisture, but now the day was hot and muggy.

She trudged over knotted vines and fallen branches and kicked old toadstools, sending up puffs of spores from the flying caps as they bounced across the ground. *Almost there.* She slid down a short embankment, careful to not fall.

The air stilled and the woods went silent, as if someone had turned off the low hum of a station-less radio. Pressure filled her ears.

What?

She gripped the strap of her pack. A squirrel scurried in the leaves nearby, chattering its distress at her invasion of its territory. She swallowed down the lump blocking her throat and sniffed.

Something isn't right.

A faint tang rode on the waves of clean air and forest pine, threading it with metallic thickness. A heavy, sharp scent that indicated one thing.

Pain.

The odor drifted from nearby, yet she hadn't sensed it before she slid into the shallow gully. The ribbon of pain looped through her mind, faint and not totally familiar. *Where?* She peered around the area. Nothing out of the ordinary. Moving closer, the smell grew stronger and blurry images, blazing red, flooded her mind.

Something was suffering, and it wasn't a bear. Her pulse thrummed in her ears at the realization. A loud screech sounded above, and she looked up to see a giant hawk circling. It soared over an area not too far ahead, bobbing on the currents of wind high above the trees.

Tawodi. Grandmother.

Warmth and strength rushed through Alicia's veins,

and she clenched her pack tighter. Always nearby when she sensed trouble, yet never interfering, Tawodi gave guidance by her presence alone. Alicia smiled. Tawodi was leading her to the injured animal.

"Thank you, Grandmother." Alicia scrambled over the loose pebbles, her boots slipping on the dusty rubble and her ponytail sliding along the ground as she caught herself. She stabilized herself and stood, then brushed off her elbows. A scrape reddened with blood, but it wasn't bad. She'd put a Band-Aid on it later.

Haste makes waste. Tawodi's voice echoed inside her head.

Alicia moved in the direction of the injured creature, her pack rubbing against her aching lower back. Deep-green briar bushes filled with tiny white flowers lined the gully pathway like drops of snow on a field of dark green. The foliage grew denser as she maneuvered closer, and twisted briars tore at her clothing.

"Shit." A thick ropy branch lashed across her legs, and she tugged it free, then the offending thorn. She held the pointed spike up in the air. Nearly an inch long and about as wide. Massive and old, the vine had probably been growing in Deep Creek for as long as she had.

Dangerous.

A flutter trilled her heartbeat. She wouldn't let anxiety get the better of her.

She almost wished she carried a gun like the rangers did. Who was she kidding? She'd never needed a gun. A battle had not happened in her lifetime, and hopefully never would again.

She continued to pull the thorny branches from her clothing as she wove among the tangle of vines, seeking the source of the odor. She stopped to hold her head in her hands as her eyesight clouded. First a tingle, then a full-on burn enflamed her eyes, and a vision flashed, clearer this time with much more detail.

A gunshot. Searing hot pain oozing down a shoulder like molten metal. Melting the skin and stripping the bullet hole to the bone. Torturous pain as muscle liquefied. An outcry, then silence.

She shivered and rubbed her shoulder, feeling for the muscle she knew to be there. Where was the animal? It needed her, and it wasn't going to live much longer without care. She tasted its injury, its fear. She scanned the forest ahead, sticking her nose into the air again, hoping to differentiate the animal's scent from everything else in the area.

Blindfolded and ears muffled, she could detect the squish of a horsefly's feet climbing over a rotting apple a hundred yards away and point to its precise location. But this scent was something she hadn't smelled before. Not exactly.

Dangerous and compelling with a hint of magic. But most of all, a drumming pain, angry and red, wove through and around him. She held her pounding head, and tightened her grip on her temples to try and ease the throbbing.

The animal's intense pain called to Alicia, but underneath his need for relief was a darkness and a sadness her empathy couldn't penetrate or interpret. She reached out with her mind and met anger that blasted her back with a force unlike anything she'd come up against.

Who was this creature?

Tawodi had known the agony that called out through the trees, and flew near to check on Alicia and give her visual guidance and comfort. Though Tawodi couldn't wield a weapon in her bird state, she could soothe fears.

And warn of danger. And maybe something else. The magic in the air was something Grandmother knew, Alicia was sure of it.

She crept closer, bracing for a possible attack from a creature blinded by its pain. Hesitation fluttered along her skin like the touch of a feather, and fear masqueraded as bravado with each step.

With Tawodi nearby, things would be okay.

Her gran had taught her to have a healthy fear of the unknown.

The large hawk shrieked, urging Alicia onward. She picked up her pace. She had to know what animal lay injured in the underbrush, and she swallowed her dread, letting her mind wander through the real and imagined as she pushed branches out of the way. Tawodi wouldn't lead her astray.

Ever.

A wall of agony hit her, doubling her over with its intensity. Her head nearly split in two with the massive force of the psychic hit, and she struggled to stay coherent. Her heart sped, and sweat broke out across her back and trickled down her legs.

No!

She should leave. Now. Get out of the woods and far from the Cave of Whispers. Bile flooded her mouth with a bitter burnt taste following. Clarity filled her mind like the chill of fresh new snow.

She knew the underlying scent. The pain had

masked the source at first, but now it broke through like a dark wet rope moving through the laces of suffering. She swallowed hard and tugged the backpack up higher onto her shoulders.

Enemy.

She shivered in the heat, the cold realization sinking deeper into her mind.

A wounded lion lay on the ground, dying, close by. Every muscle in her body tensed into knots and her psyche screamed *run*, but the sweat of fear kept her feet still. If her heart could've pounded any harder, she feared it would break her rib cage.

Lion. She'd not considered that she might come across a wounded one while she searched for bears. The lions didn't leave anyone behind. Until this lion.

Its life force weak, its pain all consuming.

He was from the pride that had killed Ria. Sen Pal. The same lions that killed friends yesterday and attempted to take the cave from the bears. He might even be the lion that took Ria from her. She stopped as a voice resonated in her mind with a sharp intensity she couldn't ignore.

Healer. Be still.

"Grandmother?" Alicia whispered. A mixture of fear and anger sizzled up her spine, lighting small fires of stress. How could she possibly help a lion? She'd spent her lifetime hating them and vowing revenge for Ria's death.

No answer came from Tawodi, but Alicia knew the expectation as she knew her own name. Tawodi had taught her the ways. Alicia couldn't discriminate. Either she was a true spirit healer or she wasn't. She didn't get to choose who she helped any more than she got to choose to breathe.

In truth, the wounded chose her, and this lion's pain had summoned her as strongly as if he'd tapped her on the shoulder. He needed her and she was to tend him, regardless of her feelings.

The odor of his blood filled the air, and his pain rang out like a beacon, dragging her closer. Begging for her help. Alicia shuffled closer, knuckles white from holding on to the pack straps so tightly.

Did she have the fortitude to help the enemy?

Broken bear bodies were piled outside the cave in a heap. The image burned in her mind. She swallowed the bile that singed her throat.

She hadn't been this close to a lion since that fateful day with Ria. Even during the recent battle, she'd been tending the wounded more than engaging the enemy. She hadn't seen much of the combat either. Being absorbed in her work had been an advantage.

She pushed the brambles away and sidestepped a large boulder on the side of the path. Whoever this lion was, he must not have been important because the other lions had run off and left him to die in enemy territory.

Or they thought he was dead.

A common soldier. Perhaps a killer or guard. No matter. They'd left him to die in the forest.

She closed her eyes and paused.

Lion.

Where was he? After turning the bend, the slanting sunlight did a better job making it to the forest floor, casting long strips of yellow across the dark dirt. Maybe he'd hidden himself to prevent being captured.

He had to know he'd be scented. No one could hide forever in the forest of Deep Creek, not with the number of shifters that lived and roamed the area.

He thought the lions would come back for him. Or maybe he was too wounded to move. She sniffed again.

Yes, definitely a *he*.

He wasn't groaning, in fact, he didn't utter a sound, so she followed the iron scent of his life force, her heart thumping. Every hair on her arms and neck rose, like electricity had shot through the trees and glanced by her.

Alert.

The faint sound of his breath, labored and uneven, a whisper on the wind. Alive. She hurried.

Healer or not, she knew better than to risk an encounter with a wounded enemy. The lion was likely unable to move given the amount of blood she scented. His injuries had to be severe, likely life-threatening.

She shielded her eyes and searched the sky for Grandmother Tawodi, hoping for reassurance and guidance on how to proceed, but the hawk had flown away. With a broken sigh, Alicia trekked nearer to the dangerous animal, tripping over a branch half-hidden in the leaves.

"Shit." She put her hands out to break her fall, scraping them on the rocks scattered on the trail. For a moment, her own pain sounded more loudly in her mind than the lion's. She stood and wiped her hands free of debris. Another mistake like that and she could be dead. An injured lion was more dangerous than a healthy one, and if he was able, he could kill her in a second.

He had nothing to lose.

Thankfully, he didn't come rushing at her from the trees. She sniffed the air again. He was so close, but where? She turned in the direction of the scent, but she couldn't see him. The underbrush was dense and summer had provided unbeatable camouflage.

She reached into the zippered pocket of her kit and pulled out a scalpel then removed the covering. Her hands shook. Not much of a weapon, but it would do enough harm in close combat. She could disembowel quickly if she had to. Knowing exactly where to cut, and how deep, was a clear advantage.

She tracked him. Pain, with a sweeter scent floating alongside it like the counterpoint to a melody. That scent…unknown and yet familiar. She was just about to undress and shift to get a better sniff when she saw his arm sticking out from under the bush, his body barely hidden, despite the full foliage.

Another step closer. He didn't move to attack.

Crumpled, he lay on his back. She studied the creature, magnificent in its manly form.

Muscular and tan, palm up, his fingers relaxed and clenched as he fought the pain that wracked his body. He suffered. She knelt to get a better look, yet stayed out of reach. The heat of the afternoon sun blazed, and a sheen of sweat covered him even though he was in the shadows.

"Go away." His voice barely a whisper on the thick summer air. "I'll kill you."

Alicia gripped the scalpel. She could slide it across his neck in a flash, and it'd be over. No one would have to know. A mercy killing, of sorts. Though she'd be lying to herself to categorize it as such.

Her grandmother's words echoed. Alicia was a healer, not a killer.

From the looks of the lion's shirt, already dark, yet now wet with blood, he might not recover even with her best efforts to save him. The scent of gunpowder and burnt flesh peppered the blood-laden air. The lions had left him to die under a bush in bear territory, shot in the shoulder.

She shook her head and settled to the ground on her knees. "I'm not going anywhere." The strength of her voice hid her fear, though he might sense it anyway. His scent was that of a strong and confident shifter, even in his current state.

He looked at her.

She blinked, trying to calm the adrenaline rush that shot through her. His eyes, mesmerizing and wide, lured her in, and she couldn't turn away. Deep green or maybe brown or even both, they were a color she'd never seen and his gaze was magnetic. Her mouth went dry.

He was her sworn enemy. Sexy, but injured.

She glanced to the sky, but didn't see Grandmother Hawk. Typical. Recently, she'd started leaving Alicia to figure out the moral decisions on her own, trusting that she would make the right one.

Part of the training.

"Shit." The scalpel had warmed in her hands, and the sun glinted off the blade in a flash of silvery-white. What would her grandmother do? No doubt, she'd help the lion. Maybe she wouldn't tell the bears, whom she was loyal to, but she'd never let a lion die if she could heal him. She'd never intentionally let anyone die on her watch.

"War is for the weak minded," she'd always said. Alicia was beginning to think she was right. Why couldn't shifters all get along?

Because the damn lions wanted the bears' territory. If they'd stayed in their own area, none of the bloodshed would've happened. Even though Alicia had heard the stories of the lions and bears and wolves sharing the cave, the actuality felt as foreign as items in an ancient history book. As remote as a fairy tale.

Fantasy.

"Go." He turned away, but she could still see the strain on his face as he winced.

His black hair, falling to his shoulders, was damp and matted. How early in the battle had he been wounded? He was bound to be dehydrated.

"I'm here to help. Like it or not." She slid the scalpel into its sheath and back into the pocket of her pack. Her earlier assessment was correct. The lion was no threat at the moment. He could barely move. The rise and fall of his chest showed his respirations were high and labored. Blood loss was nearing the severe level.

He needed help before his body went into shock.

She looked back toward the trail to make sure she was alone. If Griff or Derek found out about him, the lion wouldn't need help anymore and her time as medic would be over.

She'd worry about that another day. She had a lion to save.

Chapter Two

Will a female be the death of me, after all?

Marco peeked at the woman a few paces away. Was she real or a figment of his imagination? She'd spoken and not run away at the sight of him.

He squeezed his eyes shut and clenched his jaw, hoping to block the pain that volleyed through his body like thousands of hot needles. The skin of his shoulder was aflame, and he couldn't move his arm without sharp streaks shooting to his fingertips. He gasped for a deep breath of air, and strained to keep panic at bay.

One, two, three... Holding focus was nearly impossible.

The agony was unlike any he'd ever felt. If he could turn his head enough to see the wound, he was sure the hole was as large as a fist.

Getting shot had never entered his thoughts of how the battle would go. He'd only imagined a complete victory over the bears, having had the element of surprise. The gods had other plans.

The hot bullet slicing through his shoulder muscle had almost caused him to pass out, and perhaps he had since he didn't remember hiding in the forest after it happened. How long had he been unconscious? Had he dragged himself all the way down the path or stumbled deeper into the forest? He couldn't remember much beyond the woman shooting him and the agony that had replaced rational thought.

Why hadn't she finished him off? She'd looked right at him as she shot, and he saw fear in her gaze. She had to know he wasn't dead, and yet she let him go. The woman wasn't a warrior.

And she was *human*. And now there was another woman, a bear, hovering over him.

"Go away," he repeated. His throat, dry as dirt, closed on his words.

Exactly what were the bears up to, with humans and women fighting for them? Sure, the lions were aware that some of the human townspeople in Oakwood knew about the shifter community, but none had dared to venture into Deep Creek to fight. Maybe the spies hadn't been doing a good enough job gathering intelligence for the lions. Something was up.

A flash of iced fire blazed through his shoulder and out his back. Gagging, he held back the urge to vomit.

"Let me help you." Her voice, strong, yet sweet as fragrant summer blooms, floated in his consciousness. *Drifting...*

"No." He breathed through the pain, trying to control it at least enough to manage the moment. *Four, five, six...* His training hadn't prepared him for the depth of pain he was capable of feeling. Perhaps he'd not tried hard enough. *Seven, eight...*

"You look like you need help." The woman stood out

of reach, poised for his attack, but holding no weapon that he could see. "And I'm going to help you."

His lion paced inside, grunting and huffing at his inability to handle the situation. He couldn't attack even if he wanted to, except with his raspy words. If he weren't in so much pain, he'd be embarrassed.

He sensed how close she was, the cacophony of her emotions tumbling around him. He was enemy. She should kill him. Yet, something held her back. He stared.

Oh gods, a bear. He wasn't imagining it. She was real.

"Well?" She spoke again. Hands on her hips, she didn't appear to be much of a threat.

"Well, what?" he muttered. Maybe she pitied him. A low growl sounded from deep inside his throat. *No pity.* He wouldn't tolerate it. Not by anyone, least of all a bear. Even a bear as pretty as this one.

He almost laughed at the irony, but broke into a cough that sent shards of pain through his chest and along his arm. Only he would be checking out a female while sitting on death's doorstep. And it felt like he was about to die.

He peeked at the bear. Her brows raised, and her eyes widened, her lashes a thick frame around bottomless brown irises flecked with gold. A slight smattering of tiny freckles sprinkled across her nose, and her long red hair was pulled back. Not the red hair some of the wolves had, that brassy orange mess. No, this bear had locks almost the color of a deepening sunset, or the last embers of a campfire. Wavy and full, he wondered what it'd look like hanging down her slender, naked back.

"I'm fucking delirious," he heard himself mumble.

"Relax." Her scent had changed from fear and adrenaline to a mixture of obligation with a tinge of unease. And curiosity.

Her voice comforted him. If he were in her place, he'd have already killed the wounded animal lying on the ground. Would he have killed a woman?

Maybe.

Some lion warrior he was. To add insult to injury, she hadn't run away, afraid. In fact, he didn't sense fear in her at all anymore.

Am I hallucinating?

He blinked, and she was there, her hair flecked with prismatic golden highlights where the sun caressed it.

"Go away," he managed again, with a bit more force.

She set her pack on the ground. "I'm not going away."

Thank the gods Mason wasn't around to see the situation.

The bear knelt beside him, her T-shirt clinging to substantial curves. When she turned, he saw that her long red hair hung in a thick ponytail. Her heart-shaped face framed full lips the color of strawberries.

Her lips moved and he watched every twitch, even the sheen of sweat on her upper lip. If she was afraid, she didn't show it.

Is she speaking again? He shook his head as the vision in front of him wavered. Despite the excruciating pain in his shoulder, he looked her over.

The bear was damn fine. If she was real. And if she

wasn't, he should get points for having a great imagination while in so much discomfort.

"Wha—" He tried to sit up but the pain in his shoulder shot straight through to his back, like he'd been run through with a hot sword. He winced and fell back, his head bumping the grassy ground with a thump and sending shock waves through his body.

More words from her in the distance—either she spoke aloud or it was in his mind, but he couldn't make out what she was saying. Maybe she had switched to speaking in a language he couldn't understand. He always did have a thing for girls with an accent, but this was ridiculous.

He tried to turn over, but couldn't.

A jumble of words and sounds from her again, but he couldn't decipher them. A large bee zoomed around his face, bouncing on the air current, and she waved her hand to shoo it away.

He fought to not retch.

Two things were very clear. One, he wasn't going anywhere under his own power any time soon. If the lions didn't come, he'd likely die from lack of treatment unless the bear decided to finish him off. And two, vomiting all over the beautiful bear would not make a good first impression. Lying under a bush wounded and possibly dying wouldn't either but he couldn't change that.

"Are you talking to me?" He spoke slowly, enunciating each word. If she was going to vanish in a puff of imagination, he wished she'd disappear before he became any more enamored with her.

"Yes." Her voice remained firm, and she flicked the

rope of her ponytail over her shoulder. "Lie back, and let's move you from under that bush so I can get a better look at the extent of the wound. Here's hoping my medical training is enough."

He'd understood her words, yet he wasn't sure he believed she wanted to help, or even could. His shoulder was a sticky mess, and blood oozed from the bullet wound—he could tell by the way his shirt stuck to him. If she was a medic, she should be able to handle the injury.

He peered at her, eyes half-open, and she met his gaze. If he could shift and let his lion out, he'd scare her away in a heartbeat. But he'd lost that power with the injury. Normally, shifting came as easily as breathing but something was missing, and he couldn't remember what he needed to do or how to fix it.

Bears were afraid of him and his brother, Mason, but she obviously didn't know who he was. It'd be just like him to imagine his dream girl and have her not recognize him as heir to the lion pride.

"Come on, you need to help me help you. No reason to suffer, but I can't move you on my own, and we need to get that wound bandaged and the bleeding stopped."

"I'm tired."

"I'm going to need your help unless you prefer to lay there and die."

He blinked. Maybe she was real after all. No woman ever ordered him around in his fantasies. In his fantasies, he was already king of the pride. Always the boss.

As he should be.

"I…can't move." Wow, his voice was weak. "I don't think I can help."

He couldn't help her so she'd better go before the lions came. They wouldn't show her mercy, and though she was his enemy, he didn't want her to be injured or killed.

"Well?" she asked. "You ready to cooperate or am I going to have to insist?"

Persistent. And pushy. He watched her without replying, not sure what to make of the female. Why didn't she go on about her business and let him lie in the dirt waiting on his brother?

A brisk breeze blew through the forest, lifting her red ponytail and the tatters on her T-shirt. She smoothed stray hairs away from her forehead. He stared, unable to look away. Her milky complexion glistened in the sunlight, and he traced the contours of her lips with his gaze. She was too damn pretty to be angry with. But she needed to go while she still could. Now.

"I'll be okay. I don't need your help." Marco gritted his teeth. "The lions will come for me. You go. I'm sure there are bears that need you."

"It's my duty to help anyone who's injured, and from the looks of it, you need my help. Let me patch you up."

"Poison," Marco grumbled. He definitely hadn't had any nurse/patient fantasies. The situation no longer held appeal. Could this woman be real? He sniffed.

He could scent her. She smelled real. He scented a whiff of familiarity too, but he couldn't place it. She had a lot of anger in her, yet she wasn't showing it. But something else niggled at him.

She shook her head. "I'm not going to poison you. I don't have any medicine with me other than antibacterial ointment. Out here, I'm prepared to triage, not hospitalize."

"Good to know. This injury hurts like hell."

"I'm obligated to treat your injuries, with your consent, of course. At least get you in better shape till your pride shows up."

He smirked. If she only knew. He had no clue where Mason had gone or when he'd come looking.

"Something funny?" She unzipped her pack and pulled out her water bottle, about halfway empty. "Drink. I'm sure you're dehydrated. It's hot out here."

Her voice was sweet as honey, even when giving orders. She thrust the bottle toward him and held it as he drank long from the warm liquid. Her hand held his head up, and her soft, full breasts brushed against his good arm. The water slid down his throat so smooth, and he focused on that sensation rather her nearness.

She gently laid his head down then screwed the lid on the water bottle. "Let's get you fully out from under that bush so I can take a look at that injury."

"Can't move," he whispered, keeping his eyes closed. "My shoulder..." *Don't want to move. Want to sleep.*

"I'm going to try to pull you out. Help me if you can." She lowered her voice as she worked to maneuver him carefully from under the bush. Her arms under his good arm, tugging.

Ouch. Dammit, that hurt.

He slid across sharp rocks and jagged pebbles, yet didn't make a sound. Not aloud anyway. His one arm was completely limp, and the rest of his body felt like he'd been stomped on by an elephant. Moving wasn't something he wanted to do.

Ever again.

Somewhere in the distance he heard her talking. Was she speaking to him or had more bears arrived? He tried to open his eyes, successful for a moment.

A large hawk glided overhead, above the trees, silhouetted against the blue sky. He heaved a yawn.

"Oh no, you don't." Her firm voice pushed into his consciousness. "You aren't going to sleep until we remove the bullet."

He heard a groan and realized it was his own.

Sleep.

He closed his eyes as the shroud of pain blanketed him. If she was going to kill him, then so be it.

Chapter Three

"They're going to pay for this." Mason paced, hands clasped behind his back. He'd chewed his nails to nubs going over scenarios. The battle had not gone well for the lions. His father dead, his brother missing, and they still didn't have possession of the cave.

The one thing my father wanted more than anything.

"The bears *will* pay." He stopped and surveyed the lions that had gathered in the common room upon his orders.

None met his gaze. Their fear and grief combined in an oppressive blanket that weighed him down and set him on edge more than he already was.

The lioness, Lara, usually chin up and proud, looked down at her hands, her hair falling forward over her face in dark waves.

Mason licked his cracked lips, for the first time in his life unsure of what to do next.

Lara twisted a lock of hair into a shiny rope, her fingers expertly braiding and unbraiding with nervous energy.

He growled at his own distraction from the issue at hand. Lara had a way with him that was both annoying and interesting. How that was possible from one lioness, he didn't know.

He chewed his bottom lip, nipping it hard enough to draw blood. He owed it to his father to be the lion leader he could be. Instead of occupying the Cave of Whispers and ruling over Deep Creek, he was left alone to rally the pride into regrouping, and that's what he'd do. With Marco missing, and likely captured by the bears, he had to act soon.

"What's the plan?" Lara blurted out. "Let's hit them while they're recovering. I know they have at least as many injured as we do."

Mason looked around the room. Such a ragtag bunch of battle-worn shifters. "I'm not sure we're ready."

The remaining lions showed little fire in their hearts and even less in their posture. Defeated, they slouched and fidgeted. Some glanced toward Lara. None met Mason's stare. Many probably worried he would lead them into another attack. No, they weren't ready.

Mason tamped his rising anger down. He needed to cut them a break and remember that many were grieving too. If he wanted to be a great leader like his father, he needed to practice patience with his pride. They needed guidance.

"We've got to regroup first, Lara. Mourn my father and our losses." *Find my brother.* He had to finesse the last part. Get the lions fired up and ready to fight again.

Nothing worse than being cooped up with a bunch of whipped lions to stress him out even more. Leading was not easy. He needed to stretch his mind and his body, and fill his lungs with clean air.

If only he could take the day to run through the

forests of Deep Creek and burn off his extra emotion. His lion yearned for the freedom of a trail underfoot and tree boughs overhead with a clear blue sky peeking through. *Not yet.* A good leader took care of his people first.

He'd run soon.

A lump formed in his throat. His father, Maximillian, was dead and no amount of roaring would bring him back. And with Marco missing, everything was on Mason's shoulders.

I need my brother's guidance.

Mason's eyes stung with tears. He fisted his hands till his short nails cut into his palms. The urge to punch the wall welled, and he held his stress at the edge of consciousness. He wouldn't let it consume him.

He had to keep his cool and convince the others he was not only in charge, but had things under control, including himself. He ran his hand through his hair, snagging the tangles he'd neglected to brush out after his shower.

Deep breath.

If he'd learned anything from his father, it was that the pride needed to be guided, manipulated. Led around by their noses. If they were pushed too hard in any direction, they'd shove back, or even worse, give up or refuse to do what they were told. With Marco and Max gone, Mason would have to walk the line carefully if he wanted the other lions to obey. Marco was the tactful brother, the smooth talker.

A middle-aged lion coughed and mumbled an "excuse me," breaking the near-silence in the room.

Mason cleared his throat, and a few lions looked up, catching his gaze then averting their eyes.

Where to begin?

What would Max say? Mason paced, his muscles stiff and aching.

The tattered lions, many swathed in bandages or sporting bruises and scratches, slumped on the chairs and couches of the meeting hall. Most stared into nothingness like they'd seen the end of the world.

Lost the battle.

Maybe we did. But we won't lose the war.

"We are lions." Mason paused. "Yesterday was one of our most difficult days. We lost many, including my father. An unacceptable outcome. Yet we will overcome. We are lions."

A chorus of murmurs answered him. He waited for the room to get quiet again before continuing.

"The war isn't over. Yesterday's battle didn't go in our favor but we haven't lost." He continued to pace. "The devastation will fuel our revenge. It will make us stronger."

Mason scanned the room. Would the lions be able to live up to what he needed? Regroup and fight? Did they have the fortitude to continue what Max had started?

I hope so. "We'll kill the bears. I don't know when, and I don't know how. But it will be done. My father's memory will guide us."

And so it shall be.

Cries echoed in the crowded room, lions near-wailing at the loss of their leader. Everyone had loved Max, even though he'd been a gruff and sometimes difficult lion to deal with. He always had the lions' best interest at the forefront. No one doubted that. Without him, it would be a challenge to go on, but with his brother at his side, anything was possible.

They would avenge their father's death together.

Mason wanted to cover his ears as the pain cut deep, straight to the hole his father's death had already carved out. He pushed the hurt away and focused on his hatred of the bears. They were responsible for the pain.

They would suffer.

Mason's heart ached but he'd not give the bears the satisfaction of knowing they'd hurt him. Instead, they'd feel his wrath.

His revenge.

Another whimper sounded from the corner and he curled his lip. How had his father dealt with such weakness?

Damn, the lions were acting like pussies. What happened to the strong warriors he'd led into battle? What sat before him now was nothing more than a litter of needy babies.

He needed the lions' help to defeat the bears now, more than ever. But in this shape? *They won't be ready to fight for a while.*

Dammit. He held his head.

My father is dead.

Never again would he hear the old man's deep voice or the rough slap of a heavy paw on the wooden floor of the clubhouse. His chest tightened.

"Max would want us to fight." One of the younger lions spoke, his voice clear and strong. "Not sit around crying over our loss."

Mason smiled. "You're right. And we will fight. Are you ready?"

The lion nodded. "As soon as you need me, I will fight for the pride. I will fight for the memory of Max."

Satisfaction at being Max's son rushed through Mason. His father had been harsh sometimes, but there was no better father and role model. "Thank you. That time will be soon."

"They slaughtered him."

"They will pay."

The bears had ganged up against an old warrior, with no concern for his station or age. He'd not had the chance to defend himself with dignity. The bears behaved as poorly as Mason would expect from the Green Glen wolves. Attacking a weaker opponent, with no thought of honor.

Shameful.

A low rumble formed in his chest. He stuck his hands in his pockets and paced to the side of the room and back as quickly as he could.

Thirty-five lions were unaccounted for, as of the last assessment. Warriors. Fathers. Even some mothers. He ground his teeth. The violence had touched many.

The war had become personal. No longer only about land and retaking the cave.

Now it was about revenge.

One more trek across the room and back. Another breath.

"What about Marco?"

Mason stopped. He jerked his head toward Lara. "What?"

"Any word on where he is or if he's alive?" The lioness's question cut through the silence and pierced the depths of Mason's subconscious ramblings like a knife into his heart.

The room seemed to shrink, like a funhouse without mirrors, near-silent except for his own breath. The floor moved under his feet, shifting one way then another. Mason envisioned the last moment his brother had stood beside him, tall and strong.

Alive.

What about Marco?

His mouth went dry. The question hadn't left his mind since they were separated during battle, yet Lara voicing it brought the danger directly into the room.

Every lion held its breath waiting on his response. Mason could feel the pressure. He squeezed his temples, massaging the tight spots.

No word had come about Marco's fate, and Mason worried more than he cared to admit. Sure, he'd been jealous that Marco would be the next leader of the pride since he was the oldest, but he knew he'd share the responsibilities. And the perks.

Though they bickered, they were closer than most siblings. Twins that had a second sense about each other.

Friends. They'd lead as a team.

He opened his eyes and studied Lara. She was the most outspoken female he'd ever met, all lean muscle and smarts with a side of sexy sass. Even her dark wavy hair seemed to rebel against constraints. She annoyed him more than any other female, and more than most males.

He let a low rumble of a growl sound in his throat.

A warning she'd no doubt ignore. She was a force to be dealt with. Nothing seemed to make her back down from a challenge and that both excited and irritated him.

"I've no word of my brother's fate." He met her accusatory gaze and kept his tone level. The last thing he wanted was an argument with Lara. "Not yet. But I don't sense that he's dead. We'll get him back from the bears."

A lone gasp sounded from the corner where a cluster of younger men sat shoulder to shoulder.

One stuttered, "Th-the bears have Marco?"

"Yes." Mason set his jaw.

"How do you know he's not dead?"

"I would know. He's my twin."

Lara flicked her hair over her shoulder. "You also predicted we'd have the cave back by evening." She crossed her arms and leaned back. "Didn't happen, twin."

The growl lowered to Mason's chest but he held it in. No point in scaring the rest of the lions because he was annoyed with the lioness. She was trying to get to him and he wouldn't give her the pleasure.

"Sit." He forced the word through the air at Lara, and surprisingly she dropped into her chair. He began pacing again. "The battle was poorly planned. Not that it matters now, but we never should have waited to attack. I told my father we should go in earlier and catch the bears off guard."

And he didn't listen. Wanted to rush in at solstice because of some kind of premonition or something.

Look what happened.

"I believe you." The young lion spoke up. "Marco is alive. He has to be. And we need to rescue him."

Mason nodded. "Yes. We do and we will. The less time he's with the enemy, the better."

"We'll fight again soon?" Preston called from the middle of the seated lions. A white bandage wrapped his head and scratches slid down his cheek. "After we rescue Marco?"

"Yes." Mason kicked at the floor. "Very soon. We have to find my brother first, and if that means sending a small group to rescue him, we will. I'll bet they are holding him at the cave."

"That'd make sense." Preston winced. "They think we can't reach him there."

"They're wrong. Whatever it takes, we'll get him back."

Sharp intakes of breath sounded and a few whimpers bleated the air. Fear and uncertainty wafted off the lions in a mass of tangled emotion. The room stank. The lions needed the confidence to fight. To resist and to win.

"Are we not mountain lions?" Mason's voice rose as the adrenaline fueled his anger. "Do we not deserve our cave? Should we not avenge my father's death?"

He whipped his head from side to side, looking over his troops. Where were his fighters? Where were the lions who roared with rage at the injustice of the bears?

Lara had done well in battle, but women shouldn't be fighting to begin with. But he might need her now, given the losses the lions had taken. He snarled.

No one answered him. Instead, the scent of fear and indecisiveness thickened.

Then a lone voice rang out. "I'm not afraid. Of course we fight. We take what's ours. We get Marco back." Lara thrust her chin forward. "We'll be successful this time."

"Yes." Mason had to admit Lara was stronger than many of the lions.

Lara wiped a tear from her cheek, playing it off as scratching her face. "We'll take possession of the cave where Max's body lies. May his shifter soul run free through the river of stars." She bowed her head.

"May he run free." A lump blocked Mason's throat then he coughed it away.

"May he run free." The lions all spoke in unison.

Mason massaged his shoulder and stretched his arms. If his lion didn't get to run soon, he'd go stir crazy.

"As I told my father, we should have attacked the bears sooner. They were defending a position, not trying to take one and that became our disadvantage." He paced in front of the crowd of lions. "They knew every place to hide in the forest, every inch of that land. We didn't stand a chance. Next time, we won't make it so easy for them."

"Shouldn't we go after them now? While they are weak and while we can get Marco?" Lara didn't back down.

Now was not the time to question the leadership. If he could go after the bears now, he would. He'd rescue his brother. But the lions weren't ready.

"It'd be a suicide mission. We need a bit of recovery time and a foolproof plan. I'm not willing to risk more of you or my brother because we're impatient and unprepared."

"So what *is* the plan?" Lara stared straight through him.

"We find out where the bears are keeping Marco. We plan a rescue mission. We'll worry about revenge another day. Right now, I want to get my brother home safely."

"Let's do it." Lara set her mouth in a firm line.

"Mourning my father is important. We will hold the ceremony to honor his name tonight. After that, we'll find answers about my brother." Mason stopped and gripped the back of a chair. His chest tightened. He wouldn't cry. Not in front of the lions.

Marco will return.

"How will we mourn Maximillian if his body isn't here?" A teen cub, barely old enough to be included in the meeting, his voice trembling as if he'd spoken up among a roomful of angry parents. His tousled blond hair hung over his eyes, and he flipped it back, revealing a face full of freckles and questions. "How are we going to get him back?"

Mason took a deep breath and stared out over the room. His heart broke for the loss of his father, and he was determined to channel that emotion into anger, not sorrow or pity. The boy, untouched by battle, as he should be, sat cross-legged on the floor his face upturned to watch Mason.

Mason spoke directly to him. "Yes. The bears have my father's body. But we can hold a ceremony without his earthly shell. His spirit is already free."

"The ceremony is for our remembrance, cub," Lara

said, her voice softer than Mason had ever imagined it could be. She moved to sit by the young one. "It's for the living to remember him. Max is already walking in the river of stars with our ancestors. He's not suffering and he's not with the bears. He's also in here." She held her hand to the boy's heart. "Never forget that he is with all of us."

Mason turned away and swiped at the tear that finally escaped.

"I won't forget," the boy said. "Max will always be with me." He hugged Lara.

The room silenced and Mason turned to face his people, his emotions as under control as he could keep them. Everywhere he looked, lions were crying or suffering.

"Is it wise to wait?" another lion asked. A thin red line traced down his cheek. Perhaps a scratch from the battle. "What if they torture him? Shouldn't we try to rescue him before it's too late?"

Mason tried to think of the lion's name, but it escaped him. All he remembered was seeing the lion as a youngster, skateboarding down the compound's sidewalk. "I don't think they will seriously hurt Marco as long as they think he has information they can use. He's valuable to them alive."

"While we wait, the bears are regrouping." Lara remained seated by the boy, but her words carried in the room. "We can't forget that."

Marco pulled his gaze from her and back to the young man who'd asked the question.

"The one thing I know that is good about the bears is that they will give my father the proper burial in the cave. We've left bodies near the Sentinels, and the bears always tend the shells. Lions, bears, wolves, no matter. All shifters go to the cave, if possible, and Shoshannah guides them to the stars or greets them there. Even Evers was given a proper burial."

"Yes, sir. I'm sorry. I wasn't questioning your judgment, I promise." The young lion ducked his head.

"Good. Because we're going to do this my way." Mason stood tall and breathed away the pangs of sorrow. Time to lead. *Suck it up.*

"Good." Lara raised her voice.

Mason pushed his hair behind his ears. "Tomorrow, I'll send scouts to see if they can find out anything useful."

Lara sat up straight. "I still don't know how you know he's alive but if you say it's twin sense then fine. I don't want him to be dead. I like him."

"He's not dead. We will get him back."

The room instantly went quiet. No one moved. Then, Mason heard a hundred heartbeats, maybe more. The acrid note of fear in the air grew stronger. *Good.* Every leader should be feared at least a little.

He stopped pacing in front of the large window that looked out onto the garden. Corn was tall, and the other plants greened beside the rows. The spring rains had given a good start to the crops. Like rain, he'd need to nourish the pride back to health. Starting now. Marco was so much better at handling the lions. Calm. Steady. Mason could do it, too.

So many lions and not one of them truly equipped to fight after the failure they'd suffered. Lara had more fight left in her than most of the others put together.

How the lions had come to this, he didn't know. "You can help search, if you wish."

Lara's voice filled with a hidden smile. "I do. Tell me when."

Chapter Four

Alicia sat beside the wounded lion, out of his reach, yet close enough to hear him breathe. She'd bandaged his injury with her field kit, but he needed to be moved to a facility with more equipment so the bullet and any fragments could be removed. She might be able to do it in the cave with her full medical kit, but no way Elijah would allow her to bring a lion into the Cave of Whispers.

"What's your name, bear?" His voice, raspy from heat and pain, still hinted at power and masculinity.

Alicia sniffed the air.

Nothing unusual.

What was the harm in telling him her name?

He was barely able to move, much less hurt her. Still, wariness coiled in her gut at the thought of being so close to her enemy.

"Well?" The lion grimaced. His black hair stuck to the perspiration on his face. A purple bruise clouded his chiseled cheek.

No doubt his shoulder was on fire from the bullet wound. He tried to hide it with his banter, but he was suffering. If the bullet had hit a few inches over, he'd be dead.

It'd be better for both of us if he were.

Her cheeks burned at the hateful thought, even though it was true.

"Why do you care what my name is?" She peered into the depths of his eyes. Something about him lured her to gaze a moment too long. Linger. And the color... green, or brown, she wasn't sure. Her heart sped as he returned her inadvertent stare, opening her psyche with his piercing eyes. Between his heated look and the burning of the sun on her back, she felt like she was under the spotlight for a crime she hadn't committed.

"I'm curious." He broke the connection and turned away. "Nothing more. Small talk."

The scent of his pain intensified. "Does it matter?" She watched his face for any measure of response, but he didn't move.

Dammit, she felt sorry for him. If she had any pain medicine with her, she'd give it to him. She hated to see anyone suffer, even a lion.

Elijah would think she was weak. Hell, Griff would too, and possibly Derek.

Tawodi would be proud. Easing suffering and pain was the chief responsibility of a healer. She glanced up to the treetops to see if she could spot Tawodi flying or perched on an ancient branch, but she didn't see her anywhere.

"Maybe I want a normal conversation to help me forget about this pain. Is that okay?" He let out a long groan. "Gods, it hurts. Don't you have any pain pills? Anything?"

She shook her head. "I'm sorry."

"What kind of medic travels without medicine?"

"One who travels light and doesn't expect to be out long, much less find a lion with a gunshot. If you were a bear, I'd call for help to get you back to where I could really take care of you."

"I'm not a bear."

"And so we have another complication." Alicia scowled. "That bullet needs to come out."

"Can't you take it out now?"

She watched his eyes shift color from bright green to deep brown, his pupils enlarging then shrinking. She'd never seen a shifter whose eyes could change color. Never seen something so…beautiful in its danger.

She licked her lips. "I can, but not here in the forest. I don't have what I need, and we're hardly in a sterile or even clean environment. Maybe we should get you to a hospital. If that wound gets infected, you might not survive."

A weak laugh followed another groan. "You know I can't go to a human hospital. They'd ask too many questions, especially about a gunshot wound."

She nodded. "I know."

"Could I have more water?"

Alicia held the bottle while he drank. His lips, soft over the spout, sucked as he gulped at the warm liquid. Her face heated at the thoughts that popped into her imagination. Not the type of thoughts she normally had about patients. "Enough?"

He smiled a fraction of a smile. "Thanks. So what do we do next, bear?"

"We need to find your lions. They can help you." She set the bottle aside.

"They should've come for me already." He laid his head on the ground and gazed skyward. "I don't know why it's taking them so long."

"They must know you're missing."

He closed his eyes. "My brother ought to be here at least. He'd never intentionally leave me, especially not wounded and behind enemy lines. He must think I'm dead."

"I don't smell any lions nearby, so we're going to have to figure something else out. How far away is your nearest post? Maybe someone is there who can get you home."

"Seriously? You think I'm going to tell you where we spy?" He gritted his teeth. "No one will be there right now. They'll have returned to the compound."

"We need to do something. You don't have a lot of time. I put a patch on that wound and you're still losing a lot of blood. The gauze is almost soaked through."

What could she do with the lion? *Taking him to the cave will really cause an uproar.* She grinned at her weak pun. Didn't matter. She couldn't carry him. And if Elijah found out she was harboring an enemy, he'd kill the lion. The best thing would be if the lions came and got him. Right now, that didn't seem likely. If she went to tell the lions that one of their own was injured in the forest, they'd kill her.

A no-win situation.

"Should we wait for your brother?" She checked the tree line. "When do you think he might come?"

"That's the big question, isn't it?" He turned to face

her. "At least I have good company, even though you're a bear."

"It's Alicia."

His eyes, large for his face, almost glowed with the green as deep as the forest glen near the rocky waterfall. The color deepened as she stared and soon his mossy green gaze was as deep brown as the warm earth. She looked away, her palms damp.

What was it about this lion that set her on edge and heated her at the same time? It wasn't that he was a lion—she'd only reacted with dislike to lions before. But this one was different.

"Alicia? That's a pretty name for red-haired bear. I expected something…a little angrier." He attempted to grin. "But you don't seem angry." He forced the words out and gave her a slow wink.

She crossed her arms. "Seriously? Is that the best you can do?" Was the lion flirting with her? She needed to get him some pain medicine because clearly he was out of his mind if he thought a lion and bear could ever even think of dating. He must be delirious.

Hell, maybe she needed some pain meds herself. He hadn't said anything about dating. That was her own wild imagination rearing up and making a ludicrous suggestion.

"I don't know what you're talking about. All I'm trying to do is get home. Get this bullet out and sleep for a week in my own soft bed."

"Your home is too far away and too dangerous for me, and I can't carry you. But you can't stay out here waiting on a rescue that might not come. You *will* die." She slid her water bottle into her pack.

"Where, then?" He blinked slowly. "I'm not sure I'll be able to walk far."

"I don't think you're able to walk at all from the looks of you." Alicia's heart ached. Her mind knew he was the enemy—the same one who'd caused so much death the day before. Yet, he wasn't trying to hurt her. His suffering stabbed at her like an ice pick, again and again and deeper and deeper.

Some days she cursed her empathy.

He needed pain medicine and a quiet place to recuperate after the bullet was removed. That left two choices. Take him to his pride or somewhere she could remove the bullet herself. "You're going to grow more dehydrated out here, that's for certain. I've got to move you now."

"I'm not going anywhere with you, redheaded bear, unless it's to my pride's compound. No prison hospital for me, so don't even think about it."

"Staying out here overnight is a death sentence. Your wound will be infected by morning if it's not already. And you may have internal bleeding. Do you want me to leave you here to die?"

"I honestly don't care. No more talking about lions and bears and bullets, okay? I want to sleep." He yawned and his eyes closed. Wisps of black hair fluttered in the light breeze and his chest rose and fell.

"No, you need to stay awake." If he weren't wounded, he'd look like a model posing for a photo shoot. He was the most attractive lion she'd ever seen. A chill went through her at the thought he might die. "It's dangerous for you to sleep now."

"I'm so tired… I don't think I can stay awake. So

go away and I'll take my chances out here. No travel with doctor bear." His voice, already weak, became not much more than a mumble.

Seriously? The lion was at risk of bleeding to death, and he was worried about going somewhere with a bear who was trying to save his life? The extent of his injuries wasn't clear, and sleeping could hasten death. Staying awake was critical to his care—it was one of the few things modern medicine and Tawodi's home-opathy agreed on.

Would serve him right if she did walk off and leave the lion, but dammit she cared what happened to him.

It's my duty to care. Nothing more.

She pulled her pack up onto her shoulders. He'd nap and likely not wake up again, but if that's what he wanted, she wasn't obligated to interfere. She only helped those who wanted help. Keeping him awake would be impossible.

She still hadn't searched the entire area to see if there were any other wounded bears, and if this lion didn't want any help then why should she bother worrying if there were other lions lying around wounded?

"Suit yourself. I'm leaving. If you don't want my help, that's fine. I hope your lions find you soon."

The lion held his shoulder and the newly bandaged spot. Fixing him up had been an effort on her part, and he hadn't done anything to help her.

What she'd done was truly a patch job—it wouldn't keep him alive long. She knew it and he likely did too.

She had the scalpel; too bad she didn't think to pick up the rest of the surgical equipment. Should she do her best and operate with what she had? The forest floor wasn't clean, but she could work with what she had. She watched him breathe, breaths shallow but regular. He hadn't gone into shock. The urge to stroke his forehead overcame her and she reached out to him.

"What are you waiting on? Go." The lion squinted as he stared at her, his dark brows slanting.

Alicia paused.

"I thought you were leaving." He turned away. "So, go. I don't need your help."

She scowled. "I am definitely leaving."

"Fine. I'm tired and you're keeping me awake."

"Go to sleep then." Alicia wiped the sweat from her forehead. Summer was in full season in Deep Creek, and the heat penetrated even the deepest forest. "You know the risk."

"I know, redhead. Beats the alternative." He coughed, wincing and holding his shoulder.

"Which is?"

He choked the words out. "Being a prisoner of the bears."

Pointless.

She turned to walk away. Grandmother couldn't be upset with her. She'd done what she should do, and now she needed to make sure there weren't any injured bears left in the forest.

If the lion wanted to be stubborn, fine. She stuck her thumbs under her backpack straps and headed toward the creek.

"Wait." His voice was faint, almost a half whisper.

She stopped and faced him. "What?" Her voice was clipped and short and annoyance colored her mood.

"I'm sorry. Please don't leave me here alone."

His plaintive tone cut right through her. One moment, he was alpha lion toughshit, and the next, he was downright pitiful.

Fuck.

So he wanted help. Of course. It couldn't be a simple parting—it had to be a complicated mess where she risked her allegiance to save him. Where the hell were the lions when she needed them?

She walked back toward him. "Thought you didn't need me." She knelt beside him, setting her pack on the ground. A rosy-brown blotch bloomed across the stark white bandage and onto his skin where she'd cut the black T-shirt away from the injury. The wound still bled some, though the bleeding had slowed from a little while ago.

"I need you." He spoke the words through gritted teeth. "I don't want to need you, but I do."

Lion or man, he needed help and he'd asked. Now, she was obligated to help him. A hawk's shriek sounded in the distance, the tone shrill and clear.

The meaning even clearer.

It didn't matter if Elijah got mad—she'd have to keep things a secret from him. As long as she wasn't endangering the bears, there shouldn't be an issue— he'd never have to know. She'd get the lion back on his feet and away from the bears before there was any trouble.

Right?

If only Derek were with her. He'd help her or set her straight. He was back at the cave with Bria, where Alicia had told him to go. If she'd let him follow her into the woods, he'd be able to help her drag the lion to a safer location. As it was now, she would have to move the lion herself.

"I'm going to figure out a way to get you out of here. You're going to do what I tell you and you aren't going to complain. Clear?" She unzipped her pack and pulled out her water bottle and offered it to the lion.

"As mud."

"And no smart-ass remarks or I swear to the gods, I will leave your ass to die out here."

"Your bedside manner sucks." He broke into a coughing fit, holding a hand against his injury. "Where'd you study to be a medic? Prison?"

"Funny lion. Drink." She pushed the bottle toward him, concealing her smile.

"You can't tell anyone you found me." His eyebrows raised and his eyes widened. "The bears will kill me."

"I'm not telling them."

She put the water bottle to his lips and held it for him. He drank and a dribble of water slid down his cheek. Not thinking, she wiped it away, the heat of his skin blazing against her fingertips. She shivered at the contact. The urge to touch him again rushed through her, and she sat back on her heels, her heart thumping.

What the hell had just happened? Her stomach tingled at the aftershocks. Something about the lion compelled her to be near him, but that didn't make sense.

This guy was an ass in lion's clothing. When he was healthy, he probably knew just how attractive he was. She smirked. Her luck to have such a difficult patient.

His eyes closed, and he tipped the water bottle higher. She helped him steady the bottle as he drank. When he'd had his fill, she took the bottle. Not even a sip left. Good thing they were near the creek where she could refill. She crammed the bottle into her backpack and drummed her fingers on her leg.

She needed a plan.

A long, low moan sounded deep, and his mouth parted. He didn't move and she waited a moment. How would she move him?

She leaned closer. Was he…dead?

His chest rose and fell slightly. The tatters of his T-shirt revealed a muscular chest with lean muscle and long lines. The tan of his skin set off his strong features and chiseled lips, still damp from the water. She brushed the lock of black hair out of his eyes. His fine features hinted at Native American blood, and she was sure that all the lionesses' heads turned when he walked by.

The heat and exhaustion of the day were getting to her.

Being attracted to a lion was not acceptable. No matter what he looked like or how charming he was.

"Thank you." His head lolled to the side.

So he did have manners.

His breathing steadied. The scent of his pain had turned more acrid and piercing and throbbed in the air.

Definitely the cave. Her only option. Grandmother's house was too far away, and so was her own house in town. She couldn't lug a wounded man through the streets of Oakwood without raising a stir. Everyone was already in everyone else's business.

No way was she getting him to the cave by herself. Griff would insist on taking over and then Elijah would

find out. Nor could she leave him while she went off
to find someone to help.

Dammit.

Shifters healed more quickly than other animals, but
the damn bullet was still in his shoulder. Until it was
out, he wouldn't be able to heal completely.

She chewed her lower lip. Would Shoshannah help
him? Unlikely, given all the burials she had to oversee—
both lion and bear and even a few wolves. Her magic was
so sporadic and seemed to require time to reenergize.

If she could get him to her car, then she could drive
him to the lion's compound in Henredon and they could
tend him. If she was lucky, they wouldn't keep her as
a prisoner, or shoot her on sight.

The realization she didn't want to face wavered in
her thoughts, more strongly than before. The nagging
voice inside that kept messing up her weak will to
walk away.

Part of her didn't want to leave the lion.

She wasn't sure which part or why she felt like she
needed to be near him, but the feeling was real, and it
grew stronger the longer she was with him. She shook
her head. She was being ridiculous. He wasn't hers to
want to keep, like an injured animal found in the forest
that she could nurse to health and keep as a pet. Helping shifters was her calling, but that did not include
wanting to be with a lion.

The lion whispered and groaned, and she leaned
closer to hear.

"What did you say?"

He was becoming delirious.

"Marco," he scratched out, his voice breathy and weak. "My name is Marco."

Marco.

A sickening chill raced through her as she realized who he was. *Marco!* One of the twin heirs to the entire Sen Pal pride. Why hadn't she realized it? The dark hair... He was one of the vicious black lions, prophesied to change Deep Creek.

With Max dead, he'd be ruler of the pride. He and his brother would lead the next charge against the bears. Maybe she *should* turn him over to Elijah.

Did he know his father had been killed in battle?

The lions would come looking for him. They were likely already out in the forest tracking him. As clannish as the bears were, the lions were even more so with family, especially the pride leader.

Things had just gone from bad to much, much worse.

Chapter Five

"You can't tell anyone." Alicia pulled the soft blanket up to cover Marco to his chin then picked up the lit lantern from beside him. Kneeling beside him, she watched him take breaths laced with pain.

"I said I wouldn't." Derek stood in part shadow, near the doorway to the cave room.

Another lantern flickered near the cave wall, casting a dim light and long shadows through the rocky alcove. Coupled with the sprinkles of phosphorescent bacteria that grew on the walls in this area of the caves, there was enough dim light to see by. The remote area of the cave wasn't an ideal place to bring the lion, but it was better than leaving him in the forest to die. He'd be less likely to be found in the deep tunnels.

A lion was in the bear den.

Alicia held the lantern up. "I mean it, Derek. No one. Not even Bria. If anyone finds out he's here, we're both in trouble."

"I gave you my word. As long as he isn't a threat, I won't tell anyone."

"Thank you."

"I hope you're doing the right thing. This situation

raises my hackles." Derek stepped closer. "I don't like it at all."

"I know. But I have to help him."

Alicia laid her hand on Marco's chest and tingles raced up her arms, raising the fine hairs to attention. His body quaked with tremors even with the warm blanket over him. She brushed a lock of his dark hair aside and placed the back of her hand across his forehead. *Hot.* If infection was setting in already, she had less time than she thought.

"He's feverish." She glanced up at Derek. "We've got to hurry and get this bullet out, or there's a good chance we'll lose him."

With Derek's help, she might be able to save Marco, but the clock was ticking and the situation kept worsening. A wave of fear fluttered through her, settling in her gut. If she couldn't save Marco, would the lions think she'd killed him? Or would they believe that she tried to save him?

Not the time to worry about it. Focus.

"Maybe that wouldn't be such a bad thing." Derek stood, arms crossed, several feet away.

"You don't really mean that or you wouldn't have carried him here. Besides, my duty is to heal all creatures, not just the ones you or anyone else deem worthy." She set the lantern down and scooted closer to the lion.

"I get that, Alicia." Derek moved closer and peered down at Marco. "I still think bringing him here was a bad idea. The only reason I helped was because you asked. After what happened yesterday… Elijah will hit the cave roof if he finds out."

"I know. And I appreciate your help. You're a good friend."

"You better hope he's out of here before anyone discovers him."

"Yes." She watched Marco breathe. The decision to help the lion could be one that ended her relationship with the bears. Yet Marco was a leader in the lion pride. Healing him could facilitate the beginning of a new peace in Deep Creek.

"What are you thinking? I see your wheels spinning." Derek squatted beside her.

"Options. Paths. The many ways this could play out." Right now, she didn't have time to worry about the bigger picture. She had a sick lion on her hands. "I have to help him. I promised Grandmother. I can't discriminate."

"I don't think this is the type of situation she was talking about."

"This is exactly what she meant." She traced Marco's jawline with her finger then jerked her hand away, embarrassed. Why was she so drawn to touch him? Derek didn't notice, or at least pretended he didn't.

"Healing one of the leaders of a rival shifter group is a pretty major step in your education."

"I can handle it, with your help. I'll need you to run interference. Meanwhile, I'll work quickly to get the bullet out and treat any infection. Get him back on his feet and out of here."

Derek nodded. "As soon as possible."

"Yes."

Marco needed pain medication and antibiotics or he might not make it till sunrise. Moving him from the forest to the cave had taken a toll on his strength. If he didn't have accelerated shifter healing powers, he'd already be dead. No human would have survived what Marco had been through and shifter healing powers couldn't fight off human infections as well as human antibiotics could, so it was going to take a combination of things to give him a chance.

Marco was the biggest medical challenge Alicia had ever faced.

"Can I count on you, Derek?" She looked up at him.

"I said I'm not going to tell anyone. At least not yet. But I'm worried you're in over your head. Everything about this feels wrong."

"But here we are. Let's focus on one thing at a time. Get his meds, get the bullet out, get him out of the cave."

"What if he wakes up while we're gone? What if he wanders into the main cave and the bears see him? What then?"

"He's in too much pain to move, much less go spelunking. That's obvious, isn't it?" Alicia stood and brushed off her shorts, then picked up one of the lanterns.

"For both our sakes, I hope you're right."

Nervousness wafted off Derek like static, and Alicia took a deep breath to steady her own anxiety. She understood Derek's fears. She shared many of them. Still, Marco was here and she would take the bullet out. What happened next was up to the fates.

She turned to Derek and smiled. "This may turn out to be a good thing. Maybe helping Marco will bring good things to the bears."

"Doubtful. The lions don't care." Derek shook his head. "Well, they care about themselves and their own agenda."

"Grandmother will guide me."

"You're as stubborn as Bria. Maybe more so. I won't sleep well till there's no lion in the bear den."

Alicia nodded. "Agreed. Thank you for getting the blankets and lanterns. He might already be dead without the warmth they're providing." She lifted the lantern, letting it cast its yellow beam throughout the alcove. A poor substitute for a ray of sunshine, but it would have to do. Hope was critical, and she needed all the help she could get.

"You're welcome." Derek stood.

"I hate to leave him here with only one lantern, but I've got to get those meds and we need light too. His fever is making him cold."

"The lantern wouldn't provide heat. We need to get back now or we'll miss Elijah's ceremony. He'll get suspicious if we aren't there to see the souls recognized."

She nodded. Derek reached for the lantern. She handed it to him, giving Marco a last glance. If only she had as much faith in herself as Derek and Tawodi did. Sure, she'd had a lot of training, but she didn't feel like a seasoned healer. Some days, she felt like a charlatan, going through the motions but not really having an effect.

Healing Marco would be proof that she was truly a healer. It would be a miracle, and one she wouldn't be able to share with Elijah. He called the wolves down for saying she was a witch, but she wasn't sure how much stock he put in her faith healing either.

"Elijah will know," she murmured. "Let's get moving."

Elijah had a keen sense of what was going on in the bear world at all times. He'd notice in a flash if she and Derek were missing. How they'd keep Marco a secret from the cave full of bears remained to be seen. If Elijah decided to go on a walk, which he often did to think through things, he'd smell Marco from quite a distance away. Not much could be done to prevent it. Hopefully, Elijah would be busy handling the families of the deceased and not wandering around the cave.

If they were lucky, Marco would be gone in a few days. If they were extremely lucky, he'd be alive.

"Come on, Alicia." Derek's voice was filled with exasperation.

"I am." She took a deep breath and blew out the stress. "Thank you. This is way beyond what anyone should expect a friend to do."

"After Ria, I made a promise that I'd protect you. And I will. Right now, I'm going to have to drag you out of here by your ponytail if you don't come on."

She flashed him a grin. He'd not yanked on her hair since they were young cubs.

Marco moaned but didn't move, other than the shivering from his fever, and she bent to adjust the blanket around his neck, tucking it under his chin to keep it in place while they were gone. She didn't want to leave him, but the compulsion to remain by his side stumped her. He was a lion, not a friend.

She shook her head. She must be more tired than she realized. She'd never felt the need to be so close to someone she was healing. It was always a job, no more.

But Marco's essence pulled her to him on a deep level. One she couldn't explain.

One she didn't have time to explore.

"Now?" Derek asked, his voice strained, his face drawn tight in the lantern light. "I mean it. I'll drag you out of here."

"I'm coming."

Marco let out a low groan and whipped his head back and forth. Alicia's heartbeat quickened, and the urge to comfort him overpowered her thoughts.

"He's not going to feel better until you get that bullet out. There's nothing you can do for him now." The impatience in Derek's voice seemed to echo in the small chamber.

"I know." She sighed.

"The sooner we leave, the sooner you get back here. I'm going."

Derek headed into the tunnel and Alicia rushed to catch up. He was right. Get the meds and get back. Pray to the gods that Marco was still alive when she returned.

The small entrance led into the vast tunnels deep in the mountain far from where the bears gathered to lay their dead to rest.

The remote section of the cave had been used by native tribes for ritual and shelter. Warmer than the large area of the cave where the lake was, this deeper section held a few hot springs that bubbled away with minerals and salt.

Some bears semi-hibernated in the distant tunnels inside the mountains. The starry glow of the cave bacteria added to the mystique of this part of the cave, and bears used to spend time meditating and soaking in the pools. It had been a long time since she'd heard of anyone visiting. Since the lions had encroached, there hadn't been a lot of time to lie around.

She took a deep cleansing breath, imagining the ionized air clearing her lungs, her thoughts, her breath. Peace, calm, love and light. Tawodi had impressed on her how important it was to stay centered.

She followed Derek through the semi-darkness. She scented his concern and resolve. His normally quiet aura pulsed with stress, and she hated that she'd had to bring him into the situation, but he was her closest friend. He had always supported her in her pursuit of the old ways of healing and he truly believed in her.

Not everyone had a friend like Derek.

Believing in herself was one of the most important things toward successful healing. Self-doubt happened, but she had to learn to push it far away and trust herself.

A molten-hot rush of determination bloomed in her gut and spread outward to her limbs and finally to her fingertips and toes. If there was anywhere Marco would heal quickly, it was deep in the cave, with her help. Grandmother had been wise to show them how to get him here.

The gods had placed Marco in her hands, and she would do her best to honor them and her grandmother.

"It's beautiful." Her voice seemed detached, like it came from someone standing beside her. She was moving into the healing flow, where she could focus. It was time to gather her supplies and reach for help in the ether.

"Yes, it is. And it will be beautiful tomorrow." Derek's voice strained. "When the lion is gone."

She paused and ran her hand over ancient drawings of bears and wolves and lions that lined the rocky walls of the cavern. Slick green and brown stalactites dripped limestone from the cave's ceiling in domed areas in the distance, like a mouth full of mossy teeth. Elijah had a bunker somewhere deep in this part of the cave, but few bears knew where. Hopefully, he wouldn't be heading to it anytime soon.

"Quit lingering." Derek turned and frowned.

"Sorry." She smiled at Derek. Her anxiety had settled into a little white ball, hard and small in her stomach and no longer consuming her every breath. Marco might be the key to peace in Deep Creek.

"Trying to get to the lake before we're missed." He took off, lantern swinging in time with his long strides.

"You do know what you need to get?" He didn't stop or look back to hear her answer, keeping his pace steady.

"Slow down a bit." She hurried to keep up. "Yes. I need enough sedatives to help him rest, and something stronger to knock him out so I can remove the bullet. Antibiotics, basic wound dressing, suture kit, surgical supplies. Fine tweezers. I wish I had my healer's bag, but it's at Tawodi's house."

Derek slowed. "If you get caught…"

"Elijah isn't going to find out, I'm not going to get caught, and I trust Grandmother with every bit of my essence. She knows things we don't, sees beyond the veil into Shoshannah's realm. As soon as I get the bullet out and Marco is stitched up and able to move, we'll take him to where the lions can retrieve him." She ran her hand along the cool, damp wall as she walked.

It was hard to imagine that Marco was one of the most feared lions in Deep Creek. Was that part even true or merely a children's story?

Derek held the lantern high and maneuvered around a narrowing in the passage. "I trust Tawodi too. But we need to be careful. Marco's a lion, not a bunny rabbit."

"I know. This is the scariest thing I've ever done." Alicia followed Derek through the tight area. Circumstances had changed. "I've been angry with the lions since Ria, you know that. I've never forgiven them, but it's time for me to let my resentment go. Taking care of Marco, healing him, might be exactly what I need to be able to move on with my life. Do I let this chance escape because I'm afraid?"

"I hope you're right. I'd love to see some good come from this war. I don't think it's over."

"It's not over. It's only beginning. Unless we can do something to stop it, we're in for a long fight."

He sighed. "Though I don't agree with the risks you're taking, I support you as I always have. If we'd only been able to save—"

"We weren't able to save Ria. But the current fighting has to stop and maybe we can help by taking care of Marco. It'd be the perfect way to honor Ria's sacrifice."

"I guess there's no immediate risk since he can't get around on his own." Derek glanced back. "Not like he's going to be on a killing spree in the shape he's in."

"Exactly."

"Not at this moment anyway, but he's a shifter and that makes him shifty. He could heal without you being aware. I want to know what's happening at all times in case he gets feisty. I don't trust him."

"I can handle feisty."

"I still want to know."

"Oh, you'll be involved." She laughed and the echo filled the tunnel. "Besides, I'll need your help to move him when the time comes."

"That, I can do. There's nothing I want more than to get this lion out of our cave. Well, nothing more than peace in Deep Creek."

"Maybe it's coming."

"Maybe." He nodded, his face taut in the flickering lantern light.

Rocky projections from the cave walls cast a grim shadow throughout the winding tunnel. Alicia drew in a deep breath of the humid air. A few bits of the phosphorescent bacteria floated down like snowfall from the cave's ceiling, knocked loose by the sound vibrations of the conversation. Alicia watched it flutter to the cave floor. She'd always thought it was one of the prettiest features in a cave system full of surprises.

"Let's hope no one finds out." A bitter cocktail swirled in her stomach. Elijah could stop her from healing Marco.

She'd never known Elijah to be cruel, but with the number of bears lost in battle, there was no telling what he'd do to Marco if he got ahold of him.

"This way." Derek turned left into a narrower passage. "It's quicker." The ambient temperature was comfortable, but Derek's face shone with humid perspiration in the lantern light. He turned and moved effortlessly through the small tunnel.

Bria was fortunate to have Derek, and Alicia was happy that Derek had finally found his mate. Though she didn't know Bria well, Alicia sensed the deep connection between the human and Derek. She'd known Derek all his life, and though girls had flocked to the good-looking woodworker, he'd never really shown much interest in them.

A pang of sadness pierced her heart. She followed Derek, sending up swirls of dust in her wake.

What would it be like to have a mate? She didn't often consider the possibility. With all her studies and field training, she hadn't had time, really. It was only when her friends found their mates that it hit home.

She might never have a mate.

She lowered her voice. "You and Bria are lucky." Fated mates were always the best choice. You didn't have to be with your fated mate, but you set yourself up for misery if you mated with someone else. At least that's what she'd been told.

Would she ever find her fated mate? No sign of him so far. Did he even exist, and did she want him if he did? Did she even have time for a mate, or cubs? Being a healer was a very busy job—one that took a lot out of her.

"Yes, we are. I don't know what I'd do without her." Derek turned into another tunnel and she followed. Many paths led to the lake, but she trusted he knew the quickest one. He'd explored much more of the cave system than she had.

It seemed her duty was to remain unencumbered by a mate and wander freely as a healer in the forests of Deep Creek as her grandmother Tawodi had always done.

Alone.

Was that the expectation?

Tawodi had never married, taking the role of adoptive grandmother and sponsor of young healers who showed promise, always surrounded by at least one young person wanting to learn the ancient ways. Sometimes several people bathed in her knowledge at the same time.

Elijah never interfered with her teachings, but allowed her to practice alongside the bears. Tawodi was mother to the land and all the animals that roamed the forest, sky and river. As a hawk shifter, she could get from one end of the forest to the other quickly, and be ready to help an injured cub or wounded wolf much faster than any other creature. No one was against her willingness to help.

Well, perhaps a few selfish wolves had been, but as a whole, Tawodi was respected.

And Grandmother Hawk had said many times that she had no time for a mate. That her duty was to the forest and all who occupied it.

Perhaps that had become Alicia's destiny.

Derek looked back and whispered, "You okay?"

She nodded. "Yeah. Trying to keep up."

Alicia scanned the long, dark tunnel ahead. Maybe she should follow Tawodi's mateless path. Devote herself entirely to healing and the old ways of protecting the spirits of Deep Creek. It wasn't like her own mate had shown up on her doorstep like everyone else's in Deep Creek seemed to have done.

She grinned at Derek. Bria had appeared to him like a birthday cake. And Griff's mate had driven up from another state and rented his house. It wasn't fair.

Maybe one day Shoshannah would speak out and guide her. Not today. Today, Alicia had a concrete problem that didn't require mates or love. Today, she needed to heal a lion.

Derek picked up his pace. "Try to walk quietly. We're getting close."

"Okay." She tiptoed through the maze of corridors. A slow trickle of water ran on the far side of the cavern, glistening wet in the lantern light.

"I know where we are. Don't worry." Derek's footsteps shuffled ahead. "All you need to do is walk along the stream to the lake. It's a fairly straight shot, so you'll easily find your way back as long as you know which stream to trace."

Alicia nodded. "I can do this."

He picked up his pace. "I hope we aren't late."

Alicia kept up, though every muscle ached. The swinging of the lantern cast odd shadows of light and dark on the cave walls, and she watched the dark patches morph into lions and bear and wolves. Sometimes fighting, sometimes talking, the shapes billowing and changing in the shadowy recesses of the rocky world.

They walked in silence and the sounds of the cave came alive. Tiny splashes of water against ancient rock, the yawn of a bat, the tumble of a pebble down a stony slope. And the irrepressible feeling of weight on her from being underground. She shuddered. She'd never liked being deep in the cave for very long. She much preferred to run in the warm sunshine aboveground, not shiver in the shadows of the cold rocks.

"Derek?" She closed the distance between them.

He didn't stop walking but slowed his pace. "Yeah?"

She steeled herself against the answer that was sure to be contentious. "Why can't we take Marco to the lake for Shoshannah to heal?"

Derek stopped and held up the lantern, his eyes wide in disbelief. "Are you serious?"

She nodded and rubbed her hands together, trying to warm her fingers.

"Well, first off, we'd never get to the lake dragging that lion. Everyone would see us."

"We could try to get everyone to leave the cave. At least for a while. We could come up with a reason."

"Pull a fire alarm?" Derek grinned. "Like back in high school?"

She scowled. "No, of course not. But something. Wouldn't it be worth the chance to try and heal him fully?"

Derek began walking again, the loose gravel crunching underfoot. "Even if we did, we don't know if Shoshannah would heal Marco. She's very particular, and right now, she manifests as bear. What makes you think she'd help a lion? If she didn't help him, we'd have taken all that risk for nothing."

"She helped Claude. And he's a wolf. The wolves weren't in charge of the cave then. We were."

"That's a completely different situation."

Anger burned inside her. "How? A wolf isn't the chosen animal of the cave, and Shoshannah healed him when we took him into the lake. Sounds like the same problem we have on our hands. An injured enemy needs help. Maybe she would help. How will we know if we don't even try?"

"That situation sounds nothing like our problem." Derek picked up his pace. "In the first place, Claude was a child who'd been wounded, and not by one of us. Number two, Elijah pleaded for Shoshannah to heal him. Our leader asked. I don't think you'll get Elijah begging the ancestral spirit to save a vicious lion."

"He's not vicious. He can barely move."

"Not at the moment. But he's a killer. He's one of the most brutal lions left in Deep Creek. You know if he were able, he'd kill both of us."

"Maybe."

"There's no maybe about it. It's fact."

Alicia sighed. "Maybe Shoshannah would heal him without Elijah's request." She tugged her hair back and ducked under a low cave ceiling. "Maybe she'd pity him."

"Shoshannah has a mind of her own, but she's always deferred to the shifter that has possession of the cave. That means bears, not lions."

"That's stupid." If Shoshannah healed Marco, the whole mess would be over and he could go home. Why didn't Derek see it as a viable option? Sure, it meant risking everything to get Marco to the lake, but they'd gotten him into the cave without being spotted. At least it seemed so.

"You may think it's stupid, but these have been the ways of our people for millennia."

"It's time for those ways to change. It's time we all

learn to get along. And it wasn't so long ago that we *did* all get along and live together."

Derek ran his fingers through his beard. "Maybe so. Maybe that's a childhood allegory we were all told. All I know is that it isn't the case tonight. Tonight we treat this lion and get him out of our cave. It's bad luck to have him here."

Alicia ran her hand along the rocky outcroppings of the cave wall. With the stream on the other side, she'd be able to find Marco again without Derek. "Since when do you believe in luck? Bad or good?"

"I've got a mate to protect. I can't put her at risk because you want to play doctor."

She bit back a retort. Having Derek mad at her wasn't going to solve anything, and she needed his help, as much as she hated to admit it.

"I hope no one follows me."

"Be careful and you'll be fine. Everyone is still so shell-shocked from the battle—no one is going to be exploring the cave or doing much of anything except recuperating."

"True." She was glad Derek had come in search of her in the forest as she'd about given up on what to do with Marco. Derek had had no trouble carrying him, and with Tawodi's instruction, the path to the cave had been uneventful.

They walked in silence, Alicia a few feet behind Derek as he slipped through tunnels to follow the stream. The lantern cast circles of bouncing yellow light on areas of the cave she'd not seen in a long time, or maybe ever. The cave system was such a maze of tunnels, and there were several ways to get to the hot springs and other faraway areas.

In the distance, the echo of people talking buzzed like bees swarming a new hive. The bears had gathered at the lake.

The voices hummed louder and a faint red glow shone in the corridor's distance.

Derek stopped and turned to her. "Before we go into the lake room, I've something to tell you. I should've told you earlier."

"I'm listening." Alicia leaned against the cool stone wall.

"I didn't want you to freak out. Promise me you'll stay calm."

"Since when do I freak out?" She put her hands on her hips. What the hell was he talking about? "What is it?"

Derek stared at the floor, the tips of his hair highlighted by lantern light. "You can't tell Bria."

"Okay, I won't tell her."

He shot her a serious glance then took a deep breath. "She's the one who shot Marco."

Alicia swallowed as her mouth went completely dry. Had she heard him correctly? She moved away from Derek. How was that possible? Bria wasn't supposed to be fighting, much less shooting lions. To be the one that shot Marco, what were the odds?

Derek held the lantern high. "Marco would've killed me if she hadn't. She had the gun trained on him, and when he lunged at me, she pulled the trigger. She's still talking about how she should've aimed to kill him."

Alicia covered her mouth with her hand. Not Derek!

Lifelong friends, she couldn't bear to think of losing him. If Marco had... "If he'd killed you..."

"It could be my soul the bears are celebrating tonight. Bria could be alone."

"Oh gods, you should have told me."

"Would it have changed your stance on healing him?"

"Yes. No," Alicia sputtered. "I don't know. I guess not, but if I lost you..."

"I'm telling you this so that you understand why I'm not going to let Bria know we're helping him. It would upset her too much. She's shaken about the whole situation."

"I agree, you can't tell her."

"I love her. I can't stomach the thought of her stressing any more over Marco and the lions. Not after what she went through yesterday."

"I agree."

"I'm helping you because you're my friend and I'm sworn to protect you. But if this ever becomes about having to make a choice..."

"I understand." She walked, careful to keep her stance steady. "I can handle myself, Derek. I'll figure out when to sneak away to the storage area and grab what I need. Get this lion out of here before he creates a problem neither of us needs."

"If anyone can do it, you can."

"Hope so."

"I've got to find Bria. She's probably worried sick. I've been gone a long time." Derek's face glowed in oranges from the reflection of the fires on the lake, but his tension was still evident in his brow. "You'll be okay?"

"Of course." Alicia nodded. "Go. I'm sure she needs you."

"Let me know if anything changes, and I mean *anything*." He leaned forward and kissed her on the top of the head. "I don't trust that lion."

"I'll let you know."

He nodded then turned and began making his way down toward the lake. His hair, pulled back, stuck out in an unkempt mess. Bria was sure to have questions about what he'd been up to. He wouldn't lie to her if she asked him.

I'll have to hope she doesn't ask.

She watched Derek head toward the crowd of bears gathered on the shore. They parted to allow him through, many moving more slowly than normal, some hunched and limping. Exhaustion and grief had taken a toll.

And injury. The air was thick with the scent of wounds and bruises and pain. Even a bit of hopelessness wove through the air like a counterpoint to a melody.

Something had to be done. A war was the last thing the bears needed.

From her perspective high on the bank, the crowd looked smaller than a normal gathering, less imposing than the bear council meetings. Though the air was smoky from the fires, the smoke rose and exited through holes in the cave ceiling, keeping the air clean at the lower levels near the lake. She watched the smoky ribbons dance toward the high, rocky dome like undulating snakes on a warm summer evening. Only this wasn't a normal summer's eve.

Tonight, the shadow of much sorrow and death blanketed the bears. Many tears had been shed.

Alicia felt like a traitor. A wolf in bear clothing.

She protected one of the guilty who had caused so much death and despair. A lion who'd personally done his share of damage to her clan. Maybe Derek was right. Maybe she shouldn't try to help Marco.

But Tawodi's words slipped through her consciousness like a melody. Healing. Her gift. Her call in life—to help others, no matter their affiliation. She didn't get to choose. Any and all deserved to be honored.

Her heart skipped a beat and a burst of adrenaline pumped through her. She would finish what she'd started.

The way to improving the current climate was to do good. One deed at a time. It might not seem like one thing would make a difference, but all the little things added up, and who knew what would be the impetus for real change?

She had to do her part.

The lake burned with the reflections of molten drops from fire pits on the rafts and boats. Alight on its placid surface, each vehicle carried a contained fire or two on deck to represent a bear that had passed from this life into the starry darkness of the next. Seeing the number of bears that had given everything so that Deep Creek would remain theirs humbled her.

Each fire, a soul. Each soul, a fire.

So many. Too many to count.

The physical bodies had already been buried, but

tonight Elijah would recognize the losses and speak to the future of the Deep Creek bears. Were war and loss ever worth it?

How could it be?

What could a leader possibly say in a situation so grim? An optimistic outlook was much more complicated.

Sobs and moans echoed off the high dome of the stone ceiling and reverberated throughout the cavern like crying rain. Alicia's heart ached as she sensed the pain reaching its tendrils out to her, through her, clenching her heart in a binding that would never ease.

Brothers and sisters who'd never see each other again. Fathers who'd never open the door to a room full of family. Mothers who'd never cook another meal for their children or chastise them for playing outside and forgetting to do their chores. Grandparents who outlived grandchildren.

All gone.

The river of stars was full tonight. Maybe it would be some comfort to know that the bears were with their ancestors now.

So many fires.

She'd known the numbers were high, but seeing all the fires burning at once made an impact more than any written number of lives lost could.

All for a war that was pointless at best.

The pall of death slid through the air like a sickness shimmying over the top of the misty water, the fire's red-orange reflecting like blood spilled on the water.

Was it worth it? Was Shoshannah?

Was Marco?

Time would tell, but the price was great no matter the outcome.

Alicia headed toward the lake. Around her, her people. The people she'd vowed to protect and heal. Their presence, like a single soul, reached for her and pulled her in close. She was bear.

Family.

Sobs filled her and she stretched to steady herself, her hand landing on a firm arm.

Griff.

She looked up at the massive bear. His cropped hair and strong jawline did nothing to soften his intense personality. His face fit him. To be honest, she'd always been a little afraid of his gruffness. If he and Derek hadn't been such good friends, she'd have steered clear of him.

Amy stood at his side, her face hollow and drawn.

"Where've you been?" Griff frowned. "I went looking for you but lost your scent near the creek. I smelled lion."

Amy dabbed at her eyes with a tissue. "We were worried something had happened to you. We just saw Derek and he said you were up here."

"I… I…" Alicia stuttered. "I'm okay."

"He told us you went out looking for survivors." Griff set his mouth in a line. "Do you know how dangerous that was?" He pointed at the lake. "One of those fires could been burning for you."

Alicia sighed. "I know. I was doing my job. No different than you." She immediately regretted her words.

Griff growled.

Amy placed her hand on Alicia's arm and squeezed

it. "It's okay, honey. We were worried. Griff isn't the best at showing concern. Isn't that right, dear? You aren't mad. You're *worried*." She turned back to Alicia. "We're working on his teddy bear attitude."

Griff harrumphed and turned away.

Alicia smiled. Griff and Amy were such a cute couple. With Amy now selling her paintings at Elijah's general store in town, and with Griff's ranger salary, it wouldn't surprise her if they held an official wedding soon and maybe started a family. Well, maybe once things settled down in Deep Creek.

Life would go on after the war. One way or another.

"Find any?" Griff grunted, arms crossed.

"Any what?" Alicia raised her eyebrows. Derek wouldn't have told him…would he?

"Wounded bears."

"No." She shook her head and stared down at the small flotilla of boats. They'd mostly floated to the center of the lake, forming an oblong ring of fire, the light wavering and reflecting off the water. "Not a single one." That wasn't lying, now was it? She hadn't found any bears.

She'd found a wounded and very sexy lion. One who could completely upset her place in her own clan if she didn't get him on his way soon.

"Pity. We lost too many friends in this pointless battle. Would've been good news to hear of a rescue." Griff looked to Amy. "We'd better get back down to the lake before Elijah starts. I want to know what his plan for retaliation is. We've got to take care of those left."

Alicia's heart sped. "You think Elijah will want to attack the lions?"

"I hope so." Griff's eyes flashed with hatred.

Alicia nodded. The lions *had* attacked without obvious cause. Of course the bears were upset. Elijah was patient, but he'd been tested by the attack, and he'd lost so many. Retaliation was fair, right?

No, it's got to stop. Someone has to be first.

"I'm glad you're safe, Alicia. We really were worried." Amy patted her arm.

"Thank you." Alicia gazed at the boats, now forming a perfect circle of fire.

"We should go." Griff blew out a long breath.

"I dread it." Amy grimaced. "It's not going to be easy for Elijah tonight."

"He can handle this. He's the best leader we've ever had." Griff growled. "Never doubt his strength, Amy. He's led the bears through many rough times and this is no different. Are you coming, Alicia?"

"I'll join you shortly. I need a few minutes to gather my thoughts before I have to face everyone." She redid her hair tie, sliding the ponytail closer to her head. "I'll be there in a few. I promise."

"You know where we'll be." Griff took Amy by the hand and led her down the rocky path toward the beach.

As they were walking, Amy turned and waved, shooting Alicia a genuine smile that seemed to radiate a happiness that came from deep inside, even though her face was puffed with sadness. Alicia smiled back. If she could trust anyone besides Derek with the information about Marco, it'd be Amy. She'd help her with anything she needed. The human had blended in with the clan more easily than anyone would have ever imagined.

It was like she was destined to be part of Deep Creek, and in a way, she was. As Griff's fated mate, no one should be surprised at how well she'd adapted, once she accepted the bears. Griff had been the biggest hurdle.

Of course.

And telling Griff the truth was not an option. Even Derek agreed.

Alicia watched the couple walk away, a short pang of envy slicing through her.

Things were changing in Deep Creek. It wasn't that long ago that a human among the bears, living and being a mate, wasn't really considered. Now, who knew what the future held? Was it possible that the lions and bears would one day share the cave and live in peace, as Tawodi predicted?

After the fierce battle, Alicia wasn't so sure. Still, she'd heard tales all her life about the unification of shifters. Could it be possible?

We don't seem anywhere close.

Alicia leaned against the cave wall. Exhaustion nearly overcame her, but giving up wasn't an option. Tawodi was counting on her.

Tawodi told stories that Shoshannah had once led all the shifters as one community. Were the stories true? Everyone knew Shoshannah could take on the form of any shifter she wished, and she always took care of the dead. Maybe it wasn't a reach to think she'd try to unite the shifters again, this time under different circumstances and a modern life.

Alicia sighed and headed toward the lakeshore. For now, at least, bears and lions remained enemies.

Too many fires burned in memories tonight and that wouldn't change anytime soon. It would be a long time before the bears or lions forgot solstice and the battle that had taken so many, including the leader of the Sen Pal.

Right now, she had a very real problem on her hands.

Chapter Six

Marco opened his eyes but yellow and gray fuzziness
blurred his vision.

Am I blind? His head pounded with the worst headache of his life, and he groaned. He tried to sit up but
only made it a few inches before slamming back to the
ground, too weak to hold himself upright, compound-
ing the agony in his side.

Tears filled his eyes and he blinked them away, his
vision still blurry.

Where am I?

Pain seared through his shoulder, rivaling his headache, and his vision blacked like someone had thrown
a blanket over his head. Nausea rolled over him and
he retched.

What the hell had happened? He opened his eyes
again, slowly, and his vision swam into a tenuous focus.
In the half-light he saw the dome of stone over him.

"Holy fuck." His voice echoed off the room's walls.
At least his captors hadn't gagged him. He was a prisoner, but where?

A vision of being struck by a bullet replayed in his
mind, the force of the memory crashing into him like

a streak of lightning on a tall tree. The summer sun bearing down on him, sweat and blood and tears, the battle, crawling off to hide lest he be sought out by the bears and put out of his misery. He closed his eyes, inhaling shallowly to curtail the intense pain a deep breath caused.

Perhaps I'm dead. Or a prisoner.

Death likely wouldn't hurt, so it must be the latter. If he were with his brother, he'd be in a soft bed and getting his injuries tended by the best medical treatment available.

No, he was in deep shit in Deep Creek.

He lay still, eyes closed, assessing the situation. His shoulder throbbed with each heartbeat, and a burning heat ravished one side of his body like a bonfire. He began to shiver and shake. He couldn't stop, and the chattering of his teeth added to the never-ending headache. One by one he moved his toes in his boots. Everything seemed to work down there. Onto his fingers. One hand, fine. The other...

Shit!

The pain intensified and he stopped. Something was wrong on that side. He could move but he damn sure didn't want to. The bullet had damaged him and his shifter ability wasn't healing it quickly enough.

He listened. No voices anywhere. Not even far away. Only a trickle of water, close by, and the buzz of something. Maybe some insects.

Maybe he was unconscious and dreaming? A lantern? Someone had brought him to this place. This prison.

Where's Mason?

He wasn't close—Marco couldn't sense him any-where nearby. Had he lost his second senses? He sniffed. Nothing but dirt and a bit of organic material he couldn't place. And dust. Really old dust.

No brother, no twin sense.

Something was very wrong. His heart sped, caus-ing the throbbing in his shoulder to pick up in speed and intensity.

What good would he be to the pride if he couldn't feel anything or anyone around him? His heart thud-ded. Used to being in charge, lying on his back in an unknown place and unable to move, he wasn't com-fortable.

He was helpless.

Unacceptable.

He reached inside to find his lion so he could shift, but the ability lay beyond his reach, behind a mass of dark clouds in the distance. He couldn't get close to where he needed to be to reach his lion. He'd have to heal more first. Thankfully, he sensed where his lion lay in wait. He'd heard horror stories of lions losing the ability or forgetting how to change entirely.

He'd regain his ability. His lion was down, not out.

At least the bullet hadn't taken that away.

The bullet. He'd been shot at close range. And it'd hurt like hell.

A flash of memory and he saw the woman—a human—holding a gun. And the bear he was fighting, wide-eyed with wonder that the woman had shot the lion. The memories were barely clearer than dreams, yet Marco sensed they were real.

He'd fallen after being shot. He remembered hitting

the ground and sending up a quick prayer to the gods that death find him quickly. Sure it was coming, he'd closed his eyes and waited.

What happened after he crawled to the underbrush? He didn't remember. All he knew was that the woman hadn't shot him again and he'd struggled to get away before she changed her mind. She'd been more concerned about the bear.

A drop of water splashed on his cheek and he peered up into the darkness. He assumed condensation in the humid room had caused the drip. He shuddered, hot and cold at the same time, his teeth clacking together and his shoulder flaming with a red-hot heat that couldn't be lessened.

The one thing that could make his current situation worse would be finding out Max or Mason were dead. He pushed the thoughts away. Only positive thinking would help now. The reality of things was simple.

He had to get his ass off the ground, and make it home somehow.

Immediately.

"I can do this," he mumbled. "I'm strong."

He focused on opening his eyes again. Slowly. He blinked. Blurriness filled his field of vision, then slowly, things came into focus. Definitely in a cave of some sort. Dark and shadowy, the rocks cast long fingers up toward the ceiling. Tiny prickles of light sparkled on the rock, like glitter.

What the hell? He must be hallucinating. Caves didn't have glitter.

Somewhere, a faint yellowish glow cast up onto the stony ceiling but he couldn't turn to see where it originated. At least he had a light source. The room would be dark as pitch without it, minus the sparkle from the crystals or whatever they were that covered the ceiling like miniature stars.

Had someone buried him? Walled him into a tomb somewhere in the forest, thinking he was dead? If so, why was there a light and a tall stone ceiling? No, that didn't make sense.

He tried to feel his body with his hand, but every move brought more shivers till his teeth were clacking together so hard, he ached all over. His hand brushed over a blanket. Wincing in pain he pulled the blanket up high to try to get warm.

I wouldn't be cold if I was dead, would I?

The bears would've taken him to the Cave of Whispers if they found him dead. That was a shifter courtesy—one thing the bears had honored.

Whoever had brought him here had left light and a blanket. They wanted him to live, at least. Maybe they'd torture him, but for now at least, they wanted him alive.

He sniffed and his heart froze.

He knew that scent.

Bears. Oh my gods.

Everything rushed his mind at once.

He was in a cave. *The* cave. The thoughts and memories tumbled into his brain in a tidal wave of information.

A bear had brought him here and he, no *she*, had wanted to help. She had been kind, even though they were enemies. He closed his eyes. She had sexy curves and long red hair and full lips.

Oh yeah, and she was a doctor too.

A medic or medicine woman or something. That explained the blanket. She was taking care of him. Her voice was deep, too deep for her thin neck and curvy shape, but it fit her personality perfectly.

Oh gods, she was hot too. Like sexy dream hot. Even when she was bossing him around.

Especially when she was bossing him around.

He grinned, then cut it short as the aches intensified. He'd never enjoyed being bossed around—he liked being in control. But the sexy redhead hadn't upset him. She'd been the one bonus in what had turned out to be a very shitty day.

Why the hell had he been paying attention to her looks when he was obviously dying? No doubt he was all male. He grinned, then groaned at the sudden movement. Served him right for having naughty thoughts while his life was in danger. But that was the epitome of his and Mason's personalities.

Live on the edge or you aren't living.

Alicia.

Her name drifted back to him and he spoke it in his mind, savoring the sounds as he imagined her leaning over him, stroking his hair and caressing his cheek. He recalled the warmth of her touch, almost like a vibration throughout his body—even though he was certainly feverish, given the chills and heat that racked him.

In his delirium, had he told her his name? He was pretty sure he had. *Great.* That was a mistake. She was probably telling the bears now that one of the lion leader's sons was her prisoner.

She'd said she was going to get the things she needed to remove the bullet. Could he trust her?

He didn't have a choice.

The cave was mostly quiet except for a trickle of water and bugs buzzing near the light. He listened for footsteps coming, but heard none.

Alicia hadn't turned him in to the bears. In fact, she'd said after she removed the bullet, he could return to the lions.

Was it possible a bear could be so kind?

He shook, sure he had a fever. If infection was setting in already, he needed medicine and he needed it fast.

Hopefully, she'd be back soon.

What a blessing pain medicine would be. Right now, he'd settle for anything to ease the pain ripping his shoulder apart.

The thin pallet he lay on barely cushioned the rocks, but it kept him from being too cold. He tried to adjust his position again, but his vision tunneled.

Who knew that getting shot would be so painful? He'd always thought he was so tough that he could handle anything, but right now, he'd trade a broken leg for his bullet wound. Maybe even an amputated one.

Nausea rolled over him and he gagged as he fought for control. If he could get to his compound, there were experienced doctors there who could help him. They'd remove the bullet with more up-to-date surgical equipment than Alicia had access to.

Escape was impossible in his condition.

Gods, how he hated being weak. If he could beat his fists on the ground, he would. Instead, he'd settle for a low growl. He'd never really been truly helpless in his life—at least not as an adult.

He decidedly did not like the feeling of being out of control. He clenched his teeth against their chattering. If he got out of the situation alive, he'd see to it that he was never in a position like this again. His vision blacked then came back into focus.

He closed his eyes. If someone or something was going to kill him in his sleep, then so be it. He wasn't able to fight, so what did it matter if he was awake or not?

The bonfire licked the night sky with thin fingers of orange and gold and occasional confetti sparkles of bright white. Mason stood to the side, waiting his turn to pay final respects to his father, Maximillian. His heart heavy, he'd never expected this day to come any time soon. How the bears could've done this to his father was unfathomable. No respect, even in battle. They'd ganged up on Max and killed him.

The bears were animals.

One by one, the lions approached the fire and tossed slips of curled paper into the flames, said a few words, then moved away. Low moans and sobs filled the night air and sadness carried on the breeze. A few shifted lions hung out at the perimeter of the fire's light, basking in the warmth and mourning.

Even though the calendar said midsummer, a chill filtered through the trees and the low-lying swampy area near the lions' compound. Mason shuddered and rubbed his arms. The summer heat was in full force in the daytime, and such an evening chill was unusual.

The rest of the summer would be hot, he was sure of it. He paced along the edge of the gathering, waiting his turn. It would be the final act of memory, one he would cherish.

Despite the sad occasion, Mason took comfort in

memories. His father had been well loved and most revered in the pride. He'd been everything a leader should be and all the lions adored him, or at least respected him. As a father, he'd been strong, loving, and had guided his sons on the path of righteousness. Tonight, the lions showed their adoration in the ritual to honor Max's life and death.

Mason had hoped his father would be around till he was older and his grandcubs roamed the forest. It wasn't meant to be. Mason gazed at the assembled crowd, somber and solemn.

Will they respect me half as much as they respected my father? Or will my death be celebrated? Mason paced, waiting for the lions to pay their respects. *Will the lions prefer my brother when he returns?*

The lions took the ceremony seriously, writing their private last words to Max onto paper slips and sending the messages up in smoke to the stars.

Messages for Max. Some likely asked for wisdom, some were blessings, and some may have been prayers. All were of goodwill, Mason was sure. And Max would receive them.

Mason had given a short tribute speech before the fire ceremony and after every lion had tossed their paper, they'd sit down to a communal meal in Max's honor. A feast fit for the king Max had been. They'd dine and tell stories of his bravery and honor late into the night—maybe until dawn. Mason held his paper tightly, crumpling it in his fist.

As Max's son, he'd chosen to go last.

Lara was near the back of the line. Tears glistened on her cheeks, and she looked almost fragile framed in the orange glow of the fire. Her shoulders slumped, and her hair was pulled back, revealing a long neck.

Vulnerable. He'd never seen her look anything but tough and ready to kick someone's ass. Tonight, she appeared breakable. The urge to take her into his arms and comfort her passed through him but he pushed it aside.

Ridiculous.

Mason watched her move toward the fire. She wasn't the hostile lioness warrior. She was all woman tonight. Mourning the death of his father.

Tonight was not about Lara, and he forced the thoughts of her out of his mind.

He flattened his slip of paper in his palm. Almost his turn. He'd not written much, a few words, in handwriting his father would have chastised him for. But the words carried weight and a promise. One he intended to keep.

I will serve your memory.

He stepped into line behind the last lion, his heart aching as the weight of the moment became real. If only Marco could be with him, the ceremony might not be as difficult. He watched the ashes swirl higher.

He had no choice. Marco wasn't with the pride and he'd want Mason to proceed without him.

Tomorrow, the search for his brother would get into full swing.

Mason had sent a message to the Green Glen wolves, asking for their help locating Marco. If anyone could sniff out trouble, it was those mutts. No word on Marco's whereabouts yet, though, so facing the fire was what he'd do alone. He'd do it for his brother too.

The line shortened, and soon no one was between Mason and the fire. He took the deepest breath he could hold then closed his eyes, letting a picture of his father form in his imagination. He didn't question the memory that arose; he merely watched and waited on it to play out.

He and Marco were young cubs, and they scampered in the dew-damp green field, trying to keep up with their father, who wouldn't slow down for them. Yellow flowers tipped the long grass and bent over as they ran, getting caught underfoot and springing up behind them as they passed.

Marco laughed and jumped, and Max bellowed for them to hurry. When they came to the edge of the meadow clearing, they found themselves beside a beautiful clear pool of deep water and small waterfall surrounded by large, smooth boulders. Birdsong echoed off the stone.

They'd spent the day lounging on the warm rocks and taking turns diving into the cold water and splashing Max. They'd tried to catch fish with their paws, but were too clumsy to get close and had given up by lunchtime. By the time Max took them home, Mason had barely been able to move, he was so tired. Marco had leaned on him half the way home, and they'd supported each other as they walked, Max out in front acting like he was as fresh as he'd been when they'd set out that morning.

Mason smiled. Max would always be in his memory, a mere thought away. Accessible with the right frame of mind and a little time. He'd be waiting to relive all the good times, and the not so good ones too. The memories were there, held in confidence and sealed with emotion.

Mason flicked the paper into the fire and watched it flash as it burned. Sparks scattered from the flames, and the fire seemed to warm for a second in acknowledgment. He stepped back and waited on the fire to settle.

It was done.

Alicia sat on the rocky shore, watching Elijah move to the last boat, carrying his flask of lake water. All the other fires were out, prayers had been said, souls released. She crossed her legs and watched the somber ceremony.

Around her, bears huddled and consoled each other, the scent of loss and anguish strong in the air.

Elijah moved into the boat with the aid of the captain, who held his hand out to steady his step. She couldn't hear the words, but she knew Elijah was blessing the family for its sacrifice. Each life was precious. Each life a gift. Each bear taken in the battle, a testament to the clan's obligation to stand as one.

Her clan. Her people.

Elijah poured the sacred lake water over the small fire and the flames fizzled and went out, smoke rising from the boat like a gray vine, wending itself upward. The lone bear onboard the small boat wept openly, holding his head in large hands. Had he lost a son? A daughter? Alicia didn't recognize him, but her heart sensed his deep loss and she longed to comfort him. As he sobbed, the small boat sent ripples out from its bow.

Her heart ached to her core. Were the lions as devastated by their losses?

Surely they were.

She had a calling that ran deeper than her commitment to the bears, even. A soul-deep calling planted by the gods.

Healer.

She couldn't help the bears with their emotional injuries today. Today, she had to treat a physical wound.

No matter it was an enemy's wound.

Duty.

Tawodi had trained her to look beyond the injured to the injury, and today was the test of all her studies. Today, she would prove her heart's true intention.

She rested her head on her knees and wrapped her arms around her legs. Her ponytail nearly reached the ground as it fell over her arms, and she pushed it away. Her eyes drooped closed. Exhaustion was catching up with her and the warm air lulled her into a false oblivion where pain and bullets and lions didn't exist. She yawned. If she had the chance, she could sleep for days.

The medical supplies weren't going to retrieve themselves. She lifted her head and watched the ceremony with heavy eyes. Everyone was enraptured with Elijah's movements; it was a good time to slip away. She could be back before the final prayer.

She stood, brushed off her backside, and headed for the tunnel. She peeked over her shoulder, but no one was looking in her direction. Still, her heart hammered with fear.

What she was doing could be interpreted as the ultimate betrayal, regardless of her intention.

She wove between groups of bears away from the lake, walking with purpose and her head high.

The bears wouldn't suspect one of their own of trying to steal supplies, especially their healer. Wolves, yes, but not another bear. Guilt accosted her and she pushed it away. She was taking the supplies for a good reason.

Healing the lion might be the first step in bringing peace to the shifters. Or it could strengthen him to fight another day.

She crept along the passage, feeling like the worst traitor in bear history. The narrow tunnel was long and dark, and the medical equipment had been moved deeper to an area where they could set up triage bays as needed.

Hopefully, the area wasn't guarded.

The corridor was empty and she moved quickly, sliding her hands against the smooth rock that formed this branch of the tunnels. Carved a millennium ago by rushing water, the flat walls were cool to the touch. Sometimes the cave felt like a living, breathing organism. Maybe it was. Maybe Shoshannah was the cave. She paused and lay her head against the stone.

"Help me, Shoshannah," she whispered.

A rush of warmth enveloped her, like a hug, and she smiled. Shoshannah was in the lake with the bears, but she'd heard Alicia's plea. She knew Marco was in the cave and she supported his healing.

Alicia knew it as well as she knew she was bear.

She focused on her mission.

A simple surgical kit and suturing supplies were necessary, and a medium gauze kit, pain meds, antibiotics and narrow forceps to pluck out the bullet and any shards.

The scent of blood and the faint odor of pain still lingered in the air from triage the day before.

When she reached the alcove where the supplies had been moved, she found them unguarded. Not a bear in sight.

Thank the gods.

She went to work, gathering things from the shelves, cabinets, bins and chests. The bears had amassed a lot of supplies in preparation for war, and not everything was as organized or labeled as it should have been. Then again, no one had expected the lions' attack so soon. They'd been nosing around, but the bears weren't prepared for an all-out assault.

She grabbed a canvas bag from one of the wooden chests. She'd collected everything and closed all the cabinets and drawers and paused to go over things in her mind, when she saw it.

A white orb, bright and flickering in every hue of the rainbow, like a lighted oil slick, hovered in the corner of the room. Small, yet filling the room with its presence.

Shoshannah.

Heart racing, Alicia didn't know whether to drop to her knees or back away or run. Was Shoshannah now telling her not to help Marco? Had Alicia angered the ancestral spirit?

Why wasn't Shoshannah out on the lake with Elijah? Why had she come to the alcove at such a time, and to speak to Alicia alone?

Alicia stepped back. "What would you have me do,

spirit?" Her heart slammed in her chest and adrenaline pumped through her veins.

The orb grew larger and brighter, expanding in all directions until Alicia covered her eyes. Then the orb disappeared, flashing out in a bright spark of yellow light. Alicia blinked as her eyes adjusted. What had that been all about? She gazed around the room. Only boxes and bins of supplies. Shoshannah was gone.

Alicia saw it in the chair that had previously sat empty.

Her healer's bag.

The large tan leather pouch, fringed and beaded with the smallest of glass beads, hadn't even been in the cave earlier. Alicia had left the pouch at home, not expecting the surprise attack by the lions or the need for it in the aftermath of the battle. She'd wanted to re-trieve it, but there hadn't been time.

Though Tawodi wanted her to use her alternative training at every opportunity, Elijah preferred what he called "tried and true and modern" methods. She didn't carry the bag very often when she knew she'd be around him.

And she'd been stuck without it in perhaps one of the times it was most needed.

A pop of white light blinked in the room with a chorded chime that reminded her of the wind through thin metal, then a dark hawk feather floated to the ground in front of her, twirling as it made its way to-ward the dusty floor. it landed with grace, spinning once then stopping like a pointer, directed at Alicia.

A sharp intake of breath. Everything made sense now. Why hadn't she seen it before?

Shoshannah and Tawodi worked together.

Alicia shouldn't be surprised in the least. Grandmother Tawodi possessed a wisdom beyond her great number of years and an ability beyond even that of a mystical shifter. But she'd never mentioned she and Shoshannah had a special relationship. Tawodi was often in the caves, flying through the tunnels and bathing in the lake, but Alicia had never really thought much about it.

Shoshannah and Tawodi wanted Alicia to know they worked together. And that they supported her in healing Marco.

A rush of air filled her lungs and Alicia was invigorated. Nothing would stop her.

She grabbed the soft medicine pouch from the chair. The supplies inside would help as much as the gauze and sutures, maybe more depending on how much support Marco really needed.

She was prepared for anything.

After pausing to listen for anyone who might be coming down the tunnel, Alicia picked up the hawk feather and stuck it in the canvas bag then stuffed the bag into her healer's pouch and cinched it.

She stood tall, all bear in human form. Straight. Strong. She could take care of Marco.

Her path couldn't be clearer.

No one would question her carrying her healing bag as she walked back through the crowd gathered lakeside. The bears saw her with the bag all the time. Elijah might grouse but he was pretty busy already.

The bag contained her amulets and stones and crystals, plus a supply of herbs and special wood and other things necessary for ceremonial healing and calling spirits and cleansing. She carried a few of her personal amulets too. Carved a millennium ago, the items were some of her most cherished.

Grandmother was brilliant, and with Shoshannah's help, there wasn't much chance of failure in healing Marco.

The gods smiled on her and she would not let anyone down.

"Thank you, Grandmother Tawodi and Shoshannah," Alicia whispered.

Go to him. The words formed in her mind. *He's weakening.*

She took a deep breath, her tensions nearly gone, and headed down the corridor to the lake.

She hummed as she approached the lake, stepping out into the cavernous room just in time to see Shoshannah's light show banking off the ceiling and lighting up the air. Millions of sparkles of red and yellow fluttered from a fiery burst high in the cave, landing on the lake and floating on the water as tiny pinpoints of wavering light, like a million spinning pinwheels on the water's surface.

Shoshannah romped through the air as a sparkling white bear, half smoke, half corporeal. She sang, but the words were in another language. Tears flowed from her eyes like purple waterfalls, splashing into the lake in discordance with her beautiful singing.

Shoshannah suffered. Like the bears and lions, she'd lost much because of the battle. She couldn't possibly want the war to continue. Too many lives lost, too many people now fatherless or husbandless.

Shoshannah's purple tears drained into rotating swirls with the red and yellow lights like tiny vortices. The wind picked up in the cave, a giant hiss crossing through the air. Everyone held their ears and stared, wide-eyed, as Shoshannah screamed, the sound echoing through the caverns and piercing Alicia's heart.

The spirit was hurting for the great losses.

Alicia stared, mouth open, unsure of what to do. She glanced around. What were the other bears doing? Were any of them knowledgeable about how to soothe the bear spirit? No, everyone remained in shock. Some even hid or cowered on shore. No one wanted the wrath of the spirit turning on them.

Shoshannah's cries turned to sobs and sighs, and she pawed at her face as she wept.

No one knew how to make her feel better and her suffering reached every bear. On shore, Elijah hung his head. Shoshannah stopped, hovering over the lake, her reflection like cotton, white and pure, then she faded into a fog-shaped white bear with eyes like blue diamonds, faceted and crystalline, piercing through the dim light of the cave.

Her voice came from everywhere and nowhere as she spoke.

My bears. I love you.

Alicia crept onto the rocky beach so she could hear Elijah respond.

Elijah wiped a tear away and stared at the ground. Alicia's heart seized at the pain on his face. She wasn't used to seeing the old bear hurting. He was always the strength of the clan. The powerful force that held them all together, even during tough times.

Shoshannah blew a cool, purple wind across the lake, her form fading. *Elijah...*

"Shoshannah, we are at your mercy!" His head jerked up and he raised his arms. "Help us."

Elijah, you must find the path...

Shoshannah flew around the cave in swirl of white and the sound of rain, a trail of color behind her like a smudged painting. With a *pop* she was gone, and the only color left was the deep gray of the cave walls. The air stilled, and the only sound was the slow drip of water onto stone from an outcropping somewhere in the cave. No one moved. Alicia held her breath.

With no specific guidance, what would Elijah do? He needed Shoshannah.

He heaved a great sigh and clasped his hands behind his back. For perhaps the first time, Alicia noticed how age had caught up with him. He wasn't the youthful bear she once brought tea to or practiced bandaging while he played a board game with Derek and Griff. No, Elijah was an old bear. His stance, stooped. His demeanor, almost one of resignation.

How he remained so strong and in charge of the clan was a miracle. His shoulders slumped and his back hunched and yet he stood before them, representing all the bears who'd lost their lives, and all the bears that remained. So many would be lost without his leadership.

She didn't want to admit it, but his days were numbered. What would happen then? With Maximillan gone, the old shifter guard was changing. What would it all mean?

Griff stepped from the crowd, hands on hips. "We can handle the lions, Elijah. We need a little time to recover, but if we hit back soon, while they are still weak from this battle, we have a good chance." His face glowed with angry passion.

Amy looked up at him with a mixture of worry and love. Griff meant everything he said. He wanted to attack. Alicia recognized that look.

Elijah shook his head. "No. Though revenge is heavy in our hearts and in our minds, we have to remember that we bears did not want this war. The cunning lions along with the sly wolves have forced us to take up arms against other shifters." He motioned around the cave. "But now is not the time to be impulsive. We still have the defensible position, the upper hand. We defend, no attack."

"We need to take them out." Griff set his jaw, the muscle flexing.

"We need to stop the war. But not tonight."

A few other bears gathered in close, murmuring about the attack.

"I think the lions learned that we aren't as weak as they thought." Griff crossed his arms.

"I agree," Derek said. "We ran them off. Maybe they won't be back any time soon."

Bria smiled and leaned on Derek and he put his arm around her.

A few bears clapped. Alicia watched the crowd, seeing the fire to protect what was theirs still alight in the bears' eyes.

She tugged her medicine bag up on her shoulder and held the strap tightly. She could feel it deep inside that his healing was somehow critical to the war. He was the key to something; she didn't know what.

But she'd find out.

She slipped out of the crowd and hurried toward the corridor that led back to where Marco lay. He needed her right now, and she was on a mission that both Tawodi and Shoshannah supported.

As long as Elijah didn't catch her before she could heal the lion, she'd be fine.

Chin up, she marched down the corridor toward the makeshift triage room.

Marco had better be there.

Chapter Seven

Marco took a sharp, short breath. The pain in his shoulder shot through him with an unbearable heat, and he winced, clamping his teeth together.

His arm lay lifeless at his side, though he could wiggle his finger a bit so he knew the arm was still there. Any movement set off a pain reaction. How was he going to get to the lion compound or even out of the cave when he couldn't move without almost passing out from the agony?

Mason should have had someone come for him by now. Where was he? He must know his brother was wounded and being held hostage.

Footsteps echoed in the distance. He strained to hear, holding his breath to concentrate. One person. Small stride.

Alicia.

How long had she been gone? Hours? Days? Had she told the bears? He didn't sense lies in her words, but with the injury he might have missed what he'd normally pick up.

Never trust a bear. Especially a beautiful one.

The footsteps grew louder, closer. She was moving

quickly, but not running. He glanced around the small area to see if there was a weapon he could hide in case he needed it, but the walls were bare aside from the glowing specks of dust or whatever they were. Rock everywhere, but none that could be picked up and thrown. Not that he was in a position to throw anything.

On the other side of the cavern lay the bear's med-pack. Maybe she carried a gun. He closed his eyes. She wasn't dumb. She wouldn't leave a weapon behind. Plus, if she had one, she'd have had it out when she was making sure he wasn't going to try to attack her.

A fiery streak of pain branched through his chest like hot lightning, and he fought the nausea that came on strong enough to gag him. He willed the sensation away.

One...two...three...

The footsteps grew closer by the second. Should he feign sleep or talk to her directly? What if she'd brought someone back with her?

He held no power at the moment, and if she brought back a bear that wanted to kill him, Marco wouldn't be able to defend himself at all.

So be it. I'll fight with all I have, till the end.

Alicia stepped into the light. Like a beautiful apparition, she paused in the doorway, one hand on the rocky portal, her full lips parted and eyes wide. He caught himself staring. He shook his head to focus but couldn't stop gaping at her bright red hair and the way it flipped back and forth as it meandered down her chest in a long ponytail. Curves in all the best places, visible even in her dirty clothes.

"You're awake." She leaned against the wall, her

curves molding to fit the profile of the stone. A half smile graced her soft-featured face. "I'm glad you aren't dead."

He nodded. He was glad too.

"How are you feeling?" She looked him up and down.

Powerless was not a feeling he liked.

"I need…" Marco's voice cracked. He swallowed against his dry throat. Gods, he felt like shit. "I need to go home."

She grabbed her medkit bag and moved to kneel beside him, her hair swinging as she moved. After pushing her ponytail over her shoulder, she opened the pack and rummaged in it. For the first time, he noticed she carried another bag on her shoulder—one with fringe and beads.

Odd. The bag looked handmade, maybe Native American. He winced as his shoulder throbbed from tensing up when Alicia arrived.

"Did you hear me?" he half whispered.

"I heard you. I want you to go home too. But that isn't possible yet—we've discussed this."

She took out her water bottle. "Here, let me help you." She held the water to his lips and lifted his head with her other hand. "Drink. Slowly."

He drank, trying not to gulp. The warm water slid down his throat, washing away the dust and dryness that had gathered there.

"Better?" She tucked a stray hair behind her ear.

"Yes. Thanks."

She set the bottle beside him. "You're welcome. If you're wondering, the bears don't know you're here.

My friend Derek knows, but he won't tell anyone unless you become dangerous. He's the one that carried you here from the woods."

"I am dangerous." He coughed.

"Yeah, maybe on a good day. Now, not so much."

He growled. If a lion talked to him like this, he'd make sure they never spoke to him again. Alicia's voice held a note of teasing, and he wasn't sure if he liked it or not. A woman had never held him in thrall like this one.

A bear.

The pain in his shoulder was beginning to spread. His chest ached farther from the wound, his arm still completely numb.

I should be able to handle this pain. I'm Maximillian's son. I am strong.

"You're hurting, aren't you?" Her voice softened as she spoke.

He nodded, turning his head away from her. His pride could never know how his personal pride had been reduced to being submissive to a bear. A woman.

"I've got some medicine for you." She placed her hand on his good shoulder. "It should help."

Where her hand lay on his shoulder, heat raced through him. Not the painful searing heat from his bullet wound, but a soft heat.

A healing heat.

She gently squeezed his shoulder and he shuddered. What he wouldn't give to pull her close and hold her. The thought flashed through his mind before he could stop it, and he felt his cheeks heat through the fever.

Delirious. That had to be it.

She pulled away. "I was able to get the supplies I needed without being noticed, so I think you're safe. For now, anyway."

He tried to smile, still relishing the warm tingles her touch had brought.

"Are you going to tell them I'm here?" His heart strained at the thought. The bears wouldn't like him in the cave—even though the cave once belonged to all shifters. Given that his pride has attacked them and tried to take the cave away, he couldn't blame them. A wounded lion wasn't something that would look good in any light and patching him up would be the last thing on their minds.

"Nope. I'm not telling them anything." She pulled out an amber bottle of pills. "You need to take two of these. Maybe three. It's going to hurt when I take out that bullet." After opening the bottle, she dumped three pills into her hand then opened the water bottle with her other hand, wedging it between her knees to keep it steady.

"Thank you." His voice was so weak he didn't want to even speak. What must this beautiful woman think of him? Who could respect a man who couldn't handle a little pain?

"You're welcome." She held the pills to his lips and he opened his mouth for them. She cradled his head so he could drink from the water bottle and swallow the pills.

He winced as the medicine went down. Even the small amount of exertion exhausted him. Maybe the pills would help soon and he could gather his thoughts. Right now, all he wanted was to continue to feel Alicia's touch. She gave him…something he needed. Comfort? Reassurance? He couldn't exactly figure it out, but whatever it was, he wanted more.

She helped him lay his head down and brushed his hair out of his face. "Okay, it will take a little while till the medication takes effect. Maybe twenty or thirty minutes."

"Okay." No point in even trying to be in charge now. Marco was totally in Alicia's hands. He'd live or die by her care. All he could do was let it go and relax.

And hope.

At least Mason and the others weren't around to see him in this position.

Alicia poured water on a cloth from her bag. "Let me clean your face. It will help you feel better."

He gave a slight nod and closed his eyes. As the cool cloth stroked over his skin he relaxed, enjoying her soft touch. She wiped gently, from forehead to chin and he sighed aloud in pleasure. A fuzzy stirring in his groin snapped him back to reality and he moved his head away.

"Enough." He clenched his fist and willed away his erection.

"Okay." She set the cloth aside. "Let's take that shirt off so I can reach the wound better. I cut the shirt earlier but I need more access to remove the bullet. I hope the dried blood hasn't stuck."

She eased the shirt up his abdomen slowly, then over his head, trying to avoid touching his shoulder. Marco bit down, trying not to scream as she lifted his arms to pull his shirt off. He closed his eyes as she leaned close, her breasts brushing against his chest as she held his head and slipped the shirt off. Heat and pain mixed into a cocktail of misery and softness, and yet…he was aware of her presence. Close. She laid his head down and ran her thumb along his jawline.

"I'm sorry you're suffering."

Her words were as sincere as any he'd ever heard. Sincere enough to make him look away. She ran her thumb down his neck and lay her hand on his chest, lightly.

Those warm feelings from her touch returned in force, calming him and leaving him wanting more.

"Thank you." What else could he say? If he weren't injured, he could think of a lot of things to say and do, but at the moment, he felt pretty impotent.

She sat back and set his shirt beside her. Her gaze drifted over his naked chest, lingering at his stomach then continuing downward. He sucked in his stomach, wishing he could flex his near six pack. Mason's was much more defined, but Marco wasn't ashamed of his own either. He winced as his shoulder rebelled at his display of manhood.

Dammit, he wanted to impress Alicia.

He didn't imagine the sharp breath she took as she looked him over. Was it because the injury was so bad? Or something else? His injury wasn't below the belt and yet her stare had lingered a second longer there. His own breath hitched at the thoughts that raced through his mind.

"There, that's better. I can get to the bullet now. With your shirt off, I mean." She sat back. "The medicine should be helping soon."

He swallowed hard and gave a nod of his head to

acknowledge her words. The medicine was definitely beginning to work. A numbing dizziness floated on the edge of his consciousness, like a thick fog, and his lion napped. The fog grew closer, roiling and bubbling, coming in like a dark cloud to obscure his pain in puffs of vaporous mist.

"Have you taken a bullet out before?" The medicine fog was rolling in quickly and his tongue felt like cotton.

"No. The bears that had bullet wounds didn't live and yesterday was the first time I'd even been around bullet wounds. I've treated other types of injuries." Her tone was clipped. "And I've studied a lot."

"I'm sorry." He fumbled the words, hoping she could sense his sincerity through the drugs.

She stopped unpacking her bag. "Are you? Are you really? You lions attacked us, not the other way around." She scowled.

"This isn't the time to have this discussion."

"No. It isn't." She unfolded a towel and laid it beside her. "So stop talking so I can focus."

He watched her set out her instruments and bandages. So many metal tools to remove one bullet. The medicine fog was closer than the horizon, and his anxiety faded as he fell into the edges of the darkness. Operating in a dirt room couldn't be the best circumstances.

Somehow, he didn't care. He blinked through the dizziness and fuzzy vision. She was so beautiful. If he died, at least the last face he saw would be a beautiful one.

"Okay," she said. "I'm ready. Are you?" The color

had mostly drained from her face, leaving it pale and in stark contrast with her deep red hair. Her eyes, so wide. She was nervous; he could smell it.

Or maybe that's me?

"Do I have a choice?" Did the words come out okay? He couldn't tell. Floating on the high of pain relievers, he strained to keep his eyes open.

"Do you want to live?" She adjusted her hair back, making sure it would stay out of her way during the procedure, then slathered her hands in hand sanitizer. "This is not the most sanitary of operating conditions, but we have to deal with what we have. I'll try my best. I hope you know that. You've lost a lot blood." She avoided looking at him, but continued prepping the site with cotton dipped in alcohol, steering clear of the open wound.

"I can handle it." He continued to gaze at her face as she came in and out of focus.

So tired. He needed to sleep and his body felt like it was floating. With the pain at a bearable level, he relaxed.

Alicia paused, then rubbed his shoulder with a cold mass of gel. "Topical anesthetic." She squirted something on a cloth. "It will numb the site a bit. Nothing I can do for the inside, though. It's going to hurt when I dig out the bullet."

"Do it."

She picked up a pair of tweezers and touched them to his shoulder, near the wound. "Feel that? Or is it numb?"

Marco shook his head. "Numb." His lips barely moved. Whatever the pain med was, it worked.

He looked up at the rocky ceiling above. The lighted dots wavered in his vision.

"Relax."

A minute later, she touched him with the tweezers again, at the site of the bullet entry. A rocket of pain shot up his spine and exploded in his head, sending fireworks of agony throughout his whole body.

The world tunneled black.

Alicia moved the lantern closer. If only she could do this in an operating room or at least in a cleaner and better-lit spot. But she'd have to work with what she had.

She slipped on gloves and ran her hand over Marco's bare shoulder to examine the entry wound. He'd passed out, which was good. She wasn't sure she'd be able to continue if he screamed every time she touched him. Besides, even though they were deep in the cave, someone might hear a screaming lion.

She pressed down on his skin. No lumps where the bullet could easily be found so it must have gone directly into his flesh at a ninety-degree angle.

The mini-operation would be one of the most complicated procedures she'd done. Her stomach fluttered.

Marco was breathing. The pain medicine assisted in knocking him out. If she ended up digging for fragments, then him being still would help.

Her stomach tightened and she inhaled a shaky breath.

This is more than I'm able to handle, Tawodi.

She closed her eyes, as Grandmother Hawk had taught her, and drew in the largest breath she could take, then let it out bit by bit, imagining all the stress and trouble leaving. Blow out the stress of getting caught, of hurting or killing Marco, of another lion attack. Focus on the one task she had ahead. Removing the bullet.

Her thoughts clear, she pushed away the anxiety and forced her mind to relax.

Solitude. Silence. Serenity.

A whisper sounded, beyond her hearing, but inside her head, and she waited. Tawodi had taught her how to let things pass through her mind. Thoughts, fears, stress. She had to let everything go to move on and be ready for the task ahead.

Trust yourself, Alicia. Your destiny lies on this path.

She accepted the message as the truth. This man, this lion, needed her. She would be able to do what she needed to do to save him. Strength surged through her. She couldn't tell if the whisper came from Grandmother or Shoshannah, but it didn't matter. She knew what she must do.

Time to act. She glanced at Marco's face and truly looked at him for the first time. Rugged and handsome, he wasn't merely an enemy or lion. He was human too. And though his eyes were closed, the way he peered into her when he talked made her feel special.

Bright red, his cheeks flamed with feverishness. Infection was setting in quickly.

Angry, the skin around wound had a faint burned area and bruising where the single bullet had entered, and a black stippling pattern where the little bit of excess gunpowder had spread. She gently raised Marco and peered at his back for an exit wound but found none. He groaned but didn't come to.

A few flecks of the phosphorescent growth on the cave walls and ceiling had fallen on Marco's tan chest, giving the appearance of a constellation of stars in a warm summer sky. She blew the glowing bits away, then cleaned the area again.

Maybe the trajectory of the bullet had been straight and merely slowed and then stopped inside his shoulder without exploding into shards. Marco didn't seem to be bleeding internally, or he would've likely already died, even with his shifter healing abilities.

She pressed around the edges of Marco's wound, trying to determine if the bullet had fractured or if there were any fragments near the surface. A firm lump lay just below the entry spot, not too deep inside, against the bone it seemed.

She had no clips or anything to stave a mistake with a scalpel. He'd bleed out if she hit a large vein or artery.

Trust.

She picked up the packet that held the sterilized scalpel and tore it open. The blade reflected brightly in the lantern light.

She placed the scalpel just under the entry wound, then with a firm pressure, slid it across Marco's soft skin.

A small incision, lines of red bubbles following her blade as the skin parted. When the cut was about an inch long and the opening lined up with the entry wound, she set the scalpel onto the towel and picked up the surgical tweezers. Her hands shook and she focused on stilling them.

Marco hadn't moved, other than a random twitch or groan. His breathing was regular, almost like he was sleeping in a soft bed somewhere. He seemed comfortable. If he could stay out a little longer, he'd miss the majority of the painful procedure.

Thank the gods for small mercies. He'd suffered enough already.

She slid the tweezers in the wound, hoping to find the bullet close to the service. She twisted it and felt around with the tips of the tweezers. Blood dripped from the cut, but not too much—she'd made exactly the right incision and avoided anything too deep. The tips of the tweezers scratched against metal.

Was it possible the removal would be so easy?

She clasped the chunk of metal and tugged the bullet out.

She held it up to the light, its brass surface covered in rusty red, and its sleek casing dented. Amazing and scary that something so small could do so much damage. She dropped the bullet on the towel and sat back on her heels.

Whole!

She put light compression on the wound. Thankfully, it wasn't bleeding much and the bullet hadn't been deep enough that she needed to try to repair internal tissue. Shifter healing would take care of that.

How did they get so lucky? The bullet hadn't split or broken into pieces. If Marco had a broken shoulder, she wouldn't be able to set it, but he showed no deformity.

She cleaned the wound, put a bit of heavier compression on his chest, then checked it and decided she could go ahead and stitch the skin closed.

She pulled the curved and pre-threaded needle from a sealed pack and began running it through the flesh and cinching up the wound. Her hands weren't shaking anymore. She'd done it. Tiny stitches that would hold the skin together until he healed formed a line that followed where the scalpel had been, like a row of baby plants peeking out of the ground.

She was tying off the last stitch when Marco groaned, and moved his head back and forth. He chewed his lower lip and winced.

"Shit, that hurts." He squinted and stared at the ceiling then tried to sit up. "Where am I?"

"I took out the bullet but I need to finish stitching you up so lie back. Don't try to move."

Marco reached for his shoulder but she pushed his hand away with her forearm.

"Leave it alone. You sure are stubborn." She tied the knot on the stitch and clipped the extra nylon. The last stitch. She was done.

"It's hurting." He lifted his head. "What did you do?"

"You were shot. Of course it's hurting. You're in the cave now and I'm fixing you up, or trying to."

He lifted his head and tried to get a better look. "You're a bear."

"Yes, don't you remember me? Alicia. Bear medic risking her own safety by bringing you into the Cave of Whispers to heal you." She scooted closer.

"Thank you." He nodded. "Yeah, I do remember you. Just needed a minute to catch up. Oh, *that* cave."

"You're one lucky lion." She set the needle down then rolled up the towel with the surgical implements.

"Which cave did you think you were in?" Now antibiotics and shifter genetics could do the rest.

"How do you figure that?" His eyes, still half-lidded, searched for her. "I was shot and now I'm hiding behind enemy lines. I'd say my luck hasn't been so great." He looked around the room. "And this doesn't look like the cave I've been told about. The one with the healing lake."

"We're way inside the tunnels so the bears don't find you. As for your luck, you were left out in the woods and you would've died if I didn't help."

"I'll count my blessings." His voice quaked.

"We all need to count our blessings. The gods have shined down on us and let us live through the terrible battle."

"Yes." His voice, barely a whisper. "I dreamed my father was dead. I'm glad it was only a dream, but the battle memories have shaken me."

Alicia paused, not sure what to say. Yes, Max was dead. Elijah had buried him in the shifter catacombs deep in the cave. His spirit had joined the starry river already. Marco was in no position to handle the news yet.

"Did you get the bullet out?"

"I did. In fact, it hadn't penetrated far and I was able to remove it easily and in one piece. I was expecting to have to pull out a bunch of fragments." She smiled.

He started to sit up. "That's great news. I can go home now."

"No, you can't. I told you to stop trying to sit up. You've got to recover before you can take off into the woods. I'd find you lying on the side of the path somewhere and we'd be back to square one."

He grunted and lay down, relief wafting off him like strong cologne. He didn't fool her with his tough-guy act. She smelled his pain.

Her shoulders bunched under the pressure of the day. Good thing the surgery was over because she was sleepy and more than a bit grouchy now.

"What's next?" he asked.

"You need to rest. Also, you must take an antibiotic for a while and let your shifter metabolism heal you. Gunshot wounds are notorious for getting infected."

He licked his lips. "Did you think to grab me an extra shirt?"

She shook her head, trying not to stare. She hadn't really paid attention to the fact he was naked from the waist up, but now that the bullet was out she couldn't help but ogle his masculine form a little. Well, she'd looked when she helped him take off his shirt, but she'd been stressed by the bullet wound at the time.

No denying it, Marco was sexy.

"I was busy trying to get the medicine and supplies, sorry." She didn't want to tell him he could just leave his shirt off and it wouldn't bother her; that would be wildly inappropriate. "You should leave the shirt off for now so I can check on the wound. I need to bandage it too." Heat rushed to her cheeks. What was the matter with her?

"Thank you. I don't know why a bear would help a lion like me, but I appreciate it."

"You're welcome. Doing my job, Marco."

He grabbed her arm and held it. "Is that all it is to you? A job?" His eyes grew wide and the brown shifted to a deep green.

She couldn't look away from his gaze. "I... I heal people. Of course you're part of my job."

He squeezed her arm gently. "You've done a fine job. I know it's risky for me here. I'll be out of your hair by morning."

"Maybe you will, maybe you won't." Her arm tickled at his touch, and when he moved away, a cold chill passed over her.

"You got any food?" He glanced around the little alcove.

"You need to wait a little while before you eat, but I'll get you something soon. I do have antibiotics for you."

"Whee, thanks. Just the steak I ordered."

She rummaged through her bag and set the pill bottle beside him. "Make sure you take one of these three times a day. After you leave, I mean. I'll make sure you get them while you're here."

"Yes, ma'am." He grabbed the bottle and poured out a pill then popped it into his mouth and swallowed it. "Done."

"Don't you need water?"

"Nah."

Tough guy.

Chapter Eight

"What did you find?" Mason bared his teeth and clenched his fists. He detested having to rely on a woman to do reconnaissance work, but he had to admit Lara was good at it.

"It didn't take us long to scent him in the forest near the cave, but we didn't find him. He'd been in the area recently, for sure." Lara blew her hair out of her eyes and held tightly to the straps of her pack.

"We were *all* in the area. It's not been long enough since the battle for all the scents to dissipate. How do you know his was fresh?" He slammed his fist on his father's desk. *Dammit.* He'd hoped for better news, but at least Lara had not found Marco dead.

"It smelled fresh. I don't know. It didn't have an expiration date." She smirked.

He squeezed his eyes shut. He reached out with his mind, trying to sense his brother's essence.

Nothing.

Whatever it took to find his brother, he'd do. Even if it meant using Lara. He certainly did not have to like it, however. With the numbers of lions lost in the battle, he had no choice but to let women help. At least Lara was tough.

"Where did you lose his scent?" He glanced up and looked Lara in the eyes.

Why did she have to be so stubborn?

She looked away. She set her pack on the couch and straightened her shirt, smoothing the wrinkles. "Not far from the cave."

"Alive?" Mason raised his eyebrows. His heart rate accelerated, and he hated his body for responding to the stress. Sweat dripped down his back, and he clutched the edge of Max's desk.

"Yes. As far as we could tell."

Marco was okay. Alive. He felt it. But until he heard someone say it aloud, and then saw Marco for himself, he'd be worried.

No telling what the vicious bears would do if they captured his brother. The bears were bad news. If only the battle had gone better. If only his father had lived. He bit his lip to stop the quiver.

Things had not gone as planned and now were worse.

At least Marco was alive. Losing both his father and brother would have crushed him. He wasn't weak, but that would be a test any man would have difficulty dealing with.

"Apparently, your *twin sense* is correct." Lara pushed her hair behind her ears. "The wolves confirmed he was alive. They've been snooping around and saw Marco taken into the cave not more than two days ago. One of the big bears carried him in. We've got wolves standing by to see if they bring him out."

A sizzle of anger bolted up Mason's spine. The bears had his brother.

"Can we trust the wolves to watch for him? They aren't exactly at the top of my list for honest allies." Mason paced. "They'd turn on us in a heartbeat if they thought it'd be to their advantage."

Lara nodded and quirked an eyebrow. "So far, the wolves want to help us and as long as we keep feeding them, they'll continue to help."

"I don't like dealing with them. Owing them. They're the best option—but only till we are ready to move in and get my brother back."

"Agreed."

Mason stopped and peered at the wall over the giant fireplace in Max's den. Photos of him and Marco lined the entire length of the eight-foot hewn mantel. Pictures of them as children, as adolescents, and even as babies. No photos of their mother or even Max, save one headshot the lion had done for a portrait session he'd never completed.

Max's sentimentality and love for his sons was unrivaled and showed in every nook of his house. He may have seemed like a hardass, but he loved his twins. Mason held back the tears forming, swallowing the lump in his throat.

"There's more." Lara sat on the plush chair and leaned forward, her hair curtaining her face. "Marco is injured. We scented fresh blood that was definitely his. He was shot, from what we could tell."

"But the bears took him into the cave, alive." A sick feeling settled in his stomach. The situation was not good.

"That's what the wolves said. I assume Marco was shot during the battle and the bears found him later. Maybe they are tending his injuries."

"Maybe." Mason growled a low growl. His lion paced, panting. Wanting out. "He's the perfect lion prisoner and bargaining chip." If Marco had been well, he'd have escaped the bears and made it back to the lion compound on his own by now. The bears must have him restrained and guarded.

"Well, let's hope the bears are smart enough to realize his value." Lara rubbed her face.

"How bad was he hurt?"

Lara shrugged. "I don't know. He's alive."

"We have to get him out of there before the bears decide he's of no use to them." He stuck his hands in his pockets. The cave would be a difficult place for a rescue.

"I agree we need a rescue mission, though I think we have a little time to figure it out." Lara crossed her legs. "It's going to take a large offensive move to rescue him. The cave system is so large and we don't know it like the bears do."

"We have to try. I won't leave my brother to die."

"We can't go in half-cocked or we'll be slaughtered."

"Don't you think I'm aware of that?" He sneered.

"One more thing." Lara's voice cracked and she twisted her hands together, not meeting his gaze.

"What?" He almost felt bad at the sharp tone in his voice. Lara had found out some good information, and he shouldn't be so short with her, but his nerves were frayed and jagged.

He blew out a long breath before looking at her

again. She appeared so small, sitting on his father's chair. If times were different, he might even be attracted to the lioness. He shook his head.

Focus.

Lara's information would prove vital in recovering his brother. For that, he did owe her a thank-you at least. He softened his tone and repeated, "What else?"

She peered up at him, her features softening. "One of the wolves overheard two of the bears talking."

"Where?" He moved closer.

"By the cave. They didn't see us. They were almost arguing and didn't even scent the wolves."

"Go on." He didn't take his gaze away from her. "Tell me!"

Lara stood and walked the length of the room, clasping her hands together and not stopping to meet his gaze. "The healer bear—the one the wolves call witch. She was talking to one of the rangers about Marco. Apparently, she's the one taking care of him." She paused and turned.

He frowned, taking a step back from Lara. "I don't want that witch touching him." He clenched his fists, marking his palms with the imprint of his fingernails.

He hadn't run into the bear-witch in a long time, but had no use for her wacky ideas.

Lara shrugged. "The wolf didn't say why. Only that it sounded like not all the bears know Marco is in the caves. Maybe the witch is hiding him while she's taking care of him. That's the important thing."

Mason slowly smiled as what Lara said sank in. If it was true that all the bears didn't know Marco was in the cave, it was the best news since finding out his brother was alive. A rescue would be easier if the bears were oblivious to what was right under their noses. "Good news, indeed. They are likely keeping him deep in the cave."

"Somewhere apart from the other bears. Hidden."

"Yes. We need proof before we go in." He rubbed his eyes. "But this could really work in our favor."

"Yes." Lara yawned. "I'm glad he's okay, and I agree, we need to get more details."

Mason rubbed his temples. His head ached. Rescuing his brother would take a well thought out plan but it was doable.

"Go round up the scouts and snipers. Tell them all to meet me in the clubhouse tonight at eight. I'll have a plan to rescue my brother."

Lara grabbed her pack and slung it over her shoulder. "You got it." Hands on hips, Lara raised her eyebrows in question. "Am I going to be part of that plan?"

He stared at her a moment before replying. "Only if I don't have enough men."

"You're an ass."

"And you're a woman."

"Bite me."

"You wouldn't like it."

Lara flipped him off and stormed out. A minute later, the front door slammed closed.

Mason grinned. Lara annoyed the hell out of him but he had to admit that sometimes he enjoyed the verbal sparring. Especially when he won.

Which was almost always.

Looking out the large window, he scanned the layers of mountains that spread out in front of him like large waves on the ocean. Green with hints of blue, the landscape soothed him. High cirrus clouds puffed over the scene, on a backdrop of the bluest blue sky. Deep Creek. The lions' true territory.

The whole area would be theirs again soon, he'd see to it. His father's legacy dictated it.

As soon as he rescued his brother. A large hawk circled the lions' compound, flying low then high on the bobbing air currents. The bird shrieked as it passed over the courtyard where several lions gathered to talk, and Mason watched it soar toward the depths of Deep Creek until it was out of sight.

Flying was one thing he wished he could do.

He sat at his father's giant desk and pulled out the file drawer on the right. Though they hadn't gone into the caves in the solstice battle, Max had them study the maps ahead of time just in case. They'd hoped to take the cave from the bears, but things obviously hadn't gone as planned. The drawings of the cave system were rolled up and crammed on top. He pulled out the roll of papers, hoping to the gods that the maps were accurate. Otherwise, his rescue attempt would be a suicide mission.

He slid off the rubber band and spread the first sheet out on his desk. The caves from the east. Wiggly lines of tunnels and chambers and forks and water. Lots of water.

Somewhere in his father's pages of drawings, he'd find the key to rescuing Marco.

Chapter Nine

Alicia unwrapped a clean gauze pad and took out a roll of medical tape. Changing the bandage would help keep the wound clean.

She laid her hand on his arm, soaking up the warmth that radiated from him. "Why are you in such a rush to get back to the lions? In a couple of days, I think you'd be able to travel. That isn't long."

"I need to go as soon as I can. My brother will be looking for me." Marco stared at the ceiling. "He won't stop until he finds me, and it won't matter who's in the way. He'll kill bears until he gets to me."

"I thought you were twins?" She pulled her hand away then dug in her pack until she found the small pair of scissors she'd tossed back in after surgery. "You don't seem like the type to kill indiscriminately. Unless I'm wrong about you." She avoided his gaze.

He tensed. "We are twins. We aren't exactly alike. He's more volatile than I am."

"I see."

He cleared his throat. "I'm the heir to the leadership because I was born first, but we'll rule together. When my father passes, I mean."

She nodded. Should she tell him? *No.* He needed to rest and relax, not get riled up. She'd find a time to tell him. They'd had time to have a few conversations about growing up in Deep Creek already, but they'd avoided the bear/lion politics. She hadn't told him about Ria.

"He'll sense I'm alive, of course, and come after me. Pray the gods help anyone who gets in his way." Marco's voice trailed off.

"He sounds ruthless." Alicia shuddered. "Scary." In truth, Max had been a scary figure to her since she was young. He and Elijah were more like giants of the forest. Larger than life.

"Wouldn't you be, to save your family?" He turned to her, his eyebrows raised in question. "What's more important than family?"

"I wouldn't know." She set the scissors down and opened the tape and set it beside the scissors on her bag. "I don't have family other than an adopted grand-mother."

"Wouldn't you fight to save her?" He grabbed her arm, his thumb trailing up to her elbow where he squeezed gently. "Wouldn't you do anything to save her?" he whispered.

She slipped her arm out of his grip as tears threatened to spill down her cheeks. "I suppose so. Though I'm not a violent person." She moved closer to him and dragged her supplies. Of course she would fight, though she wouldn't want to. She'd fight for her friends too. Were the bears so different than the lions, then? Family came first for the bears, at least most of them. Yet the lions had attacked for land, not in defense of family.

"Family makes people do things they might not otherwise do."

"Yes. That's true. My grandmother is the one who taught me the healing ways. She means the world to me. I'd protect her."

Alicia took a deep breath, inhaling the healing scent of the light incense that smoked on a narrow ledge in the far end of the rocky area, its red glow punctuating the dark of that corner with a pulsating beat as it burned. The glow of the lanterns cast long shadows in the yellow light, nearly obscuring the phosphorescence dotting the cave walls. She closed her eyes and yawned.

"You're tired."

"I am. It's been a stressful few days. I need to check your wound again. I'm hoping you're showing a good amount of healing."

"It has been a long few days. I'll be able to leave soon."

"Yes."

"Your grandmother taught you to stitch up wounds?"

Alicia shook her head. "No. She taught me some things, but I had formal training too, kind of off the books. My grandmother, Tawodi, taught me the use of herbal remedies and the old way of healing. Like using the incense I'm burning over there."

Marco rose up on one elbow and sniffed the air. "It smells good but I'm not sure how it helps me heal. Unless it's magical or hallucinogenic. Though I'm not seeing any visions."

"Lie back down, please."

"Okay, Dr. Bear."

"Very funny. Hold still so I can check your shoulder."

"I'm still. I could only be any more still if I were dead."

"Now that isn't funny." She picked at the corner of the tape on the bandage. "You don't have to understand my grandmother's ways. But you do need to let me take a look at your wound."

"I'm clearly not going anywhere for another day or two, according to you." Marco pushed his hair from his face. "What's the hurry?"

"You want to get out as soon as possible? Then you need to let me take care of you. The last thing you need is a worsening infection."

"I'll be a good patient and lie here and smell the incense. Is it about time for more pain medicine? My shoulder is on fire."

"Yes, I'll give you more when I give you the antibiotic."

Alicia smiled at the thought of what Marco would think if she told him the whole story about the incense. He'd likely think, like the wolves did, that she was a witch. Tawodi had made the incense in the first fires of autumn, under a new moon, with chants that her ancestor's ancestor had once muttered over her own fire, made of leaves from the some of the same trees that still towered in Deep Creek. Tradition was strong.

"The scent is growing on me." Marco took an exaggerated breath.

The scent burned light and deep at the same time, and comforted as it helped the body heal and the spirit rejoin its place in the world of the living.

"I'm glad. Relax. This tape is going to stick a little when I peel it."

"I was shot. It can't hurt as much as that did."

"True, and now all you need is a clean bandage. You can handle it, tough guy."

Derek would be by soon with food and clean blankets. It'd been hours since she'd removed the bullet, and though Marco seemed to be doing well, she was vigilant for signs of anything going awry.

"So, I'm a tough guy?" He grinned. "I think you bring it out in me."

"Not likely. That gauze is soaked through. It will dry and stick then it really will be painful to remove."

She'd convinced him that he wasn't going to go back to the lions until he'd healed a bit, and gotten him to keep his shirt off so she could monitor the wound better, but how long would that be? The sooner he was gone, the better it was for both of them, though she had to admit, she enjoyed his company. She'd never known a lion and he seemed, well, like a normal person. A lot more interesting though.

She peeled a strip of tape from the bandaged area in a quick yank.

"Ouch." He winced. "That hurt!"

"Sorry. I tried to do it fast."

"It's okay." He spoke through clenched teeth. "I'm a tough guy, remember? I'm not going to be taken down by a piece of tape."

"Three more pieces to go. Hang on."

Alicia ripped off the second piece and Marco didn't make a sound. He stared at the ceiling and didn't even blink.

"Two more." She tried to remove the rest as gently as she could, but the tape caught in the sparse hair on his chest, and he closed his eyes as she pressed on his skin to avoid ripping the hairs out.

His pained face told her everything he didn't voice. The wound hurt even when she touched near it. It wasn't the tape removal, it was his bruised shoulder.

"Is that it?" He glanced her way.

"That's all the tape. Let me get a look at you."

"I hope you like what you see. I suffered for you to look."

"I'm sorry. I know this isn't fun. It's necessary, though." She peeled back the gauze.

Still oozing, the skin reddened with her touch as she cleaned the area. Puffy from manipulation, the incision was inflamed but didn't look too bad.

"How's it look?" Marco asked. "Will I live?"

"It looks like you've been shot. But yes, I think you'll live."

"Good to know." He placed his hand on hers. "Thank you."

"You're welcome." She slathered antibiotic cream on the wound.

He tugged at her hand and she looked up. His eyes had changed to the most beautiful emerald green with flecks of brown.

"I mean it, Alicia, thank you. You could've left me in the woods to die. But you didn't."

"Doing my job."

"It means a lot to me." He squeezed her hand then let it go. "I won't forget what you've done." His voice trailed off to a whisper, and he winced and closed his eyes.

She bandaged him in silence. How had it come to this, a bear nursing a lion back to health in the middle of a territorial war? She realized she wasn't really even thinking of Marco as a lion anymore. He was a person in need.

And he was in pain. He was alone, without his family, behind the enemy lines. Was he scared or was he really the tough guy? Maybe a little of both.

His dark hair fell over his eyes and she reached to brush it away. As she did, he opened his eyes and met her gaze. She stared, unable to look away for several moments, her mouth going dry. She licked her lips as her palms dampened. Marco's eyes, deep green…now brown…now bright green…locked her in and her heart fluttered. What was going on? Why did he turn her insides to mush when he stared deep into her—nearly reaching her very essence. She couldn't resist.

Wanted more.

He was a patient. She couldn't read more into things than that. He was grateful she'd saved him, that's all. Patients sometimes mistook gratitude for something more.

Get control.

Marco's pupils dilated, then angled into cat-eyes. She couldn't look away, nor did she want to.

"Come here," he whispered, his breath catching. "Closer."

Her heart sped as she leaned forward, brushing her lips against his, lingering a moment to enjoy the feathery softness of touching. As she was about to move away, he grasped her head with his uninjured arm, then slid his hand at the base of her neck, and pulled her to him, deepening the kiss, a low moan escaping him and moving through her in a vibration of pleasure.

She fell into the kiss, hungry for his affection. Need shot through her with such force, she would've fallen to her knees if she were standing. Her moan echoed his as she savored the contact.

Kissing him back was right and good, and she let him in, meeting his tongue with her own. His kiss was soft but persistent, and he took a breath and crushed her lips to his again, sliding his tongue over the seam of her lips and then delving deep.

Possessing her. Filling her.

She'd been kissed before. But the sparks that his tongue ignited sent electric heat down her spine and throughout her sex. She relaxed in his grip and let him lead, the ravenous energy between them keeping her in a stranglehold of pleasure and need. He moved back to look into her eyes again and she drew back, suddenly aware.

He was a patient.

On medication.

A lion, even.

Not able to look at Marco, she looked down, sure the expression on her face mirrored the confusion that consumed her. She wanted him with every bit of her being. It had to be an illusion, driven by her exhaustion and his condition.

He hadn't meant to kiss her and never would if he weren't on medication. Lions and bears...that wasn't normal. Maybe eons ago, as Tawodi had spoken of, but not now.

She'd taken advantage of a drugged patient. Grandmother Tawodi would be really upset.

She glanced at Marco, afraid of what she might see on his face. Would he be angry? Would he laugh? Would he act like it hadn't happened?

Marco smiled the biggest smile she'd seen from him yet, and she could have sworn his eyes twinkled, the irises green and the pupils narrowed into slits like a cat locked on prey.

"Why'd you stop?" He lay back. "That was exactly the kind of medicine I need to recuperate."

"I… I'm sorry. I have to go see what's keeping Derek. He was supposed to bring more blankets and some food." She stood. "I'll be back as soon as I can."

"You're running away from me."

"No, we have to have more blankets and I'm hungry." Her voice quaked with the need that still burned inside her.

"I'm hungry too."

She could've sworn he winked. "You have to take your medicine. Then I need to go find Derek." She grabbed her bag and pulled out the pill bottles containing the pain medicine and antibiotics she'd taken from the bears' supplies.

"I need more than medicine."

He enjoyed teasing her, that much was obvious. She shook out the pills and helped him lean up to take them, sharing her water with him again.

"Will you be okay for a little while? Hopefully, I can find him quickly."

"I'll be here. Not like I can go anywhere." He grinned. "I've never had a doctor with such a great bedside manner, by the way. I hope you'll treat me again when you get back." His eyes shifted color again, brown to green, the pupils dilating.

"You need to get some rest." She backed away. Marco both excited and scared her. Her own actions did the same. She turned and half ran out of the alcove.

Everything melted at Marco's touch, slipping from his fingers in long strings of molten glassy globs. He breathed molten air that tumbled, liquefied, from his mouth. He strolled barefoot across crispy grass that should be aflame, but instead glowed with an unnatural orange radiation. Heat consumed him.

The sky, painted in strips of yellows and reds and oranges, appeared ready to burst into a swirling lake of fire above him. Sweat waterfalled off his back and he removed his clothes, dropping his T-shirt, then pants, then underwear on the sizzling ground, each piece turning to ash as it hit. It didn't help cool him. Even the wind was a ferocious blast of heat, withering his energy as he struggled to go…somewhere? He needed to get to someplace but the memory glazed in the inferno of his mind.

Where am I?

He scanned the open plains of undulating brown grasses that crackled like wildfire as the stems rubbed together. He wasn't in Deep Creek. He checked his shoulder, touching the spot where he'd been injured. No sign of a bullet wound or even a scar. Sticky melting skin puttied against his fingers, and he left finger-print impressions in his own skin.

What the hell is going on?

Movement caught his attention. Dark spots on the horizon, growing larger.

A group approached on horseback. Should he run? Not a tree in sight, not a place to hide. Just burning ground and sky. He had to keep moving or he'd scorch his feet, so he ran toward the horses, his body moving in slow motion across the fiery landscape that wilted under the hot wind.

The intensity of the heat grew to almost unbearable levels but he had to know. Something inside insisted that talking to them was critical. Who were the people on horseback, and could they help him escape the nightmare?

Flaming balls of fire streaked from the sky, raining down onto the ground and igniting the grasses around him into pillars of blue-hot flame. Not much time left before everything would be engulfed.

The horses galloped closer, and their hooves didn't touch the ground as they ran. They pranced on currents of swirling hot air, billowing dust and smoke around them. Black and white, mouths foaming clouds of pure heat and eyes red-wild and roaming like unchecked electricity, they bucked and reared when their riders halted in front of Marco.

The riders, wrapped in dark cloth from head to foot, with only their eyes showing, parted their horses to allow one rider to come forward.

Before he'd even unwrapped his head Marco yelped in recognition.

Father!

Max gave him a nod. Marco couldn't hear him speak aloud, but his father's voice rang clearly in his head. The fireballs continued to pelt the landscape, thumping to the ground as Max spoke.

Son, we have little time so listen well. You and Mason are the only hope to save Deep Creek from what's coming. Do not fear the bears or the wolves. The threat that lies ahead will be even greater than the two of these. Prepare to fight with your mind more than your army. Yet you must win. You must save Deep Creek.

"What do you mean?" Marco yelled over the cacophony. "I don't understand. Where are we? Am I dreaming again?"

I'm sorry I won't be there to help you.

"What do you mean, you won't be there to help?" The weight of realization dropped like a stone in Marco's stomach.

His father was dead. He'd died in the battle.

Why hadn't he sensed it before?

Maybe the pain of injury had shielded the loss from him, but now he felt his heart had ripped apart. It hurt more than a hundred bullets would. He screamed as hot tears fell. Not his father, not Max. How would he live without him?

Son?

"I can't bear this loss!" He moved toward his father. The horses reared, blowing smoke from their nostrils and bolts of electricity from their hooves.

Don't come any closer, Marco. It is not permitted.

"Father!"

Max looked to the horseback rider beside him. The rider shook his head, his drapings moving like a dark curtain, and motioned Max to hurry.

You know I walk among the stars now. I can say no more about the coming war. But there is one other matter I will speak of.

"What is it? Give me guidance, Father. I am lost without you."

The prairie grass was mostly aflame now, and the horses shifted and whinnied, sensing the danger at hand.

Your brother will help you. You know this in your heart. And never forget I'm proud of you and your brother.

"But I need you, Father. You lead the lions better than Mason and I ever could. We'll do our best, but it won't be the same."

Max's horse whinnied, then kicked up its front legs.

Son, listen to me. Alicia is your mate.

Marco shook his head. "No! She's a bear!" Yet as he said it, he knew what Max said was true. Alicia *was* his mate. His injury had maybe kept it hidden from him but now that his father had spoken it, he knew it in his heart.

Bears and lions are equal, and you will have to work together to defeat the enemy that's coming. Max shrugged and wrapped his head again. *Learn from my mistakes, son. Don't believe what you hear from those who would keep you apart.*

Marco extended his arms. "I don't know what to do."

Hold fast to your mate, and you and your brother work together to save Deep Creek. It is your destiny.

Marco's feet were on fire, up to his knees. The burn consumed him but it wasn't pain. Heat and a crackling of nerves. Now it reached his hips, waist. Soon, he'd be ashes on the ground too.

A strong grip grabbed his arm and yanked, and Marco fought to pull away, darkness filling his vision, his father and the other horsemen fading as the heated landscape fell away and was replaced by darkness.

"Father!"

"What's he doing here?" The voice, faint, sounded underwater. "Who's his father?"

Everything was black, dark, yet still hot, like the ashen embers of a great forest fire. Where had Max gone?

Another voice, male, spoke in the darkness but the sound garbled in Marco's mind. He fought for consciousness with the pain medicine making his thoughts swim and the fire inside him tearing him apart. Heat radiated from every cell of his being, and he struggled to find his father in the vast darkness again.

Nothingness lay before him, and an overwhelming sense of nausea overcame him. The hand on his arm gripped him tighter. Marco struggled on the edge of reality and dream, trying to surface from the nightmare.

"Here's Alicia's medicine bag. What's she got to do with this feverish lion? Looks like she treated an injury." The voice was firm and gruff, from someone used to giving orders maybe.

Marco strained to open his eyes and two large blurry figures materialized.

"I don't know, but Elijah is going to be pissed when he finds out there's a lion in the cave."

The cave?

Marco's vision wavered, tunneling at the periphery into a black hole. The clarity of realization struck him hard. He was still in the Cave of Whispers, and Alicia had gone to get supplies.

Bears had somehow found him.

He'd been dreaming about his father. Marco knew he was dead and the dream had been a spirit vision. No time to analyze it—with the bears having discovered him in the cave, he was in peril.

Now he had multiple, major problems.

Not the least of which was that Alicia was his mate.

Chapter Ten

Mason surveyed the room. It was the same meeting space his father used, but somehow, it didn't feel as prestigious with him gone. The lions, many broken and still recovering, had lost much of their fire to fight. Rallying them wasn't easy, and Mason gripped the back of the chair he'd placed in the front of the room.

He could be as strong as his father. The lions needed to give him the chance to prove he could lead. It was his destiny and he didn't intend to fuck it up.

He scanned the room. Why couldn't the lions understand that the war wasn't over? Losing one battle wasn't reason to give up. One battle wasn't the whole war.

Especially with the price the lions had paid. They had to continue.

He held back a growl, not sure if he was angrier with the lions or with himself. Maybe he wasn't doing as good of a job as he should be. "We need to gather more intel. Find out where exactly the bears have Marco imprisoned."

Mason paced in front of the large whiteboard where he'd sketched out a rough drawing of the woods around the main cave entrance. He had studied the drawings of the mountain, looking for another way in, but hadn't found anything. Lara had gone over the maps too, pointing out a few places with promise, but they'd have to send scouts to check out the locations to see if there was an entrance to the cave system hidden in the depths of Deep Creek.

There had to be more than one way in.

"If he's in the cave, as you suspect, we'll never get to him," Lorne said. The hefty lion had sustained a broken arm in the fight, but was healing more rapidly than the other shifters, already out of his cast and into a sling.

"He's there. He's my brother and I'm not leaving him behind. We'll figure out a way."

"We weren't able to infiltrate the cave with our entire army. What makes you think we can go in now?" Lorne leaned back in his chair. "That cave is impenetrable."

"I believe there's another entrance, and if we find it, we'll have the advantage." Mason circled a couple of the spots Lara had pointed out as possible entrances.

"Don't you think the bears would know if there was another entrance? They'd guard it same as the main entrance."

"Maybe." Mason set the marker down. "Maybe not."

Even if they did get in the cave, finding his brother in the maze of caverns would be like looking for a cub hiding in acres of meadow grass. Nearly impossible. And the bears guarding him would be expecting some kind of rescue attempt.

"How do we even know he's still alive?" Brandon, one of the sleek and muscled lions, asked. "The bears haven't asked for ransom or a trade. Why would they simply hold on to him?"

Mason scowled. "He's alive. I'd sense it if something happened to him. He's weak. Injured." He stared out the window, scanning the bright blue sky. "They may be waiting till he's well enough to share information. Or if the rumor we heard is true, only a few bears know he's there. The witch and maybe some of her friends."

"If that's the case, we have a better shot." Lorne leaned forward. "But we'll still face bears on their own turf. It's not going to be easy."

"We'll need to be prepared to carry him out, in case he's unable to walk." Brandon slouched in his chair. "Take in a stretcher or plan to fireman-carry him. We need enough manpower for this to be successful."

"Yes." Mason scratched his head. "Smart thinking."

"If we could get the bears out of the cave for a while." Brandon stood and paced.

Fire burned in Mason's gut and traveled up to his head. "How would we do that? Some of them appear to live there."

"Maybe we could smoke them out, like keepers do to a hive of bees." Brandon looked to Mason.

"That's a possibility." Mason grinned. The lion might be onto something.

The door burst opened, and Lara dashed in, her hair pulled back into a ponytail and her T-shirt and jeans clinging to her in all the right places. Mason felt his eyes shift color at the sight. All the lions looked her way.

"We're talking about the rescue." Mason kept his

voice steady, controlling the growl that formed in the back of his throat.

"I'm here to help." Lara turned to sit on the sofa between two of the younger lions, and they scrambled to make room, blushing at her closeness. She crossed one leg underneath her then shot Mason a glare. "Got a problem with that?"

He needed her.

"No. Sit." He turned to the whiteboard and the drawn map. "As I was saying, we need to collect more information. I've studied my father's maps. I'd imagine Marco is being kept pretty far inside since we don't think Elijah knows he's there."

"Should we send out our scouts?" One of the younger lions piped up. "Maybe they can find out where he is being kept and how to reach him."

"We should send the wolves." Lara leaned back on the couch and crossed her legs. All eyes turned to her. "They have a lot more access to the area around the cave than we do. If the bears scent a bunch of lions sniffing around, they'll up their defenses and we won't have a chance. If they scent the wolves, they won't be as concerned."

"Can we trust the wolves?" Brandon asked.

"We don't have to trust them if one of us goes with them. They can be handled." Lara tightened her ponytail. "If they think they will profit from helping us, they will help."

"She's right," Mason said through gritted teeth. "Lara and a couple wolves went last time and gathered the information we have now. Let's get the wolves to see what they can find out. I'll have to figure out a payment to them."

"Claude is on speed dial." Lara waved her phone in the air.

"I'm sure he is," Mason snarled. "I'll take care of it. I don't want the whole pack hanging out by the cave. I'll get them to head out there tonight."

"They'll probably want me to go with them." Lara smiled. "Or maybe you do."

"I'll let you know as I have more information. But know this. We will get my brother back. No matter what it takes."

Alicia hurried to the alcove with a small stack of blankets. Her footsteps echoed in the empty cavern, the only other sound the screech of the swinging lantern she carried and an occasional drip of water from the cave ceiling onto the rocks below. She'd missed Marco, and that surprised her. Whether it was that she had a patient under her care or that she missed him specifically, she didn't know, but she couldn't wait to get back and make sure he was okay.

She padded along as quietly as she could, knowing she was making too much noise if any bears were around. Getting caught right now would be a very bad thing.

She thought about seeing Marco earlier. The kiss still puzzled her but she'd about convinced herself that he was confused by his pain level or maybe hallucinating. What else could explain a lion kissing her?

Still, it had been nice.

Who was she kidding? It had been wonderful and

she'd repeat it in a heartbeat if she had the chance. Even though he was a lion. And she wasn't hallucinating or on pain medicine.

Nearing the alcove, she slowed. The blankets, heavy in her arms, were bulky and the lantern added to the weight. Why hadn't Derek shown up with the supplies like he'd said he would? She hadn't seen him anywhere. After rounding the last bend in the tunnel, she stepped into the room, then stopped and dropped the blankets, her heart rising to her throat.

The pallet was empty.

Where was Marco? She held the lantern high to scan the room.

Gone.

She covered her mouth. "Oh my gods. Did he leave?" The lantern she'd left for him still burned, and her pack and medicine bag lay where she left them. He didn't have the strength to leave on his own. Not without serious help. Not yet. He'd improved a lot but still, he couldn't get out on his own, nor did he know the way.

She grabbed up her bag and pulled it over her shoulder. The pallet on the floor where he'd been resting was in disarray and his shirt and shoes were gone.

He'd run.

Anger flushed through her. She shouldn't have left him alone. The possibility he would try to escape was high, yet she trusted him to stay until he was well.

What else could she have done? And how did he know how to get out of the cave, anyway? The last of the healing incense trailed across the room, and she batted the fingers of smoke away.

"Shit!" He likely hadn't made it out of the cave. He

might have headed toward the lake and… Elijah. That would be the worst-case scenario. If Elijah found him, there was no telling what would happen to him or her. Things would be a lot more complicated.

Running down the tunnel, lantern swinging, Alicia hurried to find him. A trace of Marco's scent hung in the air. And his fear and pain. She scented bears too, but since she was in human form, the scents were faint. No time to shift, she headed toward the main cave, hoping to search the side rooms and find him there hiding before Elijah or the other bears caught him in the lake cavern.

If they didn't already have him.

As she neared the lake, a cacophony of voices became clearer. The bears had gathered again. For what?

Lots of unhappy voices in one of the rooms near the lake. Angry voices. Some shouting and many upset bears. She paused to listen to the hullabaloo. Something about a lion in the cave.

An injured lion.

Oh gods.

Marco.

She stopped to gather her thoughts. This was bad. Really bad. Exactly what Derek had warned her might happen. She had to continue—she couldn't give up and let Elijah harm Marco after all she'd done to save him.

Elijah was going to be so mad at her.

She closed her eyes and used her visualization technique to calm down and re-center. *Breathe. Calm. Peace.* If only Grandmother Tawodi was here with her now, she'd feel so much better.

She let her mind drift to emptiness, counting backward from one hundred as she stilled all thoughts. Tiny sparks flitted up her legs and arms to her heart, lighting up her insides in warm blues and purples and the wings of crows fluttered all around her.

Warmth flowed through her veins, calming her anxiety. A thousand feathers floated down on her, stroking her face, her hands, her bare feet. She floated, dangling above the ground in bliss. Then Marco appeared beside her, smiling. He pulled her close and kissed her.

She reached to hug Marco but found only air. Eyes open, she sighed.

Sometimes meditation could be a real letdown. Marco wasn't with her and he certainly wasn't kissing her. Still, she had the strength now to face Elijah and the others.

With a last cleansing breath, she headed to the gathering, prepared to explain herself and convince them Marco was not a threat. He could be the answer to Deep Creek's problems. She was fulfilling her obligation as a healer and thinking about the future of the bears at the same time.

She rounded the corner then stopped at the sight. The room was a good size but not as large as the lake room. Elijah stood toward the front, his face turned down and not lighting up when he saw Alicia. Bears filled the room, and none looked happy.

She scented the heat rolling off Marco, but she couldn't see him with all the bears in the way. Dammit, he was getting an infection. Even with the antibiotics she had given him, he was burning up from the inside out and his scent had turned acidic, sickly.

"Alicia, you've got a lot of explaining to do." Elijah

grimaced, his towering frame somewhat bent. Exhaustion filled the cave. "How could you?"

Derek and Griff were among the gathered bears. Disappointment and anger shone on Griff's face. Derek looked defeated.

"I'm sorry!" She used to be one of Elijah's favorites but now…he might never forgive her. "I can explain. I need you to listen. It's not what it seems."

Elijah crossed his arms. "You mean it's not like you hid the enemy from us, using our supplies to heal him and giving him access to our most sacred space? It's not like that? It sure seems like it."

"It isn't. Not exactly. I promise." Alicia looked around the room and was met with scowls and judgment. She couldn't expect much different. After all, the lions had attacked and killed a lot of bears. Many of her friends and peers now lay buried, their souls returned to the stars in Shoshannah's arms. Grief fueled the anger billowing in the room. Where was Marco? She strained to see around the mass of bears. He was in the room, but where?

"What the hell were you thinking, Alicia?" Griff fisted his hands. "I couldn't believe it when I saw your bag beside the enemy. I trusted you!"

She ducked her head, her face burning in shame. Letting Griff down was something she hadn't ever wanted to do.

"Griff, you don't know the whole story." Derek's voice was soft but firm. If Griff listened to any bear besides Elijah, it would be Derek.

Griff growled. "We were coming back from deep in the caves and took a shortcut and that's when we smelled the incense. We knew it wasn't normal so we followed the scent to its source. That's when we found this lion. Marco. She couldn't have gotten him into the cave alone. You helped her, Derek." His voice was measured. He was trying not to yell, she could tell.

"I did." Derek met Griff's stare.

For a moment, Alicia worried that Griff and Derek would spar, but Griff turned away.

"He had a gunshot wound." She pleaded, "Please, it's not what it looks like. I wasn't betraying the bears."

Marco groaned and all the bears' gazes went to him. As they parted, she saw Marco, lying on the ground on a blanket.

"He's got an infection. He was burning up when we found him. Did you not treat him for that?" Griff growled. "Not that I care, but if you made the choice to save him, what the hell happened?"

Oh no!

She rushed to Marco and knelt beside him. She placed her palm against his head. Burning up wasn't a strong enough description. He was roasting alive. What could be causing it? He didn't watch her or show any signs of recognition. The infection smelled foreign, unusual.

He'd been doing so well! What had happened in such a short period of time?

"What got into you to treat this enemy of the bears?" Elijah leaned close. "I know your heart is soft, but this goes beyond reason. The lions killed our people, Alicia. You can't have forgotten."

She looked up at Elijah, tears in her eyes. "I couldn't

let him die. He's a good man. My oath to heal doesn't apply to only bears. You know that."

"It should when lions are killing us." Griff's stern voice carried across the cavern.

Marco moaned as he drifted out of consciousness.

Alicia stood. "Grandmother and Shoshannah told me to help him, Elijah. Am I to disobey them?"

Elijah's eyes widened. "Shoshannah spoke to you?"

"She brought my healer's bag to me and told me to go to him. That it was my duty. I obeyed."

The bears mumbled.

Elijah studied her then looked to Marco. He paced and no one dared interrupt his thoughts. Alicia waited, her heart in her throat.

Marco's fate, and to a lesser extent, her own, hung in Elijah's hands.

After a couple of minutes Elijah stopped and pivoted toward Alicia. A scowl still filled his face and the tension in his forehead could crack rocks open.

"There's only one thing to do with this lion." The scowl on his face deepened.

She swallowed hard. "What?"

"We need to take him into the lake."

Chapter Eleven

Alicia hugged Elijah. "I know you'll understand when you can talk to Marco."

Elijah returned her hug. He walked, motioning the bears to follow. "To the lake. Now. The lion may not have much time left."

A few grumbles sounded but the bears picked up Marco and carried him. Marco cried out in pain and Alicia winced.

"Please be careful with him. He's suffering." She moved to be near Marco.

"He's lucky we aren't putting him out of his misery." Stefan spat the words.

She'd never liked the preening bear but held her tongue. Elijah was helping Marco now, but the situation was volatile.

"That's enough, Stefan." Elijah's voice echoed in the cavern.

Stefan grumbled but didn't say anything else. The bear carrying Marco handed him off to Griff, who carried the lion with ease.

"I promise, Shoshannah and Tawodi wanted me to heal him." She walked quickly, trying to keep up with the procession to the lake. "I think they know he's destined for something that will help us all."

"Maybe." Elijah huffed at the exertion. "Maybe not."

She slipped her arm in Elijah's and leaned her head on him as they walked. "Thank you."

"Don't thank me yet."

"We did the right thing, Alicia." Derek's voice was soft and reassuring. Still, she smelled his worry. He'd put his trust in her and she couldn't let him down.

Bears with lanterns marched along behind them. She could sense the tension in the cavern, as if a coiled metal was wound and ready to spring at the slightest hair trigger of dissent. Scents of pain, distrust, and even hatred mingled in the air. Her heart thundered, and she realized she didn't want anything to happen to Marco.

She *cared* about the lion. Not as a patient, but as a person. Something about the lion drew her to him. Made her crave to be near him. As odd as it was, it was true.

Warmth spread through her, and she let go of Elijah and scurried to keep up with the bear carrying Marco. The lion, his green eyes a dull shade of brown when the lantern light hit them, looked at her intently then closed his eyes.

Oh gods, please don't let him die.

"Alicia!" Elijah's voice echoed in the cavern.

They neared the lake room and the ceiling grew taller and the cavern widened. She dropped back to talk to Elijah.

"Yes? What is it?" She tried to read his face, but he obscured his emotion with his infamous scowl and raised an eyebrow.

"I sense something, and I know you wouldn't lie about Shoshannah. But I'm far from trusting a lion in our midst. Especially the one that is heir to the Sen Pal leadership." He shot her a look.

"I'll admit, there's something about him that draws me to him. But Shoshannah and Tawodi made it possible to heal him. They must have a reason beyond what I know."

Elijah paused to step over a crevice. "I'm going to try to help him, but I'm counting on Shoshannah to explain. All I know right now is that he's close to death and it's more than a simple infection from being shot."

Alicia pulled back. "What do you mean, more than a simple infection?"

"Can't you smell it?" Elijah lifted his nose and sniffed. "There's something negative involved. Ancient. I don't know what it is exactly, but it's there with the illness. This is no simple wound infection. It smells almost...familiar. I'm trying to place it."

"Why does it matter what's wrong with the lion?" An older bear pushed to the front of the group. "We know who he is and what he means to the lions. We should hold him for ransom at least."

"We should," another bear responded from behind. "He's our enemy. Maybe we can gain something from holding him."

The group entered the lake room, and the voices carried over the water. Marco appeared to be unconscious but Alicia couldn't be sure. She sniffed the air, trying to sense what Elijah was talking about. The acidic smell tinged through all the other odors.

"His father led the raid that killed my son. Killed so

many of our family members and friends." The bear pointed at Alicia. "You should be ashamed of yourself for even considering helping him. He's evil, just like every other lion. Selfish and proud, they want to kill all of us."

"Leave her alone," Derek said, his voice stern and unwavering. "She did what she was called to do. Who are we to question that?"

Alicia's lip trembled. The bears were angry. The last thing she'd ever wanted was to upset them. She'd lost friends in the battle too. "I'm sorry. I never meant to hurt anyone. I was doing what I'm trained to do."

"No one trained you to heal lions." The gruff bear scowled. "I can't believe you'd help one after all the losses we suffered."

Elijah interjected before the bear could reply. "Shoshannah wants us to help this lion, and that's what we'll do. We don't question the ancestral spirit's motives. As long as she supports us taking care of him, we will."

"Shoshannah is wrong!" the bear shouted. "We should kill him now."

The bears stopped and turned to Elijah. Alicia's breath caught. Would he defend Marco or take the clan's side now?

Elijah raised to his full height and stared the bear down. "Don't ever blaspheme Shoshannah. Ever. As long as I'm leader, you'll do as I say and you'll do it without complaint. Is that clear?"

The bear mumbled and ducked his head in submission. The tension in the cavern burned Alicia's nose. She sighed. Thank the gods Elijah was sensible.

"We'll do what's best for the bears, as we are led by Shoshannah. Right now, we need to keep this lion alive until we know what to do with him. Anyone with a problem with it is welcome to leave." He scanned the gathered crowd and none made eye contact. "Let's get him to the lake. Move. We don't have much time."

The lake lay quiet beside them like a dark glass, not a ripple on its surface. Dark, unlike the night when the spirit fires burned. Almost foreboding in its presence. What if Shoshannah wanted Marco in the lake to take his spirit? Alicia tamped down her anxiety. No, Shoshannah saw something good in Marco. Worth saving.

Alicia looked to Griff but he turned away. Even with Elijah's support, she could tell that she had overstepped her bounds with the grumpy bear.

Alicia peered around the large cavern, looking for signs Shoshannah was near. There were no signs at all. No white bear, no white light. Water seemed to flow into the dark infinity on the horizon with no interruption.

The rocky room danced with the light and shadows of so many lanterns, but the light didn't reach the corners where darkness took hold and grew to the full height of the cave. The calm lake flowed out in front of her and suddenly rippled under an unseen wind. Was it Shoshannah? No indication of what to do from the cave spirit, but Alicia was certain of her wishes.

The pall that had settled over the lake since the battle remained, lingering like a chill that seeped into every crevice and crack, and the bears lowered their voices to whispers, remembering the release of spirits and the somber mood of the fire ceremony, and forgetting the bickering and anger of the previous few minutes while they walked to the lake with Marco.

Alicia shivered and rubbed her arms. Whoever waited patiently day by day for Shoshannah's message in the quiet chamber had stamina Alicia didn't possess. The room loomed so deep and scary.

Elijah kicked at the silty dirt at the water's edge. Alicia paused, as did the bears, to hear his command. He gazed out into the darkness as if waiting on someone or something. Shoshannah, maybe. Or maybe he was going over the situation in his mind again. Alicia clasped her hands together and fidgeted.

Would Elijah really allow Marco to go into the lake? Few lions went in that weren't already dead.

Elijah turned to her. "Normally, I'd say you should take him in, Alicia." He muttered something incomprehensible to himself. "Yet I don't think you're able to carry him. Also, if he does heal and start to fight, I don't want you to catch the brunt of the attack. I'll have the young bears take him out. They'll be able to handle him if something goes wrong."

"Yes, sir." She nodded. If Marco thrashed in the water, he'd take her under, intentional or not. Yet she longed to be near him. If Shoshannah took his spirit, she wanted to be at his side.

Elijah continued. "You follow them out, but keep at a distance. If Shoshannah appears and heals the lion or gives any direction on what to do about him, you'll be there to help."

She moved forward. "Okay." She slipped her medicine pouch off and handed it to Elijah. "Can you hold this for me?"

"Yes." Elijah took the bag and slid it over his shoulder then motioned her toward the lake. "It's time to find out what Shoshannah has in store for this lion."

Alicia closed her eyes and focused on Tawodi's words. *Calm. Peace.*

Derek took her by the arm and leaned close. "I'm sorry I didn't get back to you in time. I didn't know Griff would find Marco. Still, I think this scenario is the best for everyone. Everything is going to be okay."

"Thank you." She glanced around for any sign of Bria, but she wasn't with the bears. "I hope you're right." She moved to the edge of the water, slipped off her shoes then got in line behind the young bears that held Marco.

Marco's face was flushed red, and he jabbered words that made no sense. The bacteria had spread. Elijah was correct—there was something mysterious and dark about the infection. She sensed it now. *Bad.* Shoshannah had to help.

"Okay, you boys take him in. Alicia will be right behind you. Let her have him when you get him at about four feet deep, but stay close in case the lion attacks. The rest of you, stay onshore. We don't know what's going to happen, if anything."

Everyone moved into position. The young bears with Marco walked out slowly, the water rising up their calves, then hips. Finally, they were deep enough to let Marco float. Alicia waded behind them in the cool water, her wet T-shirt and shorts sticking to her. She pulled Marco close as the cool water lapped against her. Limp in her arms, she watched him closely. He was breathing.

"Marco." She whispered his name. Nothing.

His eyes remained closed but he wasn't babbling anymore. At least the cool water would ease the fever that racked his body. She held his head out of the water and glanced back to Elijah. He motioned her to go deeper.

With the high fever, Marco would probably be delirious if he talked. Still, at least she would know he was alive. With no movement or cry of pain, she worried. She pushed him a little farther into the lake, letting the water rinse over him gently. So far, nothing from Shoshannah. She peered at the shoreline, friends and people who didn't trust her alike, watching to see if Shoshannah would bless a healing.

They also wanted confirmation that Alicia was telling the truth. How would she convince them if Shoshannah didn't show up at all?

With her wet hand, she brushed across his face, hoping her cool touch would wake him. He opened his eyes and looked at her, mouthing something.

"What is it?" she whispered, tilting her head toward him, nearly cheek to cheek. "I can't hear you."

He mouthed the words again then closed his eyes. For a moment, she thought he'd died, but he took a big breath of air.

Thank the gods.

The water around them wasn't disturbed. It was still smooth and flat and the far reaches of the lake were concealed in shadow. Alicia sighed and felt Marco's head.

Still super hot.

She pushed him a little farther out in the water, hoping Shoshannah would provide guidance. Praying she would. If the gods wanted Deep Creek to survive, Alicia knew that meant Marco had to live to fulfill his destiny. How she was so sure, she didn't understand. But something deep inside her was adamant.

Marco must live.

A small white moth flitted across the surface of the water, growing larger as it approached. Alicia watched in wonder as the moth circled and danced on the line where water met air. The moth sparkled and glowed, like a white angel, and as it neared, a deep sense of peace washed over Alicia.

Shoshannah!

Alicia looked over her shoulder to the lake's edge and saw that all the bears had shifted into their bear forms and now they paced, waiting. Even the young bears who'd helped her with Marco had retreated almost to the shoreline, giving her the distance she needed to do whatever needed to be done. Marco hadn't turned into a ferocious lion when he went into the water, and she guessed they assumed she would be okay now.

She wanted to scream that Shoshannah was near, but she didn't want to interrupt the moment.

The moth was about three feet across by the time it reached Alicia and Marco, and it lit up the whole area in a greenish-white glow. Alicia looked to the bears again, and saw a bear gasp on the lake shoreline and another on hind legs, pointing with its paw. Elijah let out a long growl of contentment.

Alicia smiled. She looked her clan-mates over,

a whole army of bears from brown to black to all shades in between. They pawed at the ground or sat and watched, waiting to see if Shoshannah would heal Marco.

Magnificent. Her own bear called out to her to let it release but she hushed it. For now, she needed to be human.

Alicia held Marco close as she watched the moth. He groaned, still not opening his eyes. Though the water was lukewarm to her, it had to be a chill to him with his high fever, yet he wasn't shivering. He didn't move at all, but floated in the dark water.

The moth grew larger and began to flicker as it beat its wings to hover just above the surface of the lake. Shoshannah's voice sounded in Alicia's head like a million musical notes bouncing against each other. Melodic, yet clear and pure in tone. With nature's rhythm sliding through the middle like the chord of life.

My child. Marco is very sick. A powerful sickness holds him and keeps your peoples apart. It will take great sacrifice to keep him in your heart.

"My heart?" Alicia whispered. She lifted Marco in the water, his eyes remained closed. "What do you mean? And what's wrong with him? Why isn't the lake healing him?"

Look inside yourself, Alicia. You'll see Marco there. He's part of you. I can't heal this ancient and deadly bacteria that has cursed him—only you can. Go to Tawodi. She will guide you.

Confusion clung to Alicia like a wet cloth, draping her and confounding her thoughts. Why couldn't Shoshannah heal Marco? Didn't she handle the balance of life and death among the shifters? Questioning Shoshannah once she'd spoken wasn't an option. The spirit knew what she meant.

"Yes, Shoshannah. I will go to Grandmother."

Do it quickly, child, or Marco will join his father in the river of stars and that will put all of Deep Creek at risk. We need him for what's coming. Go to Tawodi now.

"I will go immediately."

One more thing, child. The choice you will be given will be difficult but it will be all yours. Think hard and long and let no one decide for you. You must make the decision.

"Thank you, Shoshannah." Tears filled Alicia's eyes and she tugged Marco to her. The urge to bend her head and kiss him almost overwhelmed her but she held back. Elijah would have a fit.

Even in the water, the heat from Marco's body seared her. The moth flittered to the top of the cave and shrank in size then exploded in confetti of white light, like indoor fireworks or dandelion seeds spreading on the wind.

Shoshannah was gone.

Alicia waded toward shore with Marco, holding him tight. The bears would have to take care of him while she went to see Grandmother Tawodi. Maybe Derek could oversee everything and keep Marco safe.

Deep Creek depended on it.

And she didn't have much time.

Marco opened his eyes then closed them again. He kicked at the coverings over his legs. His head pounded so much that nausea threatened, and his whole body ached like he'd gone through a pasta roller. Twice.

"Where am I?" He posed the question to anyone who might be nearby. No one was within his field of vision.

The last thing he remembered was kissing Alicia. Ahhh. No, he was swimming in a cool lake. Was that real? Maybe he was home with his brother and everything was a dream.

"Mason?" he called. "Are you there?"

"You're with the bears. We've got you on a cot in one of the makeshift infirmaries in the cave." Alicia appeared beside him, taking his hand in hers. "How are you feeling?"

"Like I've been run over by a truck." His voice scratched out the words and he clung to her hand. So soft, so reassuring.

"Have some water." She put a straw to his lips.

He drank, long and deep, the water cooling him. He pulled away.

"Thank you." He stared up at her.

Alicia. His mate. Beautiful as always. Her red hair was braided and fell over her full breasts in a thick rope. Her large eyes held compassion for him; he could feel it throughout his body when she looked at him. No one had ever had the same effect on him.

It wasn't his fever that made him attracted to her. His father was right—she was meant for him, and he needed to tell her before something bad happened and he wasn't able to. A memory of trying to tell her flashed in his mind. He was in the lake, and he tried to speak but couldn't get the words out.

"You're welcome. To be honest, you aren't doing very well. You have an infection."

"Don't you have medicine? Do I need something stronger?"

"You've been taking a strong antibiotic since I took the bullet out. Now there's something else going on. I've got to go visit my grandmother to see about an alternative remedy."

"For what? I'm not sure I like alternative answers to medical problems." He could barely get the words out. *So tired.* Every muscle on fire, every bone aching. Even his brain felt like it was full of hot water or fluid. He struggled to stay awake to talk.

"You're very sick, Marco. Shoshannah said I need to go to see my grandmother to find the cure. It's some kind of invasive infection—she called it a curse. Apparently, an ancient one. I'm sure my grandmother will know more about it and how to get rid of it. I'll be back as soon as I can." She squeezed his hand.

"Don't leave me. The bears will kill me." He tried to rise up but couldn't.

"I have to go now. This can't wait." She brushed his hair from his face and traced his cheek. "It's the only way to save your life. You need the cure to this infection and you need it soon."

He squeezed his eyes shut and shivered. He saw Alicia's face in his mind. Her soft hair, long and deep red, and her brown eyes that held a depth he could lose himself in. It wasn't fair that he'd found his mate yet couldn't do anything to win her over. He longed for the strength he once had, if only to be able to please his mate and make her happy.

"I need to tell you something." He grimaced as a shock of pain streaked up his spine. "It's important. Before you go, please."

She laid her head on his shoulder. The small cot creaked, and he reached to cup her cheek. What he wouldn't give to pull her into an embrace and never let go. He had no doubt they'd fit together like two pieces of a puzzle. Even in his sickness, he felt the bond of fated mates and it grew stronger by the day. How he'd not recognized it before Max told him was a mystery. Now, it was as obvious as the fact he was a lion.

"What is it, Marco?" She wrapped her arm around him. "I have to go. Shoshannah said—"

"Look at me." His voice cracked.

She sat up and met his gaze. "Sounds serious."

"It is. It may be hard for you to believe. But it's the truth and I feel it from my very soul." Heat burned in every cell, and every part of him seemed to burn even hotter. "You are my mate, Alicia. I know it sounds crazy—"

"What?" Her eyes widened. "How's that possible? A lion and a bear?"

He sensed her panic and wished he could hold her till it passed. "It is possible as all things are. I've had my own spiritual journey and this was revealed to me. Before, it was hidden by my pride and maybe my injury. We are meant to be together. Don't you feel it? When you touch me, don't you sense that we are bonded?" He held on to her arm.

"I… I don't know. Tawodi told me of a time when lions and bears were mates. And I do feel something with you, like an attraction that is so strong and pure.

If that's fated mates, then yes. I never expected a mate. Usually a healer is dedicated to those she heals. No time for a mate." Her voice shook as she spoke and she turned to check the room.

"No one can hear us." He winced as another shot of pain hit him in the gut. "I had to tell you the truth. In case I don't make it. We are meant to be as one."

"Don't talk like that. I'm going to find the cure, and Tawodi will explain this all to me. But I have to go."

He nodded. Relief filled him. She hadn't run when he told her. She hadn't said he was crazy or that she hated him because he was a lion. For now, he would hang on to those things. "When will you be back?"

She kissed him on the lips. "I'll hurry."

He closed his eyes, savoring the touch of his mate on his lips. He'd hold on to that feeling until either she returned, or he joined his father in the starry river.

Chapter Twelve

Alicia tore through the brush in the summer moonlight, her paws hitting the ground in succession, claws tapping against the stones and leaving trails of dust in her wake. She traveled faster as a bear, and Tawodi's home was at the far reaches of Deep Creek.

Must hurry.

Derek had promised to keep an eye on Marco and protect him from any bears that might try to hurt him—though with Elijah on her side, Marco was about as safe as he could be. Still, if something happened to Marco while she was gone, she'd never forgive herself.

She scampered up a steep hill, the dirt sticking under her claws, and tiny avalanches of pebbles and loose soil cascading down the embankment. Fresh flowers bloomed close to the ground, dotting the green landscape with spots of bright yellows and reds.

Her bear rejoiced at being set free. It had been too long. Though aware of the urgency of getting to Tawodi, Alicia couldn't help but take in the forest of Deep Creek. Her soul sang, even as she ran.

She breathed in the night air, filled with summer greenery and the pungent tang of mating pheromones.

Occasionally, a wafting scent of blooming flowers, honeysuckle or wisteria blew by and she breathed it in.

Summer was her favorite season. Warm nights, filled with calls of wolves and owls. Young rabbits leaving their dens to explore the world on their own. Long calls of katydids as evening overtook the forest. And mates calling to each other and the sweat of love in the air.

The stress of the past several days dissipated in the night air. Sure, she had a lot to face when she returned, but for now, running through the forest gave her a respite and recharged her spirit.

She had so much to learn about medicine that she hadn't focused on the prospect of having her own mate. Then Marco appeared. As she ran, she thought about him and what he'd said.

Mate.

How could that be? On some level, deep in her gut, it made complete sense and felt as correct as her call to be a healer. On another level, it was the craziest thing she'd ever heard. A lion and a bear as mates? What would become of shifter politics if that were to happen, especially with Marco's position in the Sen Pal?

Still, the potential excited her. Even in his worst moments, she wanted to be near him. Confident she could save him from the bacteria, she hurried to Tawodi's. Maybe things in Deep Creek were about to take a drastic turn for the better.

For all the shifters.

She leapt over the small stream in her path, her back feet splashing in the cold water and slipping on the smooth rocks. The thought of Marco kissing her sent electric chills up her spine. The best kind of chills. Excitement and potential. Together, they could bring an end to the war in Deep Creek. She wasn't exactly sure how, but tonight, everything seemed possible.

As long as Tawodi helped her with the cure. Marco had appeared stable when she left and she'd get back to the Cave of Whispers as quickly as possible.

She paused to catch her breath in a moonlit patch on the path. Panting, she shook her coat, fluffing up the long fine hairs. A mating between a bear and a lion would be the biggest news in Deep Creek in a century, though stories of old said it had happened often in the past. The children of such unions usually took on the form of the mother, but not always. The scenario was certainly possible, though rarer as time had gone by.

She walked, catching her breath. It'd been too long since her bear had run free, and her muscles burned with pleasurable exhaustion.

Many from both shifter worlds would be upset. She and Marco could be ostracized from Deep Creek altogether. Where would they live? With the bears or the lions? He was a leader of the lions—could she give up the bears to go live with his pride?

So much to think about and yet, everything was happening so quickly, she barely knew what to consider first.

Trust. She had to trust that everything would work out.

She took off running again. First, she had to find out what was wrong with Marco and how to save him. The rest of the things would fall into place after that.

The last stretch to Tawodi's house wended through a

stand of silver birch trees, their papery bark fluttering in the light breeze like a million butterfly wings alight on the trunks. Alicia loped around the trees, tall and thin, nearly white yet sparkling in the bright moonlight.

Sometimes the beauty of a summer night in Deep Creek squeezed her heart with its splendor.

What she wouldn't give to run through the summer night with Marco, as lion, at her side. It would happen.

Once she left the trees, she came out into a meadow, the grass tall as her shoulders. Flower-topped grass bowed and crickets hummed in evening song. Dew had begun to form on the grass like tiny crystals, lit from within from the bits of moonlight they stole.

Pausing for a quick prayer to the gods for Marco's health, and a prayer of gratitude and thankfulness for Deep Creek and its mysteries and beauty, she dipped her head. Without a sound, as soon as prayers were offered, she moved on.

She made it across the meadow quickly. Beyond the line of trees lay Grandmother Tawodi's cabin. A tiny yellow light glowed from afar, assuring her Tawodi was home and likely awake. She burned oil lamps and would never go to bed and waste oil.

Alicia smiled as she came upon the small house. Outside, a dozen raised flowerbeds grew herbs and flowers, and new age statues and sculptures decorated the paths in between the gardens. Glass globes, rings of crystals, all part of Tawodi's healing rituals. At least fifty wind chimes of all sorts decorated the trees and branches near the cabin, some of them made from the finest metals and bamboo and some merely discarded cans strung up to make music in the breeze. One bush was filled with bottles of all colors and sizes. When the sun struck them, they made rainbows throughout the grass.

The cabin always brought joy to her heart.

She trotted up the path. The cabin felt magical, as if it protected the spirit of an immortal fairy.

Maybe it did.

Some of the best days of Alicia's life had been spent at the little cabin—sitting at her grandmother's feet listening to tales about healing or working in the herb beds or even sweeping the front porch with a willow broom. Always sweeping to the west, to discard bad intentions with the setting sun. Everything Tawodi said and did seemed to carry a weight beyond the simplicity of the task, and Alicia's gratitude for her instruction had no bounds.

Memories flooded her and she sighed. The happy times she'd spent with Tawodi brought her a contentment that would be hard to match. As she approached the cabin, her mood saddened and she grew somber. Her visit wasn't for a celebration. She was here to save Marco's life. Time to focus.

She reached the porch and began her shift to human form, her bear slipping away in protest. Tawodi must have heard her because the curtains opened, and she peeked out then dropped the curtains and the porch light flicked on just as Alicia transitioned back to fully human.

The front door opened and an arm stuck out, holding a robe. Alicia took it and slipped it on, then the door widened. Tawodi held out her arms for a hug.

"Grandmother!" Alicia fell into her arms, hugging

the frail woman. "It seems like I've not been here in so long."

Her grandmother squeezed her with more force than anyone would expect such a small creature to have.

"Too long. It's good to have you visit, child. Seeing you at the cave or in the forest isn't the same as at home." The old woman's eyes, black as coal, shone like shiny pools. "Come on inside before the night air gives you a chill."

Alicia pulled the door shut behind her and moved into the cabin's small living room. "Thank you, Grandmother."

Tawodi stoked the remains of a fire. A large pot hung over the coals and a chair had been scooted up to the stone hearth. An earth witch in every sense of the word, the old woman was always making a concoction for someone. Even some of the humans in Oakwood came to Tawodi for herbal remedies to human ailments like rheumatism and colds. Only the wolves and some of the lions made fun of her, and it never seemed to bother her at all.

"Get some clothes on." Tawodi pointed to the back room. "Your chest is still where it was. Then we'll talk about this problem you have."

"You know there's a problem?"

"Of course I do. Get dressed. Time is short and the task is complex."

Alicia bent and kissed her grandmother's dry cheek and smiled. "Okay. We have a lot to talk about." She paused.

Tawodi looked more frail than the last time she'd seen her, which wasn't that long ago. Though her hair was gray with a deep black stripe down one side, usually causing her to look much younger, something about her carriage made Alicia wonder if something was wrong.

Her posture was bent, like she carried a huge weight on her back, and her movements were slower and more pronounced. Not a vision of the majestic hawk Tawodi shifted into before she took to the air. No, she looked old and human, like she didn't have a lot of life left but was holding on to what she had with both hands, unwilling to let go.

"Git. We'll talk after you change." Tawodi interrupted Alicia's thoughts and shooed her away with a brush of her hands.

Alicia scurried down the short hallway to the bedroom. The scent of drying herbs filled the tight space, and she looked up to the rafters in the hall where the ceiling went all the way to the roof.

Hanging by twisted cotton strings, from every pocked beam and rusty nail, was a sprig or bundled herb. Most were dried, browns or deep greens ready for use. None touching each other—that would be unlucky. The combined scents formed a mixture of leafy heaven with a few floral notes and an occasional pungent herb. She smiled and turned the brass doorknob into the bedroom.

The protective ceramic amulet that hung on the door clanked against the wood as she pushed the door open and moved into the bedroom. Moonlight streamed through the wavy glass in the one window, casting a water-like glow across the patchwork quilt on the bed and the wooden floor.

With no electricity, she'd have to find her trunk of personal supplies in the near dark, or light one of the oil lamps or candles that sat on the dressers and bookshelves in the bedroom. She knew the room well, though, and opted to find her things in the blue moonlight. Her trunk still sat in the corner, piled high with spare pillows. She moved the pillows aside to open the box and grab a spare set of clothing.

She tugged on her shirt, wondering how she'd broach the topic of Marco with her grandmother. Clearly Tawodi knew some things about the situation, but she certainly didn't know Alicia was seeking a cure for a virus or infection that no one knew the name for.

Unless Shoshannah had already told her.

Did she know the cure could mean an escalation of war since she and Marco might be mates? Or was that part of the whole plan? As long as Marco lived, Alicia would be happy.

She finger-combed her hair then slipped on a pair of sneakers. How could healing become something so complicated so quickly? If the lions were already looking for Marco, they wouldn't care if she was trying to help him or not. They'd kill anyone in the way of reaching him, and now that the whole bear clan knew he was in the cave, the chance the lions would find out had gone up exponentially.

She had to get him well before the lions came for him.

Time to talk to Tawodi.

As a hawk shifter, earth witch and healer, she was much more in touch with what was actually going on than many realized. On top of that, she'd tell it like it was—no sugar coating.

Alicia folded the robe her grandmother had loaned her and set it on the bed then piled the pillows back on her trunk. With a last deep breath, steeling herself for the choice Shoshannah said she'd face, she headed to the living room.

Tawodi sat by the fire, stirring whatever the concoction was in the pot. Steam rose off the fire-darkened container and wafted through the living room. She'd lit a few more oil lamps and had a candle grouping on a shelf, casting the room in a yellow glow with shadowy long fingers reaching from the fireplace to the window on the opposite wall.

The small cabin didn't need much light and Tawodi had provided more than enough.

"How do you feel?" Tawodi smiled. "I thought your own clothing might be better than a robe."

Alicia stared at her grandmother hunched over the pot, her long hair shadowed in the darkness behind her.

"Yes, Grandmother, much better."

"I'm glad." Tawodi didn't turn to look at her. "Let's talk. I understand that there's serious trouble brewing."

"I need your help. Someone I care about is very sick, and I need your wisdom and healing powers."

Grandmother stirred more furiously and didn't speak. Then she set the spoon down and looked at Alicia.

"Do you remember the stories I told you when you were a cub? Of bears and lions and wolves all living together and sharing the cave? Of helping one another and not fighting?"

"Of course. But many of those were allegorical, weren't they?"

Tawodi sighed. "No, child. Those days were real. And the time is coming where Deep Creek has a chance to have that harmony again. I'd never have believed it would happen in my own lifetime, and yet it seems that it might occur sooner than I anticipated. If everything goes well."

Alicia sat on the couch, facing her grandmother. She tucked her feet underneath her. "Why does this worry you?"

Tawodi stared off out the window into the moonlit woods then looked to Alicia. "That's not what worries me. It's everything that must happen to get to the balance point that makes me shake with stress. Yet, we are on the way and there's nothing to come of worry but more worry. We need to address your problem. Let's talk about your mate."

Alicia gulped as adrenaline shot through her. "My mate?"

"He is your mate, isn't he?" Tawodi raised her eyebrows. "The lion you are here about."

"I… I barely know him!" Alicia's face flushed. "I like him, but I don't know what it's like to have a mate."

"Shoshannah told me."

Alicia opened her mouth then closed it. Shoshannah was pretty sure of herself, wasn't she? The more Alicia let her heart feel, the more it felt right that Marco was her mate, but what a scary prospect. Sure, she'd reveled in the idea of it, but the reality would bring so many layers of complication.

"I know your species are enemies. But like I said,

it hasn't always been so." Tawodi picked up the spoon and began to stir. "Why do you think you were compelled to help this lion in the first place?"

"Because you taught me that all life is precious and deserves to be healed." Alicia leaned back on the couch and scanned the cabin. Nothing had changed since she last visited, with the exception of her grandmother. "May I get a drink of water?"

"There's a bucketful on the counter." Tawodi nodded toward the makeshift kitchen. "With all the rain we've had, it's fresh. I cleansed it with crystals, too."

Alicia headed to grab a glass from the cupboard. She ladled water into the glass and drank. The water slid down her throat like silk, quenching her thirst from the long run.

"I don't think it was your will that caused you to help this lion, child. The lions had killed so many of your people, I find it hard to believe you'd be eager to help the lion without a further reason."

Alicia returned to the living room. "Perhaps. Let's assume that's true. He and I were drawn together. That doesn't mean he's my mate. That's a leap."

"Leaps of faith are required for love."

Alicia took a deep breath. Were Shoshannah and Tawodi playing matchmaker or was there a real shred of evidence here? "I do feel something when I touch him. But *mate* is a strong word. One I'd not really considered, given my training as an herbalist. I don't have time to tend a mate."

"It is a strong word, and one too many in this day take lightly. But you need to face the fact that destiny appears to have pushed the two of you together."

"He's hurting. Mate or not, if I don't find the cure to his infection, he won't be around for me to argue this discussion."

"We need to talk about his illness. He's very sick, and only you can save him."

"So I've been told. What's wrong with him?" Alicia leaned forward. "Why am I the one to save him?"

Tawodi stared into blankness, her eyes unfocused. "He's contracted a bacteria that once almost wiped out all the shifters. It grows in the depths of the caves. The bears are immune now because they've lived in the cave for so long. But the lion must've gotten infected."

"You mean…" Alicia's chest tightened. "The glowing bacteria on the cave walls?"

Tawodi turned to her and nodded. "You saw it, then? Like smashed fireflies on the rocks?"

"Yes, and some of it floated from the cave ceiling and landed on him when I was about to operate. Oh my gods, is this my fault?"

"No, child. It's not your fault. It's part of the greater plan. When the caves glow with a million stars, it's time for the bears and lions to work together against a common enemy."

Alicia gulped. "Something worse is coming?"

Tawodi nodded. "If we can fight it off, Deep Creek will be a near paradise again, as it was so long ago. The bacteria is a foreshadowing of what has already been set in motion. I didn't know it had spread through the caves again or… Ah, it's no matter. It's time to prepare for the greatest fight Deep Creek has seen. First, we must heal the lion."

"What can I do? And why is it me that must do it?"

Alicia rubbed her eyes. How long had it been since she slept? She couldn't miss out on the most important event of her life by taking a nap.

"Because you're his mate. Deep Creek needs Marco. Are you prepared to help him, no matter what it takes?"

"Yes, of course."

"Be careful how you answer. His illness is strong, and the sacrifice to heal it is deep and will affect you for a long time." Tawodi's tone, serious and firm, sent chills up Alicia's back. Whatever it took, she would do it. For Marco and for Deep Creek.

"Tell me what I need to do."

Tawodi leaned back. "Child, you've been a good healer. One of the best students I've ever had, always attentive and listening. Healing Marco will challenge your beliefs like nothing else has. Know this. I will not judge you for your decision. It's yours alone to make." She rose and used a potholder to pull the heated pot from the coals and set it on the hearth.

"I understand. Please help me help Marco. I need to hurry back to the cave."

Tawodi clasped her hands together. "As I have said, the shifter families in Deep Creek used to share the caves and resources. No longer, of course. But one year, deep in the caves, there was an opportunistic bacteria that would enter through open wounds and kill shifters of all ilk. It feeds on shifting ability in the DNA and isn't easy to cure. In fact, it takes quite a sacrifice to get rid of. The cure was discovered accidentally, as many of these things are. Desperation leads to many things."

Alicia covered her hand with her mouth. "Marco might really die from this?"

"Yes, Shoshannah told me that Marco picked up the latent bacteria, but I didn't really put it all together until you came. She knew the cycle was starting anew and this is the beginning of a potentially rough time for Deep Creek."

"We have to give him the cure! Whatever it is, he must have it. Then we need to eradicate the threat."

Outside, a lone wolf howled, and Tawodi cocked her head to listen then turned back to Alicia. "It's not so simple, child."

"There's no cure? I thought you said—"

"Oh yes, there's a cure. But as I also said, the cost is great. You need time to consider. I won't let you rush into it."

"When hasn't it been a great cost with Marco? I've already estranged many of my kind because I helped him. How can this be worse than feeling like a traitor?" Alicia stood up and walked to the window. The forest was dark, as the moon had set. In the trees and on the ground were every type of animal imaginable. She sensed them, hearts beating, lungs breathing, eyes ever watchful for predators. She was always more aware when she was at Tawodi's cabin, or maybe it was when she was in her aura. Deep Creek never felt as real as it did in the little house in the woods.

"He needs an elixir made from the blood of a bear or wolf shifter. From a species other than his own. Preferable from his mate because that will provide the strongest antibodies. The elixir will help counter the bacteria that are preying on his shifting abilities. He needs a boost of immunity from a shifter who's not susceptible."

"Like me."

"Like you. The bacteria almost have a consciousness. Frightening and opportunistic, there's a chance the cure won't work."

"Are my people at risk? The bears around Marco?"

"No. As I said, the bears are immune, at least we think most are. I'm going to the cave as soon as I can to check out the growth myself. I'll collect samples and see if I can't figure out what can be done to prevent this from ever happening again. I know I'm immune but I want to make sure we beat this back before it grows all over the cave."

"I can help."

"You have other, important things to do, Alicia. Once Marco is better, maybe you can help. I'll admit, I'm eager to see the bacteria in person."

"If anyone can find a way to get rid of it, it will be you."

"I'll give it my best shot. I can at least study it and maybe pass down the knowledge of what I find."

"Why him? Why is it preying on him?" Alicia tried to keep the panic out of her voice, though she was sure Tawodi sensed it.

"The germ is opportunistic and picks a weak host. I'm pretty sure Marco is the weakest susceptible creature in the cave right now."

"He is."

"So, a mate's blood, especially if the mate is from another species, is even more powerful than anything against this infection. A mate's blood has the components of immunity and also is a mirror image in many ways. It will help diffuse the infection and overpower the bacteria growing inside. Sort of like the positive and negative charges, the antibodies will cancel each other out."

Alicia turned to Tawodi. "Take my blood. That's no problem. Make the elixir and I'll take it to him."

"There's one more thing." Tawodi looked down at her hands.

"What?"

"I'll take your blood. But I must warn you, when the elixir is made, and the magic is performed to prepare it, because it takes from your shifter powers, you'll lose your ability to shift."

Chapter Thirteen

Alicia ran, the precious elixir that would cure Marco safely stored in a pouch Tawodi had loaned her. The heat of the afternoon sun on her back slowed her progress and she panted. She'd have made better time as a bear but that wasn't an option anymore. She paused to rest a minute and catch her breath. She couldn't even find her bear when she looked inward.

What have I done?

She shook off the doubts. She did what she had to, and now it was done. She hoped Marco was still alive. Grandmother had stayed up all night working on the elixir, and Alicia had helped her as much as she could. It was one of the more complex combinations she'd ever seen, and she'd left her grandmother falling into bed from exhaustion as the sun rose.

Alicia wasn't sure how much longer she could keep going herself. She'd slept two hours, figuring it was all she could spare. Getting the cure to Marco was critical.

As long as the cure worked, the sacrifice would be worth it. Alicia focused on that as she made her way through a dense patch of brush. Tawodi said the effects should start almost instantaneously. Marco's fever should fade quickly and the bacteria should die off.

Gods, let it be true.

She hopped over the small creek and scrambled up the bank on the other side, her shoes muddy but the cure safely tucked away. Not much farther to the cave now. Elijah would've kept his word to take care of Marco, would the other bears?

The small meadow before the stand of trees that concealed the cave entrance buzzed with insects. Her fondest memory of the area was playing hide and go seek with Ria in the same meadow so many years ago. Now, not only was Ria gone, but many bears had spilled blood to protect the cave.

The cave that used to belong to all shifters. Was land worth fighting over?

Marco had thought so. Who would have ever predicted the way this summer would have gone. Certainly not Alicia. Torn between sadness and joy, she tromped through the meadow. Ria would want her to be happy, of that she had no doubt. It was time for all the past sins to be washed away.

An image of Marco popped into her mind. She stepped on a twig that snapped under her shoe. She wasn't far from where she'd found him, injured and likely dying. Thank the gods she'd decided to help him. Tawodi had been right all along.

Every creature deserved care.

Mate. Warmth overcame her, and it wasn't the heat of the sun. Did she sense his presence as she neared the cave? Fated mates' attraction grew stronger as their connection developed. The blood offering she'd given had driven home how much she cared about the lion.

How much she realized they were going to be inseparable and bonded for life after the cure. Would he want her now that she couldn't shift?

What was done, was done.

Her heart ached to know that while she'd been gone, Marco had suffered. She hadn't recognized the mating attraction for what it was because she hadn't even let the thought cross her mind. A bear mating with a lion was simply not a concept she'd considered. Now, she realized how being away from him physically hurt her soul.

He was her mate and even if he refused her, he'd always be the only one. Staying positive was important, Tawodi had taught her that. Alicia would save Marco, and then they would figure out how to tame the crazy world around them.

She crunched through dried bushes in a shortcut to the cave entrance. She wouldn't tell Marco she'd lost her shifting ability yet. That wouldn't help his healing. For the time being, he didn't have to know anything about what she'd sacrificed. They could deal with it later, once he was completely well.

She pushed through the last bushes and came out near one of the Sentinels guarding the cave entrance. He nodded at her to pass and she waved. It had been the Sentinels that had spotted the lions' attack and a few had lost their lives. Grateful for their protection, she made a note to thank them for their service again later.

The tall tree that grew right outside the cave entrance waved in the wind, welcoming her back.

Finally! She headed into the cave, the change in temperature striking and significant. She shivered and waited on her eyes to adjust.

Elijah met her in the anteroom, giving her a hug. None of the bears were with him. "Any luck?"

"I have the cure in my bag. Shoshannah was right, Tawodi knew exactly what to do." She patted her bag. "Apparently, Marco has been stricken with a shifter-killing bacteria that resides deep in this cave and waits for a weakened host. Marco was exactly what it was looking for."

Elijah stiffened. "I've heard stories of this sickness. Are my bears at risk? What do we do to contain it?"

She shook her head. "The bears seem to have developed an immunity to it, unless it has evolved. Tawodi said she was coming to take samples and try to figure out how to eradicate it for good."

"I hope it hasn't evolved." Elijah motioned her ahead.

"Anyone else shown signs of illness?"

"No. Not that I know of." Elijah paused. "I wonder why Shoshannah didn't warn us. She's so mysterious. It's frustrating."

"She did point us to the cure. Or the hopeful cure, at least." Alicia debated telling Elijah about her shifting ability but decided against it. He'd be furious with her.

"True, and the bears have been fine. But I want that germ gone. As soon as possible."

"Me too." A lump formed in Alicia's throat. She had to ask. "I need to see Marco alone to give him the elixir. Is he…alive?" Her breath caught in her throat as she almost choked on the words.

"He worsened overnight, but yes, he's alive. We moved him to one of the hospital rooms with a real bed. He seemed so miserable. This way." Elijah took off down the tunnel.

"Thank you. That was kind."

Elijah harrumphed and quickened his pace.

Alicia tried to keep up, but Elijah moved faster than the big bear should be able to, and she had to near-run to stay on his heels.

He stopped in front of one of the few rooms with a built-in jamb and locking door. He motioned her inside. "He's in there."

"Thank you." She nodded to him. "I appreciate all you've done for him."

"I've done it for you, not him."

She smiled at Elijah then stepped into the room. Derek sat in the chair beside Marco. He looked like he hadn't slept. But Derek's condition was nothing compared to Marco. Marco looked like he'd washed up on shore after a hurricane.

"Alicia," Derek said. "Glad you're back. Any luck?"

"Thank you for staying with him, Derek. Yes, I have the cure. At least what we hope is the cure."

"Good." He stood and stretched. "Maybe things will start to get back to normal around here now."

"We can hope. I need to be alone with him to give him the medicine, please. We don't have much time." She heard the pleading in her own voice and hated it. Is this what having a mate did to you? Made you desperate to ensure his health and safety?

Derek raised his hands. "You got it. I'm exhausted—

I'm going to go take a nap. I'll see you later today."
He hugged her and headed to the door. "Good luck."

"Thank you again. I'll see you soon." She closed the
door behind him and flipped the lock.

She was alone with Marco now. Her mate.

He was so weak.

She moved to stand beside his bed. His eyes were
closed, his lips parted, like he was sleeping restfully,
but pain distorted his features and a sheen of sweat covered him. He'd clearly been in distress for a while and
the sickness ravaged his body. She touched his skin.

On fire.

She pulled out the medicine and set her bag on the
chair. Make it or break it time. She whispered a quick
prayer to the gods and took a deep breath.

This has to work. Has to.

She shook him gently. "Marco," she whispered, not
wanting to startle him. He didn't rouse so she shook
him harder. No response. "Marco?"

He had to be awake enough to take the medicine
without choking. She shook him again, a little harder.
He opened his eyes to slits, the irises changing from
mossy green to brown then back, recognition maybe
there at first, but then gone. He thrashed in the bed,
tossing his head from side to side like he was having
a bad dream.

She waited for him to still. If she spilled the medicine it would be too late to make more. He settled down
again, opening his eyes for a second, then drifting off
again. She had no choice. He wasn't going to wake up
for the medicine. She'd have to give it to him as he was.

She opened the medicine and held the tube to his

lips. He didn't move. She dribbled the liquid into his mouth, a little at a time. He swallowed it instinctively and slipped back into his delirium, eyes closed. It took a few minutes to get it all in him, but he took it without choking.

Thank the gods for small miracles.

She sat on the edge of his bed, waiting and hoping for a miracle. She held his hand, rubbing his fingers and feeling the skin. Even though he was burning up, his skin was soft and his fingers strong. He gripped her hand and squeezed.

Tawodi had said the cure would begin quickly. Almost instantaneously, she should notice him improving. She waited, listening and watching for any change.

He began to calm down and cool off. Bit by bit, he relaxed, never letting her hand go. Even his coloring changed, from a deep red to a more normal tan.

The medicine seemed to be working.

She rubbed her thumb against the back of his hand. His temperature went down dramatically within minutes. Truly a miracle happening. Tawodi's cure was working.

Soon, he appeared normal other than the gunshot wound, which was healing nicely and shouldn't even bother him much at all. The bears had removed the bandage to treat it, and it was healed enough to leave uncovered. Someone had removed the stitches already—probably Derek.

Marco stirred, then turned toward her. "Alicia?" His voice was almost a whisper but still stronger than it had been in days.

"Yes, I'm here." She couldn't keep the smile from taking over her face. He was aware and awake!

"Where are we? What happened?" He rubbed his eyes. "Where's my brother?"

"You're still in the Cave of Whispers, and the bears know you're here, but they're mostly okay with it."

"I don't remember much. I was...you... I was in a lot of pain." He looked around the room. "I wasn't in this room."

"No, you weren't. The bears moved you here. You had an infection from a bacteria that grows in the cave. A particularly nasty and opportunistic germ. Apparently, in the past, it killed a lot of shifters, but the bears have built up an immunity—at least we think so. But not lions."

"Why didn't I die?" He struggled to sit up, tugging the blanket around his waist.

"It's a long story, but short version, Shoshannah told me I had to get the cure from my grandmother. I went to her cabin to find out what was going on—I've told you she's a really good faith healer. She knew about the bacteria and made a cure with my help."

"Lucky me." He pushed his hair out of his eyes.

"You almost died. You *are* lucky. The important thing is that you seem to be doing better. Do you feel okay?"

"I feel like doing this." He pulled her onto his lap and kissed her.

She leaned into him, happy to be in the strength of his grasp. So much firmer than before, he held her tightly. Securely. No question, he was her mate. She didn't ever want to be without him again. Ever.

He pulled away from the kiss. "You know now, don't you? I feel it. You're my mate."

She cupped his cheek and looked into his eyes. "I think I always knew. I just hid it from myself for a while."

He pulled her in for another kiss, and she relaxed into his arms. It felt good to not be stressed over whether he would live. Life hadn't been better in a long time.

The taste of her lips on his dizzied him. Not the crazy dizziness he felt when he was infected, but a joyful dizziness, like spinning around until you couldn't stand. The righteous feeling of being with his mate. He drew her close, taking a deep breath then loosening her red hair from its band and letting the strands cascade down her back. He gripped her hair and held her to him, sure he could feel her heart beating in time with his.

"You're so beautiful, Alicia." He didn't wait for a response, instead began planting kisses along her neckline, loving the way she shuddered under his touch. He tried to memorize and capture her every movement as his lips trailed over her soft skin for the first time.

The first time of many times to come.

She tilted her head back, her hair hanging loose, all the way to the bed. He caught it in his hand, wrapping the strands around his fist and drawing her closer to his chest.

Mate. Mine. Always.

He pulled her fully on top of him, and she kicked off her shoes and wriggled out of her pants as he continued kissing her.

"I want you, mate of mine." He growled the words. His strength was returning quickly and he had every intention of using it to please his mate.

She giggled. "Hold on. I can't take my clothes off with your mouth in the way."

"Hurry up. I need you." His lion was so close to the surface, begging to be released. Pacing. It had been days since he'd felt like he could reach his other half, and his heart filled with joy that he could shift again.

But not right now. Right now, he needed his mate. Needed to be inside her, feeling her move against him. Relish her giving herself to him and him to her.

"Hurry." His voice, deep and still close to growling, surprised him. Where had this strong passion come from? This ache he knew could never be filled and need that could never be sated.

But oh, by the gods, he would try. He slid his hands down to hold her hips, squeezing her with both hands and trying to be gentle when all he wanted was to flip her over and take her hard.

When she tugged her T-shirt over her head, he drew in a breath at the sight of her, then raced to beat her at undressing without knocking her off the small bed. He only wore underwear and some sleep pants the bears had dressed him in at some point, so he was ahead.

She laughed as she unclasped her bra and let it slip off her shoulders. "Good thing I locked the door. Heck, you're lucky this room has a door. Most of them in the cave don't." She tossed her bra and shirt onto the chair beside the bed.

"I don't care. It wouldn't bother me if someone

walked in." He realized how foolishly male he sounded. How needy and oblivious to anything but her.

Her eyes rounded. "It would certainly bother *me*."

"We don't have to worry about it, do we?" He tugged her flat onto him, pressing her full breasts against his bare chest. Every part of him was aflame now, and not from fever, but a need deeper than anything he'd felt before.

"Your shoulder!" She pulled back. "I don't want to hurt you."

"My shoulder is fine." He moved under her. "You healed me, remember? Now I want to experience more of your amazing bedside manner. In bed."

Alicia laughed. She got up on her knees and slipped her panties down, then she sat and pulled them off and flung them to the chair with the rest of her clothing.

He moved under her, the feel of her soft thighs against him driving him insane, his new fever higher. She was a need he had to quench.

Now.

He had to make her his—wholly and completely.

He looked into her eyes, trying to gauge her need. She caught his gaze and held it, and his heart nearly leapt with joy and lust. Her pupils dilated as she spoke to him without words. She wanted him as much as he wanted her.

No more waiting.

He flipped her onto her back underneath him and held himself up over her. Beneath him, her hair spread around her face, framing her milky skin with a red-gold aura. In the lantern light in the small room, she seemed to be lit from within. Glowing. Soft. Perfect.

He caressed her breasts, tenderly, then ran his fingers down her stomach. She shivered under his touch.

"Do you want this, Alicia?" He paused for her answer. "Do you want me?"

Half-lidded, she nodded.

"I need you to say it. I have to be sure."

"I want you, Marco. I want you."

"Are you fertile now? I have no birth control." He ground his teeth together hoping for her to say no.

"No, I'm not. I assume lion shifters also cannot spread human disease?"

"They cannot."

"I'd say we're two of the luckiest shifters around right now."

He bent to kiss her, holding his body above her. Gentle at first he moved to more vigorous kissing until she pulled him against her, her legs wrapping around him as he entered her with a patience he didn't know he possessed. Though he wanted to take her hard and fast, something inside him needed to savor her, feel every stroke.

Whether it was because it was their first mating, or his recent illness that made him appreciate the moment, he knew he wanted to grab every second of their coming together and never let go.

He watched her face as he moved inside her. Sweat beads broke out on her upper lip as she pushed against him and grasped his arms for stability. He thrust, trying to hold back so she could take her pleasure first.

His eyes closed on their own and he moved inside his mate. So warm and so soft. He didn't know making love could feel this way. Her legs started to quiver, then she tensed and a small moan escaped. He opened his eyes to watch her pleasure cross her face.

He'd never seen anything so beautiful.

Mine.

He sped his thrusts till his own pleasure took over and consumed him in a heat of passion that blinded him with its intensity.

Chapter Fourteen

Alicia put on her shoes then climbed back into bed with Marco. "If someone comes in, at least we're dressed. No evidence. I unlocked the door too. I'm not ready to give away our secret yet. I don't know how the bears will take it."

"I don't care. But I put my pants on by your request. See?" He lifted the cover.

"Thank you." She laughed and pulled her hair back and banded it. "Where do we go from here? A lion and a bear? I don't even know where to begin."

"I don't know. It's not an easy situation, but I don't care. I've never been happier." Marco sat up, putting the pillows beside him and pulling Alicia against his arm. "We'll figure it out."

"Elijah will expect me to stay here with the bears." She watched the door. Inside the room, all was perfect. Their own little world. She and Marco had each other and that's all that mattered. Outside that door, the real world would be against them.

"I need to be with the lions. My brother will expect me at his side."

"You'll leave me?"

"I don't want to leave you, no. Of course. But my father is gone and my brother will need my help. I don't have an answer for this quandary. But we'll come up with something." He stared at the rocky walls.

"Maybe we should go to a neutral place until everyone gets used to the idea of a bear and a lion being together." Where would they go? Where were both lions and bears accepted? Oakwood? No, not far enough away.

"Maybe. Let's think about it." He touched her face. "I need to be with you."

"I feel the same way about you."

"I love you, Alicia. I know we've not known each other long but we're meant to be together forever. I feel it." He stroked her hair. "But logistically, this is a nightmare."

She nodded. It was. Somehow, they had to figure out how to be together in a world that wanted them apart.

The door burst open, knocked from its hinges by a makeshift battering ram.

Alicia scrambled backward as several lions, unshifted and wearing gas masks, poured into the room. Why hadn't they just knocked? Her heart pounded and she backed toward the wall. How had the lions gotten past the Sentinels? How had they found Marco?

"Don't hurt her!" Marco yelled as two of the lions pointed bows at Alicia. The lions who had the battering ram dropped it and rushed to Marco's bedside.

"Brother!" Mason strolled in and flipped his mask up. "You're alive! The wolves said you were—I'm so glad this wasn't one of their tricks."

Alicia blinked. An almost exact replica of Marco in

physical form, Mason's scent was different. The twin was not like Marco. She pressed her back against the rocky wall. Mason, dressed in black, was surrounded by a strong aura of power. She felt his presence as larger than he physically was.

Marco held his arms out to Mason and they hugged. "It's good to see you," Marco said. "I was worried you had perished with Father."

"I'm fine. You're not injured?" Mason glanced over Marco's body. "We had reports you were shot."

"She healed me." He pointed to Alicia. "I'd have died without her."

Mason bowed. "Many thanks to you, bear."

"Y-you're welcome." She didn't trust this lookalike.

"Come, brother, we have to go before the bears wake up. We've gassed them to sleep with gas grenades. A brilliant idea from one of our lions. We only have a few minutes to get in and get out before we cause a major war that we aren't prepared for. The gas has already dissipated and the bears will begin to wake any minute. Thankfully, we found you quickly."

"Very humane. Father would be proud." Marco moved toward the lions.

"Let's get out of here, Marco. We can talk about all this later. We need to go *now*."

"Where are you taking him?" Alicia rushed to stand between Marco and Mason.

"Home," Mason said. "Where he belongs. Thank you for healing him but he belongs with us."

At that moment, a huge brown hawk flew into the room, its wings beating fast, like a hummingbird.

"Tawodi, no!" Alicia yelled. "Fly away!"

Too late. The lion by the door pulled his bowstring and shot an arrow at the hawk.

"How in the hell did that creature get in here?" Mason stepped back from the bird, its wings barely moving now. One wing had an arrow through it.

Alicia looked at Marco. His face reflected her shock. She fell to the ground and covered Tawodi's body.

"Leave the bird alone, brother." Marco put his hand on Alicia's shoulder. "I'm so sorry. They didn't know."

"We were attacked by a hawk in a cave where a hawk doesn't belong. What's there to know?" Mason stepped toward the door.

Alicia started to pull the arrow out, but Tawodi's breathing was erratic and she began shifting back to human form.

Alicia leapt up and rushed at the lion, but Marco pulled her back. "Don't," he said. He wrapped his arms around her in a hug. She fell against him.

"Marco, we need to go now. Before this turns into a bloodbath." Mason's voice grew louder. "Now. And I'm sorry about your bird. We didn't know she was a shifter."

Tawodi lay on the floor, human, curled into a fetal position, the arrow stuck in her upper arm.

Alicia looked to Marco. "Are you leaving me?" She wasn't ready to make a decision. Everything was happening too quickly. Without enough time to think.

"I have to go help my brother. I told you the lions needed me. Come with me. They'll accept you. My mate."

"I can't leave now." She nodded toward Tawodi. "I have to take care of her."

Mason sputtered. "You have a bear mate? Are you sure you didn't hit your head?"

"She and this hawk healed me. I'd be dead without them."

Mason put his hands on his hips. "Healer is one thing, and I'm eternally grateful for what she's done. But mate? That's an entirely different thing."

"I hear a bear stirring, or someone. Down the corridor!" One of the lions looked out the door.

"We have to go right now, Marco!" Mason grabbed him by the arm.

Marco pleaded. "Please, Alicia…"

"I have to take care of her. No one else can." She shook her head, tears flowing freely down her cheeks.

"You know where I'll be, Alicia. I love you. We'll figure this out."

A shout echoed deep in the cave.

"They're waking up!" Mason motioned the lions. "Go, now!"

Marco nodded. "Let's go. The gas won't affect us?"

"No, it's already dissipating. Another minute and the bears won't let us leave at all. We'll all be killed. Hurry."

She couldn't leave Tawodi. Not after all she'd done.

Marco kissed her on the cheek and stared into her eyes. "Come to me when you're done. I'll be waiting."

Alicia didn't reply. She hadn't even told him about not being able to shift. She watched the lions leave, feeling as if her heart were running out the door without her. She dropped to the floor to check on Tawodi.

Right now, her mate would have to wait. Tawodi needed her.

Chapter Fifteen

Marco flipped over in his bed, pushing the sheet off his bare chest. The lightweight blanket already lay on the floor. Even though the air-conditioning was running full blast and his room was cool, dreams of Alicia kept his blood hot, though she wasn't anywhere nearby.

What had he done? Why hadn't she come? He was sure she would, once Tawodi was well. But he'd had no sign of Alicia. Didn't hawk shifters heal quickly?

He'd let the one person who'd believed in him one hundred percent—his mate—walk out of his life. No, that wasn't accurate. He'd chosen to leave her—when she was most vulnerable. He'd put her on the spot and made her choose to leave her people and go with him into the unknown. No time to think, no time to prepare.

He'd tried to make her choose. What a mistake.

Then he'd doubled the mistake by walking out.

He wiped at his forehead. He'd not heard from her since that moment he'd left the cave. Three days had passed with no message, no sight of her in the edges of the forest.

Mason didn't want him going far for fear of him being recaptured, so he sat at the edge of the complex and peered into the forest for hours, hoping to catch a whiff of her or see her red hair glint in the late summer sun, or her speckling of freckles move when she smiled.

He'd thought she would come to him at least to visit.

The line between duty and love had never been an issue until he met Alicia. Now, he ached to be with her daily and his duty to the lions drifted away. He loved his brother and the lions, but things had to change. He needed his mate at his side—wherever they were. The pride, the cave, or somewhere else entirely.

No more war.

The bears weren't as bad as the lions thought.

Max said he had to prepare for the next battle. One that would have a new enemy. He had told Mason about his visions but he wasn't sure his brother believed they were real. Mason thought maybe Marco was having hallucinations instead of dreams. Regardless, things needed to change.

He needed Alicia. He would go to her, whether Mason approved or not. Once Mason got to know her, Marco knew he'd care for her and understand. Mason didn't have a mate yet, and for that, Marco pitied him.

Marco's heart noted every second that passed, and each beat sent a pang of pain through him, reminding him of what he'd done. He kicked the sheet to the floor and sat on the edge of his bed, naked. The moonlight through the lone window cast a blue light into his room, and he stared. The moon waxed and soon it would be full, and the wolves would run wild through Deep Creek, preying on rabbits or anything else they could overpower. That's what wolves did.

Mason had been busy planning another attack even with Marco's opposition. The wolves weren't ready, and the lions hadn't recovered. Marco worried that if he left Mason alone while he went to find Alicia, Mason would do something stupid like attack the bears again.

He had to figure out a way to get to Alicia. He loved her and needed her and he was sure she was mad at him for leaving. He needed to explain things to her. Still, the thought his brother might lead an attack while he was gone hung over him.

He pushed his hair out of his face and watched a small cloud drift over the moon's disc. Then, a large bird sailed by. A huge hawk. He watched its silhouette as it caught a thermal and lifted in front of the bright globe, its wide wingspan seeming to cover the moon from his perspective.

Hawks usually aren't out hunting this late at night. The hawk flew closer and Marco saw it was alight with purple and blue flames. He watched as the bird sailed straight up then around the shape of the moon, then in a flash, disappeared.

Tawodi.

She was checking on him. He had to get to Alicia. Figure out a plan to balance his mate and his brother.

Marco rubbed his eyes and lay down, tucking his legs under him then reaching to pull the sheet off the floor. He needed sleep or he'd be hallucinating more. Tomorrow, he had to figure out what to do about Alicia.

Time to act.

He'd screwed up. He needed to fix it. No matter what Mason said. No matter that she was a bear.

She was *his* bear.

If she didn't want him, then he'd have to deal with it, but he wasn't making progress by doing nothing but lying around wishing. His body relaxed, almost at once, like every muscle was in agreement with his decision.

Sleep, then he'd find her. The rest would be in her hands and the hands of the gods.

Alicia sat on Tawodi's porch steps in her nightgown, a cup of warm sassafras tea in her hands. Tawodi had completely healed, at least physically, since Marco had chosen to go back with the lions. Still, Alicia couldn't bear to leave her alone. She'd come so close to losing her.

Tawodi was out flying tonight, under the full moon, and Alicia waited on her return. She'd all but moved into the basement of the cabin, setting up an old bed and staying close by until she knew Tawodi could take care of herself again.

Why had she picked that time to come check on the bacteria? Alicia had known Tawodi was anxious to get a sample, but the timing had turned out to be horrible.

Alicia wasn't sure she was cut out to be a healer anymore. The emotional pain of healing Marco and Tawodi had cut her in two, and she wasn't any closer to healing herself. Her mate had walked out. It hurt.

She watched the moon. It'd be full the next night. So close right now. The Thunder Moon. Appropriate.

She sipped her tea, savoring the bite of the herbs. She'd sleep well tonight, once Tawodi returned. No nightmares, she hoped. Every night, she hugged a spare pillow, pretending it was Marco. And every morning, she'd woken up to the reality that he had chosen to go with his brother instead of staying with her.

She took another sip of the warm tea. Already, she was relaxing and beginning to slip into a pre-sleep, slowing-down phase. She yawned. Tawodi was staying out late.

Maybe she'd go see Derek and Bria tomorrow or even Griff and Amy. They'd visited her and Tawodi the day before, but Alicia craved their company now more than ever. Tawodi had been clear—Marco had to decide which path he'd take. Alicia, or war with the bears. Until then, Alicia needed to wait.

Three days felt like an eternity.

She missed him. Across the meadow, the reflective eyes of a night hunter popped up for a moment then were gone. Even most insects had gone to sleep.

All Tawodi's talk about taking care of everyone and working to bring the shifters together had done her no good in the end. The lions didn't care. Marco didn't care.

She had believed him when he said she was his. Yes, he'd told her to come to the Sen Pal complex, but the fact he'd left in the first place was hard for her to understand. Especially since he knew she needed to take care of Tawodi's injury.

The whole mess could've been prevented if she'd not treated Marco. Now she didn't know if she could even continue to heal others. Tawodi thought she was cut out to do it, but it sure didn't feel like it. She couldn't even shift anymore.

Right now, she felt like she'd failed her grandmother, her bears, and most of all, herself.

She stood and stretched, then sipped the last of the tea. The moon loomed high above the treetops now, round and bright. The branches of the tallest trees silhouetted along the horizon like a jagged saw blade, ready to cut the sky from the land.

Alicia turned to go inside.

To add insult to all the injury the situation had caused, she really missed Marco and the way electric shocks skittered up her arm when she touched him. Hearing his voice again, whispered against her neck as his lips brushed her earlobe…she shuddered…she wanted that again.

They were mates. How could she let that go?

He hadn't tried to contact her or get a message to her at all. He'd left her. Not called for her to join him, nothing. He'd asked her in the moment to join him, and she hadn't answered quickly enough for him.

If that was what mate meant to him, she didn't want any part of it.

She'd tried rationalizing his behavior. He hadn't seen his brother. The bears were waking up from the gas. He had to choose quickly, and he had.

At first, she thought it was because his brother was there. She got pretty intense vibes from Mason. He was more impulsive than his brother—she could tell that from the brief encounter and how he handled both Marco and his men.

Mason seemed like someone you really didn't want mad at you. But was he keeping Marco from contacting her? Alicia doubted it. Marco said that he and Mason handled things in the pride equally, though they had different strengths.

No, if Marco really wanted her, he'd show it. He could find her if he wanted.

With a nod of good-night to the moon, Alicia padded inside and was just about to close the door when Tawodi swooped down onto the porch.

"About time, Grandmother." Alicia held the door and the hawk hopped inside and down the hall to Tawodi's bedroom.

Alicia locked the door and took her cup to the tiny kitchen. Tawodi was home. She could sleep now. She flipped off the lights and headed down the basement stairs.

Every cell in her body wanted to find Marco in her bed but when she opened the door, the bed was empty. Like the night before and the one before that. She tugged her hair elastic out and picked up her brush and starting raking out the tangles.

Her medicine pouch sat on the dresser across from the bed. It hadn't moved since she brought it here the night he left. She paused brushing.

Maybe Tawodi had a concoction for a broken heart.

"Like that would be real," she murmured. "And as if things could be that easy. Not my luck."

She attacked her hair with full force then dropped the brush on her nightstand, flipped off the lamp and flopped down on the bed. She tugged the thin quilt to her chin and cried.

Tears for the loss of Deep Creek as she once knew it.

Tears for the loss of the bears.

Tears for the loss of her healing drive and her shifting power.

And finally tears for the loss of her mate. A mate

she wasn't looking for or expecting, but one that had forced himself into her life and changed her from the very first touch.

The haze and fog billowed over the path through the densest part of the forest. Marco couldn't see two feet in front of him, though his lion scanned with precision, watching for any movement or any change in the scenery that might indicate where he was. He didn't recognize this part of Deep Creek, yet the area felt like home.

His muscles burned. Tawodi's cabin was on the far side of Deep Creek, and he hadn't taken the most direct route, getting lost in thought as he walked. The path, never changing, the mist growing denser with a slight chill in the nighttime air. He didn't remember leaving the lions' compound or climbing the steep hill into the forest. He had walked and walked, alone, for hours and his paws were sore. Compelled to go…somewhere.

The sun should've been up by now, warming the land and lifting the mist, and the forest should've been alive with birdsong, warning small creatures of his presence but instead it was quiet except for the crackle of his paws on the rocky pathway.

He stopped. Compulsion had pushed him onward but he wanted to go to bed. Sleep away the rest of the darkness. Tomorrow, he'd find Alicia or at least deploy a plan to get her back. Whatever this nonsense was would stop and he'd regain control of his destiny.

Another half mile and he'd convinced himself to go back when a warm light lit the whole forest. His lion mouth hung open, his tongue lolling at the bright spot ahead.

The light intensified till it outshone any definition in the trees or anything in the natural world. He ducked his head to protect his sensitive eyes.

"Marco," a voice called. Familiar, yet out of place.

He looked up. Shoshannah stood before him, enrobed in the brightest white light he'd ever seen. She was a lioness, her long back curved with muscle and her strong head spiked with teeth of steel. His eyes watered at the brightness of the sight and yet he couldn't look away. She looked like she was made of the finest crystal or diamonds, yet living and breathing, organic.

Beautiful beyond measure and deadly beyond proportion.

Shoshannah. He couldn't speak aloud in lion form but he knew she could hear him.

She smiled and the light around her wavered like a pebble had hit a serene lake. "Find Alicia. Deep Creek needs you two together for the battle that's coming. Your father warned you of this. It won't be long. Shifters must be ready."

Coming? We've already lost so many. We can't fight much more. He paced, his tail dragging the ground. What did Shoshannah want him to do? *I don't feel like fighting a war.*

"The war is nigh. The question is not if you will fight, but how prepared you will be. Deep Creek will need you and Mason to fulfill the prophecy. You need Alicia by your side."

"She may not want me back. I abandoned her."

"Son."

His father, Maximillian, stepped out of the fog.

Large as a spirit lion, his voice reverberated through the air like the crackling of a bonfire.

Father! Marco shrieked in his mind. He began to rush to him but Shoshannah nudged her nose in the air for him to stop. "We only have a few minutes while the veil is thinned. Don't waste the time." Her tone left no room for argument.

Marco stopped, wanting to hug his father but not wanting to ruin the chance he had.

Marco gazed from one to another. What did all this mean? Shoshannah and his father, together? Had he died and moved into the river of stars himself?

"No, you aren't dead, Marco." Shoshannah attempted to hide a lioness's smile. "Listen. Your father has come to talk to you."

Max smiled and Marco noticed his bad eye had healed. His father's lion had always been impressive, but now, it was young and large and strong.

Perfect.

"Son, you have many choices ahead of you. Stay true to your heart or you won't survive. Find the girl. The bear. I can't emphasize how important it is that you listen to me." Max frowned. "I was wrong about so many things. You and Mason need to correct the problems I caused. It's your legacy."

Wrong? You, Father? You guided and led the lions as a leader we were all proud of. Our hearts are all broken that you are gone.

The lion's shoulders slumped then he straightened. "A man is more than the power he holds over another, son. One thing I failed to teach you and Mason is tolerance. Other beliefs, ideals, ways of living—they all have merit if no one is hurting anyone else. I selfishly pushed for my goal—to take the Cave of Whispers— without thought of the costs. And the costs were dear. So many have joined me in the river too soon."

We understood. The cave belongs to the lions.

"The cave belongs to all shifters." Shoshannah slid from lion, to bear, to wolf, then back to lion, swiftly shifting and changing until all the creatures seemed to morph into one. "The shifters belong together." She was a lioness again.

No?

Shoshannah nodded. "I think you know that, Marco. You sense the thread that ties all together. That thread is unraveling more quickly right now but you must find a way to tie it back together before it's too late for Deep Creek. Your brother will help you."

What do you mean? I don't understand.

"You and Mason are fated to change Deep Creek. The time is almost upon you. You will be tested beyond measure but you are our only hope."

Cold fear washed through Marco and he padded a few steps to the right then back, his tail swishing. *We need your guidance, Shoshannah.*

Shoshannah twitched. "You and Mason will lead the final battle, along with the other shifters and humans you can recruit. You must bring everyone together. The bears. The wolves. Everyone. Or Deep Creek will be no more. I will be no more."

Max looked up, his eyes wide. "We have to go—the veil is closing. I feel it."

But I have so many questions.

"You will find your answers as you seek the truth." Shoshannah scanned the forest. "Hurry, Max."

"One more thing, son." Max's voice intensified. "You've been selfish. You've not treated your mate well."

I know, Father.

"She gave up one of her dearest treasures to save you, and yet you left her."

I will try to ease her pain.

"Talk to your bear mate. Learn what happened. You must make everything right before it's too late."

I will try. Marco's head spun. So much information yet so little to go on. What could he be talking about? What had Alicia given up?

Max stepped forward and nuzzled Marco's neck. "I love you, son. Never forget that. Find your mate and, with your brother's help, begin to heal Deep Creek and prepare for what's coming."

I will make you proud.

"You already have."

"Go now," Shoshannah said. "Run. Time is short. They are coming."

Who? Marco fought to control his emotion.

Shoshannah shook her head. "We'll help all we can, but the living must save Deep Creek." She and Max grew taller and larger as the fog swirled around them and the scent of mint spread through the air.

I love you too, Father.

Marco walked on, his black fur slicked and the night breeze sending a chill through him. He stopped and looked back. Shoshannah and Max were gone already, like they had vanished. The mist was gone and only a deep darkness, darker than a moonless night, lay on the path like an omen.

Chapter Sixteen

Marco awoke drenched in dampness, naked, with the window in his room wide open. The night sounds of insects buzzing and chirping drifted in with the breeze. Had he dreamed the experience in the forest? Seeing Max? What about Shoshannah?

He'd felt his father's warm nuzzle, sharing love and comfort the same as so many times when he was growing up. The ground underfoot on the pads of his feet, damp with the forest's mist, was real. Pine and summer wildflowers, the cool breeze, the ache of heated muscles…all too intense to not have happened.

A star-walking vision?

He'd heard of them but never experienced one before, or had he? He vaguely remembered one when he was shot. His father had been there, too, and told him of his mate. Yes, this was his second vision. How blessed he was.

Was Marco to now experience star-walking regularly?

His father told of star-walking once when his mate was pregnant with Mason and Marco. Shoshannah and a great-great-grandfather had appeared to Max and prophesied the twins' role in saving Deep Creek. Max had told of the experience and how clear and vibrant it was—unlike anything he'd ever experienced. Marco had been enthralled as a child, but as he'd aged, he'd not put much belief in the vision, thinking maybe it had only been a dream.

It wasn't like he and Mason had actually changed Deep Creek or that the prophesy had come true.

After what happened recently, he wasn't so sure anymore. In the vision he had walked the veil-line between the dimension of the living and the dimension where time didn't exist, at least not normally. The other side of the veil where the ancestors lived had been right out of reach but palpable. Max was proof of that. Marco had stood on the banks of the starry river all shifters were born from and where they eventually returned.

Now what?

He'd walked the starry path, been called to action, and now he had to act. Finding Alicia was more important than ever, and apologizing would be the first step. Deep Creek's future might depend on how he handled it.

And he wanted his mate back.

He slipped on gray sweatpants and a T-shirt, socks and tennis shoes. He had to get to Alicia, convince her he'd been wrong. He tied his shoe and tucked the laces inside. How would he find her, when he had no idea where to begin to look?

He'd run as a lion if he didn't have to worry about getting caught, but it was too dangerous if night turned to day when the park was full of visitors who'd be interested in a black lion, so he'd travel as man.

If she was at the cave, he wouldn't get close enough as a lion before being shot by the Sentinels—and he didn't want to go through that again. He rubbed at his shoulder. Even after healing, he remembered the searing pain too well. Getting shot was horrible.

He tied the second shoe. Where else could she be? The whole time he'd known her, she'd been in the cave. He didn't know where she lived. She'd never told him, or if she had, it was when he was feverish and out of it. Maybe she had a place in Oakwood or even Henredon, though he doubted that. She loved the forests of Deep Creek too much.

Help me, Father. He closed his eyes and cleared his mind, hoping a piece of forgotten information would resurface. A clue. Anything to help him find her.

He replayed the vision in his head. Shoshannah as the magnificent lioness, his father large and healthy at her side, the mist descending like a curtain of clouds.

An image of a cottage flashed in his mind, remote yet quaint. Overgrown and surrounded by herbs and untended gardens, scarecrows and wards meant to keep out spirits. He remembered the hawk flying near the moon. Tawodi had been giving him a hint to where Alicia was. She'd be with her hawk grandmother.

Of course!

Tawodi needed medical attention and she'd likely been moved from the cave to her own home to heal. Alicia wouldn't leave her alone. She was a true healer, putting her all into every patient. It made sense, and he knew exactly where Tawodi's cottage was.

Most shifters stayed away from her home, calling it the witch's lair, but rumors didn't bother him. He had a fondness for the old hawk, despite her odd ways, and she'd helped Alicia save his life.

Besides, anyone his mate cared about, he should also care about. Yes, he'd go to Tawodi's house first. If Alicia wasn't there, he'd figure out where to look next.

A rap came on his door, firm and solid, and he debated ignoring it and pretending he was asleep. It was Mason, and he'd try to talk him out of going to find Alicia. Mason wouldn't want him leaving the complex alone and he certainly wouldn't approve of him going to Tawodi's house. Since when did his brother boss him around?

It was time to resume his place as eldest lion twin. He grinned at the challenge.

Mason pushed the door open and poked his head in. "Brother? I heard you up."

"I'm going for a walk."

"In the middle of the night?"

"Yes, I'm restless. I need to think." Marco tried his convincing voice.

"Don't lie to me, brother. I know what you're doing."

Marco sighed. "And what would that be?"

"You know as well as I that you're going after Alicia. You've been pining for her since we rescued you." Mason stepped into the room and closed the door. "Are you sure it's the right thing? She's a bear. We're at war." Mason put his hands on his hips. "I know you think she's your mate but is that really true or was it part of your delusions while you were in pain? It's been known to happen—making that kind of mistake. If you go to the bears now, you could die."

Marco stood. "I'm not going to argue with you,

Mason. She's my mate and I never should have left her behind. I made a rash decision, and I need to make up for it. I was wrong. I'm going to get her. If she won't come with me, then I'll stay with her." He'd not used such a strong voice with Mason in many years. "You can support me or not, but I'm going."

"Okay, if that is what you want, I won't stand in your way." Mason held his hands up in mock surrender. "I'm trying to protect you, that's all. I almost lost you once and I don't want to be in that situation again."

Marco's voice softened. "I know that, brother, and I appreciate it. I do. But you don't know all that's happened to me. I'm only beginning to process it myself."

"What happened?" Mason's eyebrows rose in question.

"I had another star-walking vision."

"Seriously?" Mason sat on the bed. "You're kidding. Are those even real? I figured the one you told me about was purely a feverish delusion."

"I'd wondered myself. You know our father insisted he'd had one. Well, I'm convinced now. Shoshannah and our father came to me."

"When did this happen?"

"Tonight. I can't describe how real it was, Mason. I felt Father. I saw the look in his eyes and felt his arms about my neck. I have no doubt it was real. He came out of the river of stars and through the veil to talk to me. With a message for both of us."

Mason shook his head. "Did he want us to attack the cave again?"

"No. He and Shoshannah told me to find Alicia first. Then they said that Deep Creek will come under attack soon, and we'll need to ally with the other shifters to save the forest. That it's critical that Alicia is by my side and that you and I lead the effort."

"That's a lot to expect. And who is this unknown foe?"

"They didn't say. Only that Deep Creek and Shoshannah will be destroyed if we don't work to defeat this enemy. I can't imagine who it could be, but I believe them. Why else would they appear to me like this?"

Mason scowled. "Sounds fishy to me, but what do I know?"

Marco ran his hand through his hair. "I realize it sounds crazy. Like I said, I'm still trying to understand it myself. Working with all the shifters toward a common goal—seems unfathomable, and yet we know there was a time when we did all live together in peace."

"Like the bears would trust us enough to work with us. That's ludicrous."

"Seems so. But Father was intent. He said he should have taught us to be more tolerant of others. Not be so focused on taking the cave."

"That doesn't sound like Father." Mason crossed his arms over his chest. "He wanted the cave, maybe more than anything."

"I know. But it was him. Perhaps returning to the starry river has afforded him wisdom he didn't have while here on Earth."

"And perhaps you were dreaming, not having a vision."

Marco shook his head. "This was so real, I wouldn't

have been able to tell the difference between it and us sitting here now. Whatever is coming, we'll need to prepare. I don't know how long we have, but we need to take Shoshannah's word that we'll be needed."

"Who could be possibly be formidable enough to threaten us?" Mason smiled. "We are powerful. Even threatening the bears would be a mistake. I don't know what shifter clan thinks they can come take Deep Creek, but they don't have a chance. Not from what I can tell."

"I don't know. I'm taking them seriously though, and you need to as well."

"I'll do it for you and the off chance that you really did have a vision. But I don't understand what's going on. It's hard to worry about such a nebulous threat. Right now, we need to get our lions all battle-ready anyway, so I don't suppose it matters if it's for the bears or another threat."

"Agreed. But we won't be attacking the cave again." Marco paced in front of the bed. "I need to go now. I have to find Alicia. We have a lot to work out. Promise me you won't lead the lions into battle without me."

"I promise. We need your help anyway."

"Thank you. I'll be back soon, and we can start working on this larger problem Shoshannah and Father talked about."

"I wish you all the luck and joy, brother. Be safe."

"Thank you." Marco stepped past his brother then turned. "One more thing."

"Yes?"

"In the vision, they said 'they are coming.' And it's happening soon. We're going to have to save Deep

Creek." Marco stared into Mason's eyes but saw no recognition.

"We'll be ready."

"We have no choice."

Alicia tossed and turned. The old bed was comfortable, until thoughts took away all sense of sleep. The herbs had failed her. She couldn't sleep.

Memories of Marco kept popping into her mind. His touch. His eyes. His kiss. And the way he wrapped her hair around his fist and tugged her to him.

She was his, and his alone. She needed him.

It felt right and good, and yet she lay in the bed alone. Life had thrown her some serious curves in the last few weeks. She wouldn't recognize the bear she was before the battle. Even Derek and Griff had noticed the change. Bria had accepted Marco and forgiven him for attacking Derek, but would Marco ever know?

Would she see him again before they both swam in the stars?

She heard a rustling outside the bedroom window, and she realized her window was open. She rose to shut it. The walkout basement faced the side yard and two windows flanked the door. She peered out the window.

At the edge of one of Tawodi's beautiful flower gardens stood a lion. A black lion. Mason or Marco.

The lion growled.

Marco!

She unlocked the door and flung it wide. She didn't care that she was in a T-shirt and underwear. Marco was outside. He'd come for her.

"Hello." He'd shifted into a man.

A very naked man.

"Hi." She rushed to him, throwing her arms about his neck and holding him close. "Oh, Marco, I've missed you."

He kissed her cheeks, her nose, her forehead. "I was waiting on you to come to me. I worried you were angry because I left. I knew you had to help Tawodi. My brother needed me and didn't want me to be captured. I waited at the compound with the pride, then I realized I was being selfish."

"Shhh," she said, covering his mouth with a kiss.

He backed her inside the cabin and shut the door. "Before we go any further, we need to talk. It's important."

Her heart sank. Had he come to tell her she was no longer wanted? She picked up the robe off the couch and tossed it at him. The same robe she'd worn when she visited Tawodi and given up her shifting ability for this man.

He pulled the robe on and it barely came to his knees. His arms stuck out longer than the sleeves. She giggled.

"At least I won't freeze," he said, smiling. "I've been thinking a lot about our situation. I need to ask you some things."

"Okay." She sat on the bed.

He sat beside her, straightening the robe. "You aren't going to lose me. I made a huge mistake leaving you behind in the cave. I wasn't thinking clearly and everything was happening so fast. It's still my fault and I hope you can forgive me."

"Of course I forgive you." She nodded. "You did

what you had to do. Mason needed you. I understand that. I've been in that position before."

"No, I was selfish. Can we stop there? I was wrong. I've spent every moment away from you wishing you were at my side. Every single moment."

Alicia examined her fingernails and refused to meet his mossy gaze. "So have I, Marco. I've wished you were here in this bed every night."

He reached for her hands, and she let him take hers in his larger ones. His skin, warm, but not hot with fever as he'd once been.

"How is Tawodi? I should've stayed to help you."

"She's well. Her healing was uneventful." She squeezed his hands. "Tonight, she went for a long flight. I'm amazed she healed so quickly."

"How are you doing?" He leaned close.

"Healing others takes a part of the healer's soul. Mine is hurting." She pulled her hands away.

Marco sighed. He rubbed his face then looked up. "That's my fault."

"No, it's part of my education. I need to learn to distance myself. Not be so involved."

"You mean like you were with me?"

She paused. "No, Marco. I gave you my all because you're all mine."

He hugged her and she relaxed in his grip. No denying it, she belonged in his arms. After a minute, he pulled back, his face serious.

"I need to know something, Alicia. I had a vision where Shoshannah and my father spoke to me. They warned of the dark things coming to Deep Creek."

Alicia looked at him. "Tawodi told me the same."

"They said we need to unite the shifters and prepare for a greater enemy." He met her gaze.

"Yes. Tawodi said Deep Creek was at risk. I'm tired. I don't want to fight anymore."

"I don't either. My father said this battle can be won with intelligence. I hope that's true. I'd be fine with never carrying a gun again."

She nodded.

She watched his eyes change from green to brown and back to green. Few shifters held the power of spirit that Marco did. It was probably why he lived as long as he did with the bacteria in his system. If he'd been weaker, he'd be dead.

"They also said I needed to talk to you about what you gave up, in saving me. They found it important that I know, yet they said you would have to tell me." He leaned closer.

"It's nothing, Marco." She looked away. Part of her wanted to tell him the truth. Let him see how much she'd sacrificed for him to walk away. Part of her didn't want to hurt him with the truth.

"Tell me. You are my mate and I love you. Please don't keep secrets. We need to face challenges as one. We can't do that if you won't tell me the truth."

"You mean…"

"I want to perform the mating bond tonight. Why wait any longer to be one? Seal the deal and prove my love for you."

"Oh, Marco. I want that, too."

"First, I want you to tell me what else you lost." He scooted closer on the bed.

She took a deep breath and let it out slowly. Maybe

he did deserve to know. They couldn't mate-bond without her telling him. He would sense she couldn't shift. "When I came to Tawodi's to get the cure for the shifter bacteria, I had to give her blood to mix in. To help counter the bacteria's havoc on your system."

"Yes?"

"There's more." She fiddled with the edge of her T-shirt. "I had to give up my ability to shift so that you could live."

He reacted like she'd slapped him. "No! Why would you do that?"

"It was my gift to give." Her lip quivered.

"Oh my gods, Alicia. Oh my gods." He held his head in his hands. "I can't believe you would give up something…something so critical to your being."

"It was my choice and I stand by it." She stood and walked to the door.

Marco rose from the bed and swiftly made his way to her. When he yanked her into his arms, there was no doubt who was in control. She surrendered to him.

"I love you, Alicia. You're mine no matter if you can shift or not."

He kissed her on both cheeks then picked her up.

"What are you doing?"

"Carrying you back to bed. Once you tell me you love me, that is." He bounced her in his arms.

"I love you. So much." She leaned on his chest.

He tossed her on the bed and it squeaked as she bounced. She laughed. This wasn't a dream. Marco was really with her.

"You want to mate for eternity, Dr. Bear? I need to

know. The bond won't take if we both aren't sure." He untied his robe.

"I've never been more sure of anything than my love for you." She stripped off her T-shirt and panties and dropped them on the floor beside the bed.

His robe followed.

He was on her so quick, she barely had time to catch her breath. His hands roamed all over her and she reached for him, feeling every muscle and indentation on his body. Her hunger for him dizzied her, and she closed her eyes as he nipped at her collarbone then kissed each breast.

"Time for slow lovemaking later, love." He spoke through his panting. "Right now, I need to claim you before life throws us another curve. Are you ready?"

She looked up into his eyes. They glowed with a green she hadn't seen before and his gaze bored into her soul. She nodded. "Take me, Marco. Make me yours. Forever."

He growled and pulled the elastic from her hair. She sat up and shook her head, loosening her locks and letting them fall over him. He tugged her to him, brushing her hair aside so he could nip at her shoulder.

Chills of the best kind raced over her skin as he nipped and licked. She giggled as he hit a ticklish spot on her back then winced as he bit a little too hard on her bottom.

"Marco, please—" She panted, her heart hammering with excitement.

She didn't have to say it twice—he pushed her back and was above her in a flash. He grinned, then kissed her deeply. She responded with her tongue on his, her hands roaming his body, feeling every hardness and every plane of muscle.

"Are you ready?" he asked.

"Oh gods, Marco, I've been ready."

He nudged her knees apart and was inside her quickly. She tried to keep pace with him but soon lay still to feel him sliding in and out of her. His thrusts built and her pleasure did, too, soon blooming throughout her abdomen and between her legs.

Her orgasm hit sharp and fast, and his teeth were on her shoulder, biting hard. There was no pain, only extreme pleasure. A moment later, he was coming inside her with a guttural moan so raw and pure, she'd never forget.

He had claimed her. For better or worse, they'd walk life's path together from this moment on. Whether it was saving Deep Creek or raising a family, they'd do it together.

He collapsed on her chest then looked up at her and smiled. "I love you, mate."

She tousled his hair. "I love you, too."

Chapter Seventeen

Alicia awoke with Marco beside her. The sky outside her window was barely turning from deep night's purple to early morning's red. Her heart filled with happiness. It hadn't been a dream. Marco was really with her and they were bonded.

She closed her eyes and replayed the lovemaking from the night before. Not just the mating ritual, but the three other times Marco had held her close and pleasured her. She'd never felt so satisfied and happy and content.

He let out a soft snore, and she pulled the covers up to his shoulder where a small silver crescent reminded them both of the circumstances fate had cast them in. The bullet that had almost ended his life had brought her the greatest happiness she'd ever had.

She traced the curved line with her finger, marveling at how well he'd healed from the bullet wound and the bacteria. Barely a blemish on his skin.

Incredible.

Her bear snorted, coming close to the surface of her mind. Alicia sat upright instantly, her heart fluttering.

Her bear had been gone since she'd given up shifting

for Marco's cure. Why did she feel her so close now? Was her bear back?

What was happening? Her bear pawed to get out with a yearning that made Alicia's heart ache. She reached inside and could feel her bear just below the surface, ready to come out and run.

Begging to run.

Marco sat up. "What's wrong? Aren't you tired?" He rubbed his eyes and yawned.

"You aren't going to believe this!" The delight in her voice roused him and his eyes widened.

"What?"

"I think I can shift again! My bear...she's here."

"Really?" He sat upright in a flash. "Are you sure?"

"I think so. I feel her and she wants to run. She's begging me to let her out. Maybe our bonding gave me back whatever it was I needed. Whatever I gave up, it seems like you've given it back when you performed the mating bite."

He pulled her into a hug. "That's the best news ever."

"Can we go run? Before the sun is too high?" She rubbed his chest and snuggled against him.

"Race you to the door." The green of his eyes deepened.

She jumped up and dashed, naked, to the door.

Before she could unlock it, he was on her, pushing her against the doorframe.

She stared up at him. "Outside!"

"After you."

She opened the door and the early morning sun's warmth bathed her skin in oranges and yellows. She ran out into the damp grass, letting her bear roar to the surface. She stretched, her arms lengthening and shifting and her body morphing as she inhaled the morning air. She reared up on two legs, savoring the feeling she thought she'd never have again.

Her bear was back.

A laugh sounded and she looked back to Marco. He smiled so big, her heart nearly burst with love.

"Race you to the trees?" he called. He dropped to the ground as his body changed and moved into his lion.

She didn't wait to see his lion fully form, but her bear giggled as she loped toward the trees, well aware he'd catch her before she was halfway there.

She ran as quickly as she could, but within a few seconds, she heard a playful growl behind her. In a flash, Marco had tackled her to the ground and they rolled through the dew-filled grass, laughing as only a bear and lion could.

* * * * *

Acknowledgments

Many thanks to everyone who helped me with this book. To my awesome editor, Anne Scott, for her enduring patience and skilled red pen, thank you! To Barclay Publicity and especially Danielle Barclay and Alicia Wheeler for keeping me organized, many thanks! And to my friend Lia Davis, for keeping me (mostly) sane through the process, thank you!

Thanks also to the entire Carina Press team, who helped me get this book to press.

SAVING HIS WOLF

Chapter One

Streaks of pain seared through Olivia's ankle as she slipped on the sharp rock. She bit her lip to stifle a yelp, but a weak moan managed to escape. If she didn't keep quiet, the rest of the wolves would find her. She was already at great risk in human form since she wasn't able to shift, but it couldn't be helped. Never had she wished for the ability more than as she trudged down the path tonight. She batted away the snowflakes freezing on her eyelids.

Being blind hadn't ever been more dangerous than it was now.

The icy snow gave way underfoot, and she began to slide down the embankment she'd fallen over when she stumbled off the path.

Despite the snow, she'd had to leave the pack.

She grasped for anything within reach that would break her descent, but the slush and ice covered everything in a glaze of slippery wetness she couldn't hold on to, and she continued to slip down the hill, her ankle twisting loose from the rough rock that had broken her initial fall.

From what she could tell, the rock was more of a

boulder, perhaps one that had sheared off recently and left jagged edges more damaging than a serrated steel trap against her skin. Her ankle pulsed as her boot tightened around it, a sure sign of swelling. She'd be lucky if her ankle wasn't broken.

Arms spread-eagled, she tried to slow down. She whimpered, snow edging under the hem of her coat and damming against her abdomen.

She grabbed at the ground as she slid, her gloves snagging on something twisty and knotted. A root or branch of some sort stuck out from the ground, and she clutched it with both hands, her throbbing ankle now useless as an anchor. Tears burned her cheeks as she dug her other foot into the snow to hold herself steady.

"I had to leave," she whispered, laying her cheek on the cold snow for a moment of rest. *No choice.*

Staying with the Green Glen wolves wasn't an option since Alfred had decided to take her as one of his mates. He'd made the announcement, and no one had spoken up in protest, not even those she called friends. Everyone was afraid of him. He was the cruelest creature she'd ever known and she could never love him, even if he was the last wolf on Earth. He'd threatened to force her to mate, and he meant it. Everyone knew it.

She shuddered.

Blind and lost in a snowstorm with an injured leg was better than being with Alfred. Freezing to death, alone, was better.

A long, low howl sounded in the distance, and icy fear slid up Olivia's spine and gripped her in frozen panic. She clung to the root tighter, her knuckles aching at the tension.

Alfred.

No mistaking that howl. Part monster, and part… something else, his howl strangled her soul, and made her wolf want to curl into a ball and hide forever. She pushed her hair from her face and listened. How close was he?

And more important, how long did she have before he found her? Maybe he would stay on the trails while he looked for her. He'd never believe a blind wolf would dare leave familiar ground. Not that she'd planned to, but the snowstorm had messed up her internal map, and she'd gotten off the path and gone right over an embankment. She adjusted her toehold in the snow. She was stable for the moment, but she needed to come up with a plan.

Alfred howled again, but sounded no closer.

Other howls answered. One, then another, and another. All different, all long and low and piercing. Deferring to him. They sounded out from different areas of the forest, yet converged as they overlapped and echoed through the snowy tree boughs.

They're searching for me.

And they'd find her on the embankment, as they triangulated her position methodically. Wolves hunted in packs and they always found their prey. They'd drag her back and she'd be Alfred's forever. Once back at the pack compound, he'd make damn sure she'd never have the chance to escape again—telling everyone it was for her own safety but, in reality, using her blindness to control her.

Alfred took advantage of weakness and used it to gain and maintain control. That went for anyone the wily wolf came in contact with, be it wolf or human or shifter. She'd scented his *modus operandi* the first time she met him, and it'd grown stronger as he'd matured. His younger brother, Claude, might be the head of the pack in name, but it was Alfred who reigned.

She shivered, more from fear than cold, though the slow seeping chill of her damp clothing pressed against her skin and sent goose bumps racing over her stomach and chest.

She'd be hypothermic soon if she didn't find shelter and warm up. She almost laughed. She didn't know where she was or how far she was from Oakwood, so the chances she'd make it to town were slim.

The snowflakes stung as they hit her cheeks and forehead, and the wind tossed her hair across her face. The shivering had become almost rhythmic and her teeth chattered. Her leg ached from holding her body weight on the snowy hill, and her other ankle had gone completely numb.

If only she could shift. Then she could run, despite having one gimpy leg. But that wasn't meant to be. No, she was going to have to get out of this predicament like a human.

She tried to push herself up with her good leg but couldn't get traction, and she was growing more tired by the minute. Things could be worse. The wolves weren't howling, so they weren't close, and the snow would mask her scent a little.

At least for a while. Eventually, they'd find her. The question was, would she be alive or have frozen to death?

I want to live!

She yanked at the root to readjust her grip and punctuate her feelings. The wood gave way in her hand, pulling loose from the embankment.

With no time to scream, she covered her eyes and let go, hoping she wasn't about to tumble off a cliff. Her ankle bumped and banged as she rolled, and snow flew in her mouth and nose as her braid slapped her in the face.

She hit the flat ground at the bottom of the hill with a thump, the fresh snow cushioning her fall enough to keep her from getting the breath knocked out of her. On her back, she lay still, listening, her heart slamming against her chest wall as adrenaline flooded her system like a warm cappuccino.

Alive!

She could've just as easily slid down a bank and dropped a couple hundred feet to her death. Her moment of gratitude was short-lived. The wolves howled again, the low voices almost lost on the wind or blocked by the cliffs.

Alfred wouldn't give up. Once he had his mind set on something, he kept at it till he had what he wanted. And he wanted her. She'd gone against his wishes and he'd make her pay.

The snow had picked up, and it bit into her face as it fell faster and the wind whipped it against her. She imagined the flakes as little spears swirling in puffs of air then attacking her bare skin. She had to move before she froze. Willing her legs to move, she lifted them one by one, her injured ankle sending aftershocks of pain up her leg to her thigh.

She sat up, feeling the ground around her body with

her hands. Her wet gloves stuck to her palms, and she mashed her fingertips against the ground, trying to figure out where the ground ended and a cliff began.

One wrong move and she could fall to her death. She pulled her hood around her face, the faux fur trim tickling her cheek. The flush of adrenaline was wearing off and the shakes set in.

Do or die moment.

She slid to the right, dragging her bum ankle, which had numbed to a hard block of flesh. Feeling the solid ground again, she inched a bit more. A few more times, and sweat had formed on her back, though she still shook from the chill of wet clothes and falling snow. She tugged her scarf tighter, trying to keep her neck protected from the elements.

Hope I'm going in the right direction. If she could get to the embankment she had tumbled down, she could figure out how to climb it. Moving incrementally, she continued to slide toward what she hoped was the hill. The wind whistled as it swept around the cliffs and through the trees.

The wolves had gone silent.

Her wet pants, soaked through from sitting in the snow, began to stiffen. Warmth filled her legs and she closed her eyes.

The darkness was blacker than usual. She yawned.

She breathed deeply, scenting the pine amongst the snow. Always a peaceful scent, and one that reminded her of her mother. If she were alive, she'd never have allowed Alfred to lay claim on Olivia. She'd have fought him herself if she had to.

So tired.

The shivers and shakes were continuous but she ignored them. The embankment had to be close.

There!

She touched the incline. Steep at the bottom, it would take a lot of energy to haul herself up. And she was exhausted.

It's not so cold anymore.

Was that a wolf howl? Or a bird call? She leaned against the bank and listened to the muted sounds in the snowy forest. The air had warmed. When had it gotten so warm? She could take a little nap before trying to climb the embankment.

Yes, a short nap. A few minutes.

The crunch of heavy footsteps sounded, and Olivia struggled to stay awake, her heart picking up speed at the thought of Alfred.

"You there. What are you doing out here in this blizzard? And all alone at that?"

The voice, a man's, was commanding and firm.

And not Alfred's.

"My ankle," she whispered.

"What?" More footsteps. "You're injured."

His voice melted over her like warm honey, and she waited to hear him speak again. She could listen to him forever…she took a long deep breath and the world silenced.

"Oh no you don't."

The voice jerked her back into wakefulness. No longer cold, she couldn't remember why she'd even worried.

"I need to rest for a few minutes." She curled on her side. "I'm so sleepy."

Chapter Two

What the ever-loving fuck was he going to do with an injured wolf? Powell dropped to his knees and pushed a long strand of the woman's blond hair out of her face. He yawned and tugged his toboggan over his ears.

Yawns really are contagious.

He could use a good nap himself, but he was on patrol duty for most of the month while the other park rangers rested, and of course all the excitement happened on his shift. Finding an injured wolf wasn't on his agenda for the day. Yet, here she was, and her wolf was so close to the surface; the sensation was almost palpable.

The scent of her washed over him like a warm wave of summer air, and he breathed her in and savored the feeling for a moment.

But she was *wolf.* He scowled and peered closer. Not one of his normal rescues, that was for sure. Wolves were dangerous and conniving.

Her full lips mouthed something, then her head lolled to the side and she went limp. With skin almost as pale as the snow, save the bluish tint of cold around her pink lips, she might be in serious danger.

"Dammit." He scooted closer.

Was she still alive? He placed two fingers on her neck to check her pulse. Slow, but then again, she was a wolf, so that was somewhat normal. Hypothermic, he was pretty damn sure of that. He wiped the falling snowflakes from her face.

Why the hell was she out in the woods alone during a blizzard so bad he could barely see six feet ahead of him? And in human form too. The wolves weren't known as the brightest creatures, but this was a pretty dumb move. Shifters healed more quickly in their animal form, yet here she lay, all human, sprawled in the icy cold.

He shook her gently, but she didn't respond. He'd heard the wolves howling—maybe they were looking for her. They'd sounded agitated as their howls reverberated through the snow-laden forest, and that was never a good thing. If they found her with him, injured and passed out, they'd leap to conclusions that could be extremely dangerous for a lone bear. He couldn't take on numerous wolves at once.

He sniffed again, pushing through the honeyed warmth that wafted from her, to the deeper scents. *Blood.* Faint, but he smelled it. She said she'd injured her ankle. The snowstorm obscured most scents from his sensitive nose, but the metallic trace of blood pulsed in the crisp air.

Fresh.

If he didn't get her help soon, she'd die.

A long lone howl sounded in the distance. The sky was already darkening as dusk approached. It'd get dark more quickly in this snowstorm. He shook her, again, more forcefully. No movement. Her puffy coat was saturated from melting snow, and her body temperature would drop quickly if her skin got wet. He moved her wet scarf from her face.

Wolf, dammit!

He fisted his hands. Continuing his patrol and letting the wolves find her would be the right thing to do. If she died, well, that was on them for not keeping up with their own.

What did he care if there was one less wolf? He was always dealing with them stealing sheep and chickens from farms that neighbored Deep Creek, and they often sided with the lions and lied to the bears. They told people what they wanted to hear then did as they wished.

A wolf's word wasn't worth the breath that it was uttered on.

Not one good reason he should help her.

She moaned, almost too faint for him to hear.

Duty.

"Dammit." He'd never live with himself if he didn't try to help her. As a park ranger in Deep Creek, he couldn't leave her to die. Maybe he could move her to a more obvious place, like back on the trail she was following. Then, her pack could find her more quickly.

A compromise.

After unzipping his parka, he slid it off and over her, then scooped her into his arms, pulling the coat around her like he was wrapping a baby in a blanket. Limp in his arms, he held her close to his chest and headed back toward the path that led around the embankment.

Why she'd tried to climb the hill when she could've

made her way out more easily along the lower path, he didn't understand. The snow must've been falling more heavily when she took the tumble down the small hill.

Maybe she'd hit her head.

Another howl sounded, this one closer, more plaintive and piercing. Then another. The wolves weren't happy.

His breath caught in his throat and he scanned the forest.

No wolves except the one in his arms.

His boots crunched with every step and he moved quickly through the forest. Snow muffled most sounds, and the world turned into a peaceful place when Deep Creek was alight with the glistening ice of winter.

Powell preferred patrolling in winter. He rarely saw another bear. Occasionally, a buck would gallop through the brush or a hare would thump the ground, but mostly he was alone.

And he loved it.

He paused on the path, the snow well over his ankles and still piling up. If he was going to leave her on the path, now was the time to do it. The snow had picked up, and a chill settled over him and was working its way into his core. He had to get to shelter soon or he'd also be hypothermic.

"Shit." No way he could leave her. If he could carry her as a bear, he would, but she wasn't able to hold on to him in her current state. She wasn't heavy, but if they ran into the other wolves they'd be in trouble.

A screech owl hooted and its echo multiplied through the trees. He crunched over a dead limb and trudged on. He'd take her to his cabin for now. Figure out what to do with her after he warmed up. With the forest on the verge of nightfall, he didn't have many choices.

He trudged on, sniffing the air for male-wolf scent and hoping he'd make it home before the forest was completely dark. The female wolf hadn't stirred. Her long hair, mostly in a braid, swung like a pendulum as he walked. He adjusted her in his arms.

Not much farther. His arms burned under the effort of carrying the wolf, and his face stung from the icy cold air and falling snow. Most of the bears would be napping now, content and warm under their blankets. Snoring.

He smiled at the thought. Glad that the Deep Creek bears didn't fully hibernate, yet happy that the long gray winter was a time of rest and rejuvenation. Much of the park was closed to tourists and only some roads were open. A glorious time to hike and run free.

A howl, much closer. Then another. Powell sniffed the air, his pulse racing and breath coming in cloudy bursts. Not much range for scenting with the snow heavier than before. Hopefully the wolves were having the same trouble. Sharp yips sounded. Then repeated.

Too close for comfort.

He pulled the injured wolf up over his shoulder in a fireman's carry so he could move faster. Sure the wolves were behind him, he took a big breath of cold air and ducked into the wind, the snow pecking at his face and eyes. His cabin porchlight shone in the distance, like a yellow firefly in a mason jar. Thighs and back burning, he jogged toward home, careful not to bump the wolf's injured leg.

Sweat dripped down his back as an icy gust pierced every pore of his exposed face.

He'd never been more glad that he'd taken the most remote ranger cabin when it became available. Tonight, that decision probably saved his life.

And hers.

The snow had accumulated several more inches since he left, and his footprints from the cabin were mere hollows now. He tromped up the steps to the wooden porch, hand on the rail as he fought to maintain his balance on the slippery stairs.

A lone howl sounded from the forest, this one an octave higher than the last, and farther away.

Good. The wolves were not following them. He reached into his pocket, grabbed his key and pushed it into the lock.

Finally, home. The door swung open and a blast of warmth rushed over him. His cat, Narcissus, meowed in protest, fur askew in the chill.

"Not now, Nar."

The cat hopped onto the sofa back and padded his front feet. Powell pushed the door closed with his foot then carried the wolf to the couch and laid her on it. She was still out of it.

After removing his gloves and hat, he locked the door. They'd made it and the wolves hadn't caught up with them.

Thank the gods.

He moved the fire screen out of the way so he could get a fire going. He'd learned a couple of winters back to prep a fire in the fireplace before he went out on patrol. Coming home and lighting a match was a lot easier than building a fire from scratch. He lit the wadded paper under the kindling and stood back a moment, making sure the fire spread throughout.

Nar rubbed against his legs. "I'll feed you in a few minutes, buddy. We have a guest. I need to tend to her first."

The cat meowed and purred.

Powell gave him a quick pat on the head. The cat had kept his loneliness mostly at bay. He'd found Nar as a kitten, flea-infested and scrawny, wandering around the Dumpsters in Oakwood. Taking the little thing home hadn't even been a choice.

He couldn't leave him to die.

Powell glanced at the couch. Seems like he was developing a habit of rescuing lost and wounded animals.

This one isn't staying.

Powell moved to unwrap the wolf from his parka. Despite having her coat on, he could feel that she was thin and lean, like a dancer. After unzipping and slipping off her coat, he set both coats near the fire to dry. He set her scarf beside it.

The wolf still hadn't woken, though she was breathing.

He headed for the bedroom. Maybe he should call someone, let them know about the injured wolf in case the other wolves made an issue out of it. Griff was likely awake, but Powell hated to take the chance and wake him and Amy both up.

Powell sighed and dragged some clothes out of the laundry basket of clean clothes he hadn't gotten around to folding. If she was still around in the morning, he'd let the bears know. No point in making a fuss tonight.

Not like anyone would be getting out in a blizzard to come see her. And he could tend to her ankle.

He quickly pulled off his boots and changed into a T-shirt and flannel pants. After he slid his slippers on, he grabbed an extra pair of socks and padded back to the living room.

She hadn't moved.

She lay on her back, eyes closed, her arms draped over her chest. Powell set the socks on the couch beside her then added some larger branches to the fire. Nar had curled up near the hearth already—warmth replacing food as his comfort.

He went to take off her boots.

Which ankle was it she hurt? He sniffed. Though the wound wasn't bleeding anymore, he scented the tang of blood. He unlaced the boot closest to him and pulled it off. Her sock was soaking wet and he peeled it free. He couldn't reach her other leg as easily, so he kneeled by the couch and reached carefully over her and slid her pant leg up, revealing a long scratch that disappeared into her boot top. The blood had dried but the cut needed attention. He untied the laces of her boot and loosened them.

He winced as he tugged at the boot. It had to hurt. Her foot had swollen and the boot didn't budge, so he unlaced it completely then wiggled it to and fro till it came off. She groaned as he pulled the sock down, but didn't stir. Better that she not be awake while he tended to her ankle and the long cut.

Examining her ankle, he found no evidence of an open fracture, but she had a lot of swelling and some purplish blue spots forming around the anklebone. The cut ran the length of her shin.

Powell washed her foot as gently as he could, then put antibiotic ointment and a bandage over the cut. She'd heal quickly as a shifter, but no need to risk infection.

Her ankle needed compression bandaging, and he wrapped a dressing around it to help support the swelling, careful not to wind the fabric too tightly. When he was done, he pulled her into his arms to adjust the pillow underneath her. Her body stiffened in his arms.

She awoke and attempted a scream and flail, but he held on. Her voice cracked and she coughed, her body shaking.

What was he going to do now? His mouth went dry. "I'm trying to help you."

She looked up at him, long lashes surrounding pale blue eyes, wide and cloudy with a hazy fog covering her irises.

"Who are you? And where am I?" Her voice, weak and shaky, shot straight through him.

No! It can't be. A warm rush of adrenaline burst through his core.

Mate!

Chapter Three

Olivia struggled against strong arms that held her tight, but not painfully so.

"Take it easy. Everything's okay." His voice warmed her from the inside out, like a shot of fine, aged whiskey. Smooth with a slow burn.

Exhaustion gripped her and the day's tension had tightened every muscle in her upper back and neck. Something about the man comforted her, and slowly she relaxed in his arms until she went limp, unable to hold her own body up or fight against the unseen any longer. If he was the Big Bad Wolf, then she'd not be able to fight him today.

No, he wasn't Alfred. Her legs dangled off the edge of a soft chair or couch or something, and her ankle was numb. She'd never been so tired, and so confused. Surely they hadn't gone all the way to Oakwood. Her luck had never been that good, and there was no reason to think it was going to change today. Besides, even a shifter couldn't have made it so far in the bad weather.

The air warmed her, and there was no wind slapping her hair on to her face, no sound of twigs snapping under an icy load. The lack of noise was deafening. He must have brought her inside.

Somewhere.

"Who are you?" She sniffed, her breath catching in her throat. *No!* Sniffed again, scenting bear, not wolf. The chill returned to her gut and she shook. Bears and wolves had a tenuous peace, and she'd heard plenty of stories about what the bears did when they wanted something.

They took it.

Not sure whether to be afraid of the bear or happy he wasn't Alfred, she licked her lips and waited for his response. At his mercy to some degree, she listened for anything that might help her escape if she needed to. An opening door or a piece of furniture she could hit him with if he tried to hurt her. Blind, and with an injured ankle, she was at quite a disadvantage.

"I'm a park ranger here in Deep Creek." The man's voice, strong yet worried, resonated inside her. "You can trust me."

"Says who?" Her voice came out weak and uneven. Dammit, the day hadn't gone as planned.

"I didn't hurt you. I found you."

"I wasn't lost." She pulled from his grasp too hard and fell backward, then quickly sat up. The cushions were soft, like a couch. And there was a fire—she hadn't noticed it before but as the heated air brushed against her skin, ripples of sensation crawled up her arms. She turned her face to the heat, palms out, closing her eyes for a brief moment to savor the warmth. The room echoed with the crackling and popping of the fire.

Still so tired.

The bear harrumphed. "Well, excuse me. What were you doing, pretty much face down in the snow? Checking for buried acorns?"

She felt his weight lift off the couch then heard his footsteps cross what sounded like a wooden floor. Where was she? A house in Deep Creek, maybe. But where? Could she escape? The mocking tone in his voice set her nerves aflame and tears filled her eyes. She wouldn't cry in front of this bear. Typically, she held it together well, even with Alfred picking on her.

This bear was no match for what Alfred could inflict, but she was so exhausted, she didn't have the strength to continue the banter with him.

So what if he rescued her? She didn't owe him. The next thing he'd tell her would be that he'd called Alfred and the wolf was on his way to claim her. Her chin quivered and she couldn't stop it. Her whole body shook, and her muscles ached.

Had she planned and escaped only to be turned back to the pack? She'd spent too much time figuring out when to leave—when the wolves were busy and less likely to notice. The only miscalculation had been the weather.

It may have cost her everything, and she should've taken into account that the weatherman was often wrong about how much snowfall Deep Creek was going to get. She should've waited till later in the season to leave, but the fear that Alfred might set a wedding date sooner than later had been enough of a catalyst that she wanted out as soon as possible.

How long had she been lying in the snow before the

bear found her? She'd heard footsteps as she closed her eyes. That must've been him approaching. She was lucky he'd seen her, or scented her.

"What were you doing face down in the snow?" he repeated.

"Obviously, I fell."

"So you needed me." The grin in his voice was as apparent as the scent of masculinity that flooded off him.

She sniffed again, and the smell of bear, and fire, and wood permeated her senses. No wolves had been in the room in a long time, if ever. Maybe Alfred didn't yet know where she was. The hope was almost painful in its intensity.

"I didn't say that." She fought against the urge to cross her arms and chew her bottom lip. The last thing she wanted to appear as was a petulant child.

The ranger poked at the fire—she recognized the sound of metal against wood and the scrape of coals on the hearth. A blast of heat washed over her as the fire was stoked higher. "Well? Why were you out in the snowstorm in the first place?"

She smirked and crossed her arms anyway. If he was going to prod her, she was going to push back. "None of your business." Her tears dried on her cheeks.

"Fine, I'm merely trying to help."

"You can help me by telling me where I am. I need to get to Oakwood."

"I brought you back to my ranger cabin. Wrapped up your ankle and treated a nasty cut on your shin." His back was still to her—she could tell by the muffled tone of his voice. His voice grew louder—he must've turned around. "I got some warm dry socks out for you, if you want them. I was about to put them on your feet when you woke up."

"Yes, thanks." She nodded, teeth clattering. Once she got warm, she could go back to being perturbed at him for taking her to his cabin without her consent. "I'd like some warm dry socks."

"Don't think you'll be heading to Oakwood tonight. Not on that ankle and not in this heavy snow. I wouldn't go out on ranger duty unless it was an emergency."

Who did he think he was? The Deep Creek park rangers were always messing in the wolves' business. She felt beside her for the socks.

"They're right there..." His voice held a question.

Cold dread settled in her stomach. He didn't know, but he was figuring it out. Quickly. And he was probably pointing to where the socks had landed. Could she fool him? She felt for the socks on the cushion she sat on, acting like she was merely pulling at the hem of her shirt.

Her hand warmed when he covered it with his own, and tingles shot up her arm at his soft touch. She jerked her hand away like she'd been burned by fire. She could sense his presence, close. He didn't move away and she breathed in a deep breath, unable to stop herself from scenting his intoxicating manliness. The dread in her gut spread and bile burned the back of her throat.

She was the enemy.

Injured or not, he probably didn't like that she was wandering through the forest on the bears' turf. The wolves were as territorial. It was as if Deep Creek were divided by magical lines delineating territory. Bears, wolves, lions.

He towered over her—she felt it. Yet, he didn't say a word, which made things worse. How could she respond to something when he stared at her without questions?

She swallowed hard. "What is it?" she whispered.

The socks were shoved into her hand and she clutched the thick ball of fabric.

"You can't see, can you?" His voice was warmer than the fire and low, full of empathy. Compared to Alfred's shrill whine, the bear was downright soothing. She wasn't used to anyone feeling sorry for her. Most thought she was a drain on pack resources and were glad she was going to be wed to Alfred, put to use providing heirs. In their eyes, she was finally giving back.

She was the disabled wolf among a pack of warriors and thieves.

He cupped her cheek, his rough thumb tracing the line of her jaw, then he pulled away.

She shook her head. Now what? Would he take advantage of the poor blind wolf? Her heart fluttered in fear, and she tugged the sock on to her good foot in silence, the popping and crackling of the fire the only sound in the room. Maybe she should've expected as much. The wolves always did say the bears were barbaric.

"I'm sorry." His words no more than a whisper, his fingertips trailing up her arm.

"Not your fault." She turned away from his touch, unsure of what to think. He'd felt comforting, not frightening. But that went against everything she'd learned. She eased the other sock over her tender ankle, wincing as it passed over the bandaged area. Surely, her shifter ability was already helping it heal faster.

Not quickly enough.

Maybe by morning she could escape.

"Meow?" Then a bump against her leg.

A cat? Olivia froze, then sniffed the air. Yes, she should've scented it immediately. Sure enough, the bear had a cat.

How unusual.

"That's Nar. As in Narcissus. And I'm Powell."

Powell moved away, and she cooled from the loss of his presence. The shivering returned, and she ran her hands along her pant legs—her clothes damp from the wet snow.

Despite her discomfort, she smiled, though she hid it as much as she could. The idea of a huge bear taking care of a little cat amused her. She didn't know why. Who was the alpha? Wasn't the cat usually the one in charge? She ducked her head to suppress a giggle and smoothed the oversize socks. Her feet already thanked her for the fuzzy warmth, though her injured ankle began to throb as feeling returned in the thaw.

After straightening the other sock over the bandage on her ankle, she tugged her shirt straight. How much should she tell the bear? Sure, he'd rescued her, but that didn't buy him her trust. For all she knew, he'd take Alfred's side. "Olivia. I guess I owe you my life. You're right, I wouldn't have survived long out there, so thank you."

"I thought you wanted to be out in the snow." His words carried a smile. "I can dump you back out there if you want, but I don't think you'd make it through the night."

"You wouldn't dare."

"Try me. Is that what you want? I can arrange it." His levity spread.

"I don't want to leave right now, but soon. I have to."

"You aren't going to be able to walk for a while. Even with super shifter healing power, it's going to take some time."

"It won't take that long." She'd show him. Maybe she couldn't see or shift, but she'd always healed quickly.

"We'll see." His voice held plenty of skepticism.

"I heal fast."

"So do I, but there's a massive snowstorm outside to complicate things."

"I won't be here long." She tugged the elastic hair band from her hair and finger-combed the braided tangles. Yeah, the snow would be a problem, but she'd worry about that when it was time.

"You can stay here at my cabin while you heal. I'll sleep on the couch."

"I guess I don't have much of a choice, do I?" She shifted on the couch, rubbing her hands together. Her skin was so dry. "I appreciate you bandaging my ankle." He must've removed her gloves while she was passed out. And her coat and scarf.

"I could still toss your backside out in the snow." The humor returned to his voice. "If you don't want to be here."

"I'll stay inside." She wouldn't give him the benefit of a smile. "Where it's warm."

"Let me get you a blanket and some coffee or something to eat."

"A blanket would be great. But I'm not hungry."

"Maybe later, then." He walked away and she heard a sound from the other side of the room. The cat jumped up onto something, small thuds followed by claws on wood.

"Maybe." If she had her way, right now she'd be sleeping not eating. She yawned.

"Get down, Nar." Powell came close, and then she was surrounded by a heavy blanket on her shoulders.

"Thank you." She tugged the blanket tight. Whatever had happened—whether she'd hit herself on the head and knocked herself out or what, her current situation could be a lot worse. Would Alfred find her at the ranger cabin? She turned in the direction she assumed Powell was standing. "Where is your cabin located?"

"In Deep Creek. On the fringe of the southwestern edge of the forest. We're pretty far from what you'd call civilization now that there's so much snow, and until it lets up, we aren't likely to be going anywhere."

"We aren't near Oakwood?"

"No, not at all. Why? I have plenty of rations. We won't starve."

If she waited for Alfred to show up, he'd kill Powell. Alfred didn't want anyone to be near her. With Powell alone, he was vulnerable. "I have to go." She stood then immediately fell back onto the couch, streaks of white pain shooting up her leg.

She cried out.

"Silly wolf. Why'd you do that?" His hand was under her elbow, guiding her into position on the couch.

"I need to get to Oakwood."

"Not tonight."

"But—"

"Sit still. You can't walk yet, much less to Oakwood. Let me get you some coffee and pain medicine. Then you need to rest."

She set her mouth in a line and sighed. Staying and waiting for Alfred to come pick her up was not acceptable. She had to be proactive and get away from the cabin, and into Oakwood. The prospect of hiking in the snow wasn't pleasant, given what had happened already. Still. She needed a plan.

"Where are my boots?" She asked.

She heard the tinkling of silverware and glass. He'd walked away.

"On the floor, but you can't put them on till that swelling goes down in your ankle." He bumped around in what she assumed was the kitchen area. "Relax and get some rest. Tomorrow we can call your den. Find someone to come get you if the snow isn't too deep. If that's what you want."

"You haven't called anyone?" She tucked strands of hair behind her ears, sure his gaze was piercing through her.

"No, I'm sorry. I've been busy tending to you."

The aroma of brewing coffee wafted through the cabin. The cat hopped up beside her and curled against her leg. She stroked his head and scratched under his chin, and he purred. A crack sounded outside, and she whipped her head toward the noise, though she couldn't see it.

Was it Alfred? Another burst of adrenaline shot

through her. She'd run from Alfred until she dropped dead if she had to.

"I need to go." She gripped the edge of the couch.

Powell was right. She wouldn't get far in the dark and in a snowstorm. And with a bum foot, it wasn't likely she'd make it to Oakwood in three days much less one. Staying in the bear's cabin meant they were all sitting ducks in a game where she was both the target and the prize.

"Not tonight, you don't. We can talk tomorrow. Tonight, you rest." He approached her, his footsteps soft on the creaking floorboards. "Here, take these."

He took her hand, opened her palm, and dropped tablets into it.

"What are they?"

"Ibuprofen. And I've got a glass of water. Let me know when you need it." His voice soothed her, though she didn't want to be soothed. She wanted to be away. Out. In Oakwood where she could figure out how to get to Florida where her aunt lived or anywhere but Deep Creek. Anywhere away from Alfred.

"How do I know you aren't lying?" She turned her face toward his voice. He could poison her, and that would be it. Or sedate her to turn her over to the pack.

"I guess you don't. But I've done nothing but help you. Take the medicine and let me get some more wood on this fire. And stop this nonsense about going out in the snow tonight."

She held her hand out and the cool glass was shoved into it. She popped the pills then chased them with a gulp of water. Then another. Thirsty, she drank the rest then held the glass out. She felt Powell take it from her hand.

She listened to him return to the kitchen area and set the glass down then come back and heft a larger piece of wood onto the fire. Lots of sputtering and popping as the wood hit the flames, and a blaze of heat seared her.

"That ought to last a while." He sat beside her, but at the other end of the couch. "Coffee will be ready soon. Then we can go to bed."

Her blindness couldn't hide her embarrassment. Powell snickered.

"Don't worry," he said. "I'll sleep on the couch."

"Fine."

"I can tell you're anxious. I'll protect you while you're in my care. I promise."

She didn't respond. What would the bear expect in return for all his *kindness*?

"You haven't told me what's up with the wolves but the howls didn't sound happy."

"Is it that obvious?"

"Yes."

"Don't call them, okay?" She hated the pleading tone to her own voice. Nothing worse than sounding weaker than she already felt.

"If you don't want me to, I won't."

"I don't."

Nar meowed from somewhere across the room.

"What does he want?" She turned her head in the direction of the sound.

"He thinks I'm going to let him out in the snow but I'm not."

"It's too cold outside for a cat." She fought to stay

awake. Her clothes, now dry and warm, plus the heated air, combined to make the day's exhaustion set in hard. So much more comfortable than being outside in the cold. She yawned.

"Yes." He stood. "He can go out when it's daylight. Are you ready for coffee?"

"No." She shook her head. "My ankle aches, and every muscle I have and some I didn't know I had hurt like crazy. A good night's sleep will help."

"You didn't hit your head when you fell?" His voice held the serious question. "No chance of concussion?"

"No, just my ankle. I'm so tired, I want to sleep."

She heard Powell yawn. "I am too. I agree. Rest tonight, fresh start tomorrow. Hold on."

Arms slipped under her and before she could protest, he'd swept her up and was carrying her...somewhere. Part of her wanted to lean against him and let him take care of things and part of her wanted to punch him in the nose for being so presumptuous.

Before she could decide, he dropped her on a soft bed.

"The cabin is small, but adequate. This is my bed. There's a bathroom right here to the immediate left."

She wasn't sure what to say. The bear was being super nice to her. All the stories she'd ever heard were about how bad the bears were, with few exceptions. "Thank you," she managed.

"Lie down."

She obeyed and the covers settled over her. He tucked her in all the way around, then laid a heavier blanket or a quilt over her. The bed seemed to sink in and the warmth from the blankets soothed her aching muscles. *So comfortable.*

"I'll be in the next room if you need anything." His footsteps retreated. "We'll deal with everything else in the morning."

"Okay."

He paused at the bedroom door and it squeaked as he started to pull it shut. "You realize how lucky you are?"

She nodded. She needed sleep, so much sleep.

"Not much longer out in that weather and you'd not be alive."

She yawned. "Thank you, again." She tugged the covers higher around her chin, and the scent of him washed over her, setting her insides jumbling. Of course a bear would give her a stomachache.

"I'm going to feed Nar and turn off the coffeepot." The door squeaked closed after his whispered words. "Stay put till morning. We'll get you home."

She didn't answer, though. The wind rattled the windowpanes nearby, and she listened as ice crystals pelted the glass.

Thank the gods, she was inside, safe and warm. Even if it was in a cabin somewhere unknown in the forests of Deep Creek. A good night's sleep would help a lot before she continued her journey.

A howl began, far away then seemingly nearer, its purpose and intent clear. Olivia belonged with the Green Glen wolves. She belonged to Alfred. Unless she found a way to get into town with an injured ankle, she'd need to hide out. Shifter healing had already begun, but she'd messed her ankle up and it would take some time for it to heal enough for her to be on the move again.

She wouldn't be running the next day unless she had to.

Alfred bayed again, insistent. Persistent. The sound trilled on the wind and through the bare tree branches, which clicked together like secret code in the icy wind.

Olivia...where are you?

My Olivia...

Chapter Four

How long had he lain awake, thinking about the beautiful wolf in his bed? How many times had he fed the fire
in the night? He wasn't sure when he'd finally fallen
asleep, though the pinks and oranges of dawn had lit
the room in a pale glow. Now past midday, he needed
to get moving. Powell sat up and pushed the blanket
away. She was exactly what he liked in a woman. A
little sassy, with a sense of humor to match his own.

And she was his mate.

Dammit.

He didn't want a mate. He'd never wanted a mate.
Mates were for other bears like Griff and Derek: bears
that wanted to settle down and have cubs and a house
in the woods with a split-rail fence and flowers growing along the walkway; bears that were much more
emotionally equipped to take care of a female and not
screw things up—not forget how to love or what to do.

He rubbed his eyes and studied the remains of the
fire, the embers glowing like crusted lava with feathers
of blue and yellow flame flaring up occasionally. He
could whip the fire back into a blaze if he wanted—
there were enough coals—but it was still plenty warm

in the cabin already. Besides, poking around in the coals would mean breaking his reverie, and he was enjoying the quiet reflection.

Delicate as the fine branches that sprouted from the trees in spring, Olivia had charmed him immediately. Her lips, so pink and wet, begged to be kissed, and he wanted to wrap her hair around his hands and clasp on to her as he moved inside.

I've got to stop thinking about her as a lover. She's a wolf.

As long as his mate remained a daydream, he could handle her. Reality was another thing entirely. The risk was getting daydreams and reality mixed up. If he was honest with himself, he'd admit he needed to feel her in his arms. His very essence ached to protect her, hold her, comfort her. And yes, make love to her.

Muted sunlight reflected off the bright white snow banks into the living room. The sun had definitely climbed to midday, and he needed to get up. He moved to the window and pulled the curtain back to look out. Birds pattered everywhere, enjoying the peanut butter and birdseed logs he'd made for them and set up along the narrow fence that lined the walkway to his porch. Cardinals and a couple of blue jays and tons of little nuthatches and sparrows pecked and bartered over the feast.

Patchy clouds blotched the sky, and snowflakes swirled and danced on a much lighter breeze than the night before. His snow gauge measured twenty inches, but the snow drifted much higher in places and another round of snowfall was expected in the late afternoon, though the gravid clouds of precipitation hadn't rolled in yet. He dropped the curtain into place.

He loved the way winter hugged the forests and mountains of Deep Creek and brought a peace over the valleys. Most of the bears stayed inside even when awake in the cold weather, but he took long hikes in the fresh air to enjoy the blanket of solitude the cold brought to the park.

Time to wake Olivia. He'd been waiting, hoping the extra rest would help. Her ankle needed to be re-bandaged. The cut was probably already healed, but in case, he'd check it and dress it again if necessary. Maybe the swelling had gone down some, too. He walked carefully to his bedroom and rapped on the door.

No answer.

After calling her and knocking louder with no re-sponse, he turned the doorknob and pushed the door open.

An icy blast burst forth, punching him in the face. The room was still dark, as all the shades were drawn closed. Why the hell was it so cold?

"Olivia." He used his loudest whisper. He didn't want to startle her, but something wasn't right.

He moved closer to the antique bed and reached to tap Oliva on the shoulder. When his hand hit the lump of blankets, the fabric collapsed onto the mattress.

Olivia was gone.

"Dammit!" His yelp was loud enough to be heard in the kitchen. He closed his eyes to breathe through the rage that filled him. Gods, the woman was stub-born as hell.

Worse than he was.

What made her think she could travel in the snow that had washed over the forest overnight? Not only was she blind, her ankle was injured. She'd barely be able to move, much less trek through deep snow on one leg.

Stubborn.

He checked the window. She'd mostly closed it, but that had been her escape route. The window was close to the ground and it would be easy to slip out. Had she gone out in the snow without shoes?

Dammit. He'd slept through her escape.

His bear paced, huffing in frustration. *Mate in danger.* The urge to shift almost drowned him in nausea. The pull, so strong, to find her and bring her back. Now he understood how Griff had done what he'd done to Evers. Having a mate was nothing to joke about, and a bear would do anything to protect her. Anything.

Mate is life.

After slamming the window shut and locking it, he went into the living room and stripped and dropped his clothes on the floor then headed out the front door, sliding into his bear as he pulled the door closed behind him. He paused on the porch, where the icy chill blasted him as his body shifted.

Breathe.

His bear fought to surface, pushing aside man with a growl that reverberated through his body. Never had his bear been so eager to take charge.

Mate.

Blues and hues of purple swirled in front of his vision as he relaxed and let his body take on its natural bear form. Fur warmed him and long strong legs formed like columns. His head ached with the stretch, and he gnashed his teeth, nipping at the spiraling snowflakes that filled the air. Curved claws raked through frosty air.

A growl sounded from deep in his gut as his eyesight cleared to a precision unmatched by human vision, and his hearing sharpened. A thousand twitters of birdsong rang in his ears, and close by, the pattering of a rabbit heart sped by.

He swung his head left then right, scanning his fence where yard met forest. In some places, snow drifted almost as high as the four-foot posts. He growled and loped off the porch in search of Olivia. She couldn't have gone far in the deep snow.

He rounded the cabin to the side where his bedroom window perched a few feet off the ground. She'd put on his boots, apparently, and dragged a quilt with her, by the look of the tracks in the snow—though the tracks had filled in a bit, which proved she'd left in the morning. He glanced up at the sky. Gray storm clouds swirled and now covered the sun.

It'd start snowing again soon.

Footprints led to the west, and he hurried to follow them out of his yard and into the deeper part of the forest. He paused to sniff a tatter of his quilt that had caught on a branch and torn off.

Smells of mate.

His bear heart thumped with the sudden rush of blood. He never felt as alive as he did when he was all bear. Snarling, he moved on. He'd find her and bring her home.

The wind whistled as it bore down on the forest, tipping ice-laden branches into graceful curves and crystallized evergreen boughs arced almost to the ground like tunnels of magic. In the dim light, the snow sparkled. As soon as the forest thawed, the trees would spring back upright, tall and majestic.

Resilient.

Mouth open, he panted then paused to sniff the air. No scent of Olivia or any other wolf. Where could she have gone? The footprints into the forest were less defined, and Powell moved more slowly as he tried to track her.

The steel-gray sky began to spit snow, and chunks of ice wedged between the pads of his toes and clumped to his claws. Bears knew better than to be out in this weather for long. Though he had a warm coat, eventually the cold would penetrate to his skin. He shook, sending a shower of loose snow flying in all directions. Everywhere he looked it was white, with interruptions of brown and an occasional green.

No Olivia.

He reared onto his hind legs and scented, again.

Pine. Birds. Some small mammals. And a faint hint of frigid water crashing over smooth boulders in one of Deep Creek's many streams.

No Olivia. Following the fading tracks was his only option.

He continued onward, unable to get a fix on how long it had been since she passed through the area. The snow came down hard now, no longer light flurrying action. He picked up his pace.

Rage fueled his movements and he growled as he

ran. What a dumb thing for her to do. She could easily die of exposure. Hadn't she learned her lesson when she fell down the embankment? Hell, he would've helped her get to town if that's what she wanted. She didn't need to feel like she had to do it all herself. She didn't need to run from him.

Women!

This type of behavior was the exact reason he had never wanted a woman of his own. Or, if he listened to how Griff or Derek described it, a woman would own him, regardless of what he thought. Sure, he'd still protect her and take care of her, but her wish was always the man's command. His bear snorted. Either way, it was too much trouble.

He didn't need the stress.

The fur down his back bristled. No, he was a single bear and intended to stay that way. Just because he had met his mate didn't mean he had to marry her. Besides, she was a wolf and didn't seem to have any clue that he was her mate.

Maybe it didn't work that way.

Maybe he was wrong.

Maybe wolves didn't know who their mate was at all. Olivia had shown no sign that he was anything more to her than a man who'd rescued her.

And would rescue her again.

He padded on.

He shook his head, his ears flapping as the snow went everywhere. *Mate.* Whoever came up with the idea of a fated mate needed a head check. Commitment was for the birds. Too much trouble, too much work. He slowed his run, tired and achy, and ready to leave Olivia in the woods and hope someone else came across her.

Serve her right.

A pang of guilt stabbed him the moment the thought crossed his mind.

Of course he wouldn't dare leave her alone in the snow. He wouldn't leave anyone to die, much less Olivia. He'd only known her a day, and mate or not, she'd consumed about every waking thought and had walked in his dreams.

His ears pricked.

Hey, what was that?

A red round object peeped from beside a large elm tree ahead, and Powell slowed to check. Maybe a woodpecker. Whatever it was, it stuck out like a stop sign in the white snow. No, it was something that he'd seen Olivia wearing—her scarf! She must've limped into the living room to get it before she left. Her coat must not have been dry since she had left it behind.

Or she didn't want him to notice it was gone.

Sure enough, it was her. She leaned against the tree, the quilt wrapped around her and a pair of his boots bulky and loose on her feet. He picked up his pace and rushed to her. Why the hell was she in human form? She hadn't shifted into wolf—and she could've frozen to death because of it.

He nosed her in the side.

She screamed.

Dammit! He'd startled her.

He'd forgotten she couldn't see. He nudged her again. How scary to be in the woods alone, cold, and lost—and not be able to see. He couldn't imagine. An all-encompassing urge to protect her washed over him.

"Powell?" Her voice weak, shaky. She reached for him, taking his head in her hands. "I'm so glad it's you."

He leaned against her, hoping she felt some security in his touch. She trembled with cold. Good thing he'd found her. The quilt was covered in a layer of snow, and the precipitation continued to fall at a steady rate. They needed to get to the cabin.

She climbed on his back, groaning as she moved her leg, and laid her head on him, her arms around his neck, still clutching the quilt. He waited on her to stabilize herself and turned toward home. Shocked that she trusted him to carry her, he headed back to the cabin, careful to balance her and not let her slip and fall. The warmth of her on his back and the slight weight of her body felt right. His bear hummed in approval.

Mate.

The sky had almost completely darkened with clouds, though it was only late afternoon by the time they got back to the cabin, and he eased her onto the porch. She slipped off him and entered the cabin without a word. As he morphed back into his human body, he wondered if she was sneaking out the back door while he shifted. Surely not. She'd seemed genuinely glad to see him. The cold air hit his exposed skin like frozen needles, and he rushed inside to get warm, shutting the door behind him. She wasn't in the living room. He grabbed his pajama pants off the floor and pulled them on.

Olivia limped out of the bedroom with Nar in her arms.

"I don't know what to say." She stroked the cat.

Her hair lay around her shoulders and down her back in a mess of wet tangles, and her cloudy eyes stared into oblivion.

He pulled his T-shirt over his head and down over his abdomen. Anger bubbled in his gut, but it was mixed with relief. She could've died.

"Sit."

She felt around and hobbled over to the couch then sat. Nar lay beside her, and she pulled the blanket over her legs. "I thought I was healed enough. I could walk, somewhat."

"Did you think so?" He poked at the embers and added some small wood and sticks. "Because I thought it was pretty obvious that you weren't ready. It's a long walk to Oakwood, and correct me if I'm wrong, you don't know how to get there from here."

She didn't respond.

He jabbed the tool at the embers, sending sparks up the chimney. For someone who seemed so damn smart, she had done something pretty stupid. Twice in two days.

Nar hopped up onto the hearth and swished his tail, eyes questioning the anger in Powell's voice.

"Meow?"

"Yes, I'm working on it." He petted the cat on the head then scratched him behind the ears. "It'll be hot in here soon."

"Working on what?" Olivia asked.

He looked back to her. She'd pulled the blanket up to her chin, shivering. It was a wonder she hadn't caught a cold by now. Or gotten frostbite. If she'd been human, she would've, for sure.

Being a shifter had saved her life.

"Building a warmer fire." He grabbed the last log off the hearth, a small piece of wood only about two inches in diameter. "I need to get more wood off the porch. We're out in here. It's starting to get dark, so I want to have enough for the night in case the snow piles up more."

"I'm sorry for dragging you out in the cold. I didn't expect you to come after me."

He sighed and put his hands on his hips.

Seriously?

"Of course I'm going to come after you. I'm not going to let you freeze to death." He set the log on the fire with the tongs, then moved to sit beside Olivia on the couch. "But I don't understand why you felt like you had to sneak out."

She shrugged but said nothing.

"Why can't you wait a couple days? I'll take you to Oakwood. And why didn't you shift into a wolf to stay warm? Why stay in human form when you could fight the elements so much better as wolf?"

She turned her face away. "It's a long story."

She'd tensed up and locked down, her knuckles white from tightly grasping her shirt hem.

"I've got time. Tell me. It makes no sense why you wouldn't shift. Unless you thought the wolves could track you more easily? I've kind of guessed that you're running from them."

She shook her head.

Nar jumped up between them, and Powell petted him till he purred and flopped onto his back. "I think I deserve to know why you left a perfectly warm house and went out into the freezing cold with an injured ankle. Are you psycho? If you are, I'd like to know it."

She smacked him on the arm and smirked. "No, I'm not crazy."

"Then why not shift? What reason could you possibly have to go out in the cold by yourself? In a blizzard—blind and injured?"

She pushed her hair behind her ears. "I'll give you the short version, but you have to promise not to pity me."

"I promise." He scooted closer, her scent filling his nostrils and wending through his brain. Pity was the last thing on his mind.

"I'm engaged to Alfred."

It was as if she'd given him a lobotomy with an ice pick.

"What?" Had he heard her correctly? She was engaged to that scrawny asshole? That red wolf without a conscience? What the hell?

"It's not by choice," she added. "The pack thinks it's what's best. No one would want me. I'm damaged goods. And Alfred, well, he can have more than one wife since he can take care of more than one and well, they decided I wouldn't be a burden to him—" Her voice hitched in her throat.

"That is the most ridiculous thing I've ever heard of! Isn't polygamy illegal? Especially forced polygamy?" Anger surged through him, and the desire to rip Alfred's head off consumed him like a flash flood. He fisted his hands and tamped down the feeling, gritting his teeth so he wouldn't scare Olivia. "What the hell is damaged about you? You mean because you are blind?"

She nodded. "That's part of it. There's another reason."

"What?"

She squirmed, her chin quivering. What had Alfred done to her? Powell would kill him.

"I can't shift." She turned her face to him, her milky gaze full of tears.

"Oh." He wiped the tears from her cheeks and pulled her to him, her head on his chest. "Why can't you shift? Did something happen?"

"I've never been able to. It's probably because I'm blind." She sniffled. "At first, I agreed with the pack about marrying Alfred. I figured I'd be taken care of. But then I heard about his sexual sadism, and I can't…"

He gripped her arm and took a deep breath. "And you won't have to. I'll see to it."

Not sure whether her inability to shift or her betrothal to Alfred upset him more, he gritted his teeth. No wonder she was scared. Alfred was an asshole.

"But the pack is strong. They'll find me and drag me back. I won't have a choice."

A long, low howl sounded outside and Olivia tensed in his arms.

"Shh. They aren't close. It'll be evening soon and they are out hunting, that's all. They don't know you're here, and there's no reason to think they will find you, especially with the snow piling up and covering scents. I'll protect you, but you've got to trust me and give me the chance to figure out what to do. We'll handle this together. I need your promise to stay put and let me work up a plan."

"Okay." She relaxed into him.

He stroked her hair. "Everything will be okay. We'll get some dinner and rest."

A loud buzz sounded followed by a snap—then everything went dark in the cabin except for the orange glow of the fire and the faint light coming in the windows from the setting sun.

Chapter Five

"What was that sound?" Her heart thudded and she gripped him. Was Alfred on the porch? *Oh my goddess, no.* He'd kill Powell without hesitation, and she'd be back with the Green Glen wolves before she had a chance to do anything.

"The power went out." Powell's voice held a hint of wariness. "That's all. No need to worry."

"I'm scared," she whispered. And she was. Her palms dampened. Was it possible that Alfred had cut power to the cabin? Would he and the others attack while the power was out and they had the advantage of darkness, killing Powell and taking her back to the pack?

"It often happens when there's a storm. It's gone out quite a few times." He patted her knee. "The power lines get heavy with snow and ice and snap, or the transformer blows. The cabin is so remote, it doesn't take much to cause a problem. And we've gotten a lot of snow. We have a fire to keep us warm, though. We'll be fine."

"Are you sure that's all it is?" Her voice caught. She chewed her bottom lip. Nothing worse than feeling helpless. She was so tired of having to rely on others to take care of her. If only she could shift, she could fight.

"Yes, of course. What else could it be?"

"Alfred." Maybe she should return to the pack and stop all the stress. Be Alfred's wife. Maybe she didn't deserve more. Who would want to be with a blind wolf who couldn't shift, anyway? She'd always be a burden.

"No offense, but he's not that clever." Powell rubbed her arm.

"I wouldn't put it past him. When he wants something, he's pretty insistent."

"He's not going to get his paws on you unless it's what you want."

She shook her head. As much as she didn't know what she'd do, she didn't want to be under Alfred's control. "No. Definitely not."

"Good. I don't want you with him, either." He squeezed her hand and stood. "I need to get more wood from the porch so we can keep the fire going all night. We'll need it to stay warm since the heat is out."

"Okay." If he could tell how frightened she was, he didn't show it. "Do you have enough wood set aside?"

"Yes." He laughed. "There's enough wood for a semi-hibernating bear to sleep away the winter by the fire. Not a little fire, either. A roaring bonfire. Plenty of wood."

She let out a breath. Maybe things would be fine. "If you say so."

"I do. Once the fire's going, we'll find some food. I'm sure you're as hungry as I am. I'll be back."

She pulled the blanket higher, rubbing the softness against her chin. "Please hurry. I don't want to be alone."

"I'll be right here in the living room stacking the wood as I bring it in. You aren't alone. Nar is here too."

"Meow."

The cat rubbed against her, purring. Olivia smiled. She'd never have guessed that she would befriend a cat, ever. Wolves and cats usually didn't get along. But Nar was different. He wasn't all scratchy and bitey like the few other cats she'd met scavenging around the pack fringes. Nar liked her.

She patted him, running her hand down his back. Being a wolf, she'd not had much close-up experience with cats at all, though she'd heard that black cats were even more unlucky than other kinds. A wolf had once told her that the color black was what she saw all the time—the darkness she lived in. It was the absence of color. Surely Nar was different. He was too nice to not have color. One thing was certain, petting him calmed her in a way not much else did.

Powell made several trips in and out, dropping arm-loads of wood on the hearth and floor, and she listened to the wood hit the ground and roll or crack as it landed. He brought in a lot, surely enough to last the whole night. She'd not realized it took so much to keep a fire going. With the door opening and closing, the warm air had escaped, and now the living room was freezing.

Powell hadn't pushed her about shifting.

What had he thought about her inability to transition to a wolf? Did he feel sorry for her? More than he must already because of her blindness?

The blanket wasn't enough to keep the chill away,

and she shivered as she tried to cover herself. As she bent her leg, her ankle ached. So frustrating. She never should've tried to go out in the snow. Healing was likely slowed down, and she'd have to wait longer before she could hike to Oakwood, not counting the stupid snow. If she could shift to wolf form, the ankle would heal much more rapidly. She sighed.

The late day was full of reasons to feel sorry for herself. Powell must take his ranger duties seriously for him to take her in and tend to her injuries.

She was lucky he had been the one to find her.

He tugged the door shut with a thump and clasped the lock.

"That should do it." He coughed. "I think the snow is letting up. But it's pretty deep. Good thing we don't have to get out."

Icy air hung in the cabin. Nar walked across her lap, pausing a moment before jumping down.

"I want to go to Oakwood as soon as possible." She leaned forward. "You shouldn't have to take care of me. I know I'm a burden."

"You aren't a burden, and it's not a problem. It's my job to take care of people lost in the forest, remember?"

She heard him toss another log onto the fire and poke at the flames. A burst of heat raced across the room. So that was it. She was a duty. An obligation to Powell. Nothing more than another lost soul in the forest who needed tending.

The realization made her heart ache, but she didn't know why.

"I'm sorry. You shouldn't have brought me here."

She held her head in her hands. The sooner she could leave the better.

He sat beside her and pulled the blanket over them both, his thigh warm against hers. "Olivia, what's wrong?"

She turned away. How to explain to someone what it felt like to never feel wanted? To never be good enough? To always be the one holding everyone else back?

It sucked.

Hot tears filled her eyes, and she set her chin, trying to keep from breaking down. That would be the topper to a great day—crying in front of her twice-rescuer. He surely couldn't pity her any more than he already did.

"Olivia?" Powell's voice, calm and warm, seemed to come from inside her.

She wiped her eyes. "What?"

"I don't know why you're so upset, but I hope you aren't mad at me."

"No." She paused. "Why would I be upset with you?"

The fire popped and crackled, and the scent of pine filled the cabin. He must've put a fresh pine bough on the fire.

"I don't know. But you are on edge, and I don't know why. I wondered if I'd done something to upset you."

She smoothed the blanket over her legs. "No. I'm sorry. I must seem ungrateful. Thank you for rescuing me. Twice."

"You're welcome. Happy to do it. But please don't leave, again. The snow has reached dangerous levels out there."

"I'm concerned about Alfred. He won't be happy if he finds me here. And he's mad that I left. I'm sure it made him look bad that one of his promised wives ran away."

Powell took her hand, and she savored the warmth of his palm seeping into her skin. So strong. So firm.

A man who knew what he wanted. Yet...one who didn't force his will on others.

"I don't understand why Alfred is being assigned wives and in the plural. Since when are wolves polygamous?" He rubbed her hand with the pad of his thumb.

"They aren't. He's taking all the unwanted girls in marriage. It's supposed to be a mutual thing. He takes care of them and they...take care of him."

For once, she was glad she was blind and couldn't see his reaction. She was ashamed she'd considered the proposal. From the outside, it was absurd. At the time, most pack members made her feel like she was lucky to have Alfred. Now, if she went back, she'd be shunned. If Alfred still wanted her, she'd be punished.

"How many wives does he have?" Powell's voice remained low and unaffected.

"Oh, only two right now. I would've been number three." The fire's heat warmed her cheeks. "He's the only wolf that has more than one partner, though. Because his family is in charge, though I think most of us know that Alfred runs the pack. Claude is weak."

"That's ridiculous, you know that?" He squeezed her hand. "Having more than one wife—and not being in love, that's my assumption?"

"Oh, he doesn't love anyone but himself." She tried to pull her hand free, but Powell held on, gently squeezing.

"What about true mates? Love? Hasn't he heard of that?"

She shook her head and relaxed in his grip. "He doesn't believe in fated mates." Her heart pattered at Powell's proximity. Why did he have such an effect on her? He was a bear, for goodness' sake. But every time he was close, she broke into a light sweat and her heart did mini flips. And she craved his closeness.

He cleared his throat. "Unacceptable. True love and fated mates are…essential beliefs."

"That's why I left. I want more. Well, and I don't want to be a burden."

"You deserve more. Much more. You won't have to go back, I'll make sure of it." His voice picked up an urgency she hadn't heard before. "You aren't a burden to me, Olivia."

Every bit of her essence wanted to believe him. But how could he help her? He was a bear. She was wolf.

A damaged wolf.

They didn't share the same urges. On the cold nights of winter, she ran with the moon and he napped by the fire. She wiggled away, pulling her hand free. Napping by the fire was something she could get used to.

If only…

She sensed him before she felt him. Warmth then soft lips touching hers, his hand sliding behind her head and pulling her toward him. Off balance, she inhaled deeply, filling her lungs with his scent and tumbling head over heels in her mind as she reached for something to grab on to. Her wolf howled inside like it had been set free from a trap.

He tugged her close, planting kiss after kiss on her

lips and cheeks till she responded, sliding her tongue along the seam of his lips. He welcomed her tongue and met it with his own, thrusting with a strength and passion she'd not imagined was possible.

After a moment, she pulled back. He didn't speak. What was he thinking? What cues would his facial expression provide, if she could see?

"I'm sorry." He offered no other words but pushed the blanket away, then stood and walked away.

Chapter Six

Powell shoved the iron poker at the fire, lining up the burning logs with precision. The flames surged and sputtered. What the fuck had he done? He couldn't bear to look at Olivia. She'd trusted him.

He'd betrayed her trust. He was no better than Alfred, forcing himself on her.

Blind and injured, she was his responsibility. Not because he was a park ranger, but because he was her mate. Even though she didn't seem to sense they were mates, he was sure they were. Hell, maybe wolves didn't know when they met their mates. Maybe it took longer than a first touch for them to know.

It didn't matter. He'd taken advantage of someone in a weaker position and that wasn't his style. Kissing her when she was in such a vulnerable position had been out of line.

Dammit.

Sorry wasn't enough, but what else could he say? She was stuck in his cabin for the foreseeable future unless they got out the snowmobile and tried to get to town. With her injury, the last thing they needed was to have to deal with an accident. They needed to wait until the snow stopped before snowmobiling, that would be safer. He'd gone out on rescues when the snow was pouring down, of course, but he didn't want to risk his mate.

He peeked at her.

Blond hair splayed across her shoulders, blanket pulled up under her nose—she looked like a child hiding from a scary movie. Yet he knew how strong she was. The fact that she'd set out, blind, not once but twice, into the forest to get away from an unimaginable fate with her pack proved that.

She'd had a rough couple of days.

The flickering fire their only light, she was bathed in oranges and yellows, more beautiful than any girl he'd ever seen. Knowing she was his mate cast her in a different light, for sure, but he'd dare say she was gorgeous inside and out.

He'd kissed her because he couldn't resist. He'd never been in that position before.

Way to go.

Now he felt like a first-class asshole. Never mind that she'd kissed him back. That might have been habit from dealing with Alfred, responding out of fear of repercussion if she didn't. Anger rose in his gut.

If that damn wolf had harmed her, he *would* kill him. It wasn't an idle threat. The bears had dealt with the wolves before, and Powell already knew what a scheming jerk the red wolf was. He'd used his own injured brother to gain the bears' sympathy and scope out intel to take to the lions. Probably had been paid well too.

He breathed out slowly. Getting ahead of himself and letting his imagination run wild wasn't going to solve anything. He didn't know the truth about Olivia's relationship with Alfred, other than she didn't want to marry him.

She hadn't said the wolf had done anything to her or physically harmed her, though clearly he'd been emotionally abusive. Powell shouldn't leap to conclusions until he knew the whole story. Still, he couldn't help but want to rip Alfred's throat out for thinking about touching Olivia.

His bear reared up inside, pawing and begging to be released to go after Alfred.

Having a mate was complicated. Being a bear and having a mate that was a wolf?

Impossible.

For now, he'd have to make the best of things with Olivia. She'd be staying with him for a little while, until she was healed enough to get around on her own. No more trudging through the snow with a bum ankle though—he'd see to that.

"How about a sandwich for dinner?" Lame, yes, but practical. Plus, fixing dinner gave him a chance to think and maybe figure out a way to redeem himself. A way to apologize. He had to start talking to her again, somehow.

"Sure, that sounds good." She pulled her legs up onto the couch, gently easing her injured ankle onto the pillow. "Thank you."

No mention of the kiss. And she was talking. Good signs.

"Give me a minute to set the table." He placed the fire poker back into its holder. "Peanut butter and honey sandwiches okay? I know I have both."

"Yes, I love peanut butter." She kicked her legs forward and started to rise then winced and fell back into the couch. "I'm sorry I'm not much help."

"You relax and let me fix dinner. You're injured. I can make sandwiches." Relieved she didn't seem mad, he headed toward the kitchen.

The open-floor plan of the cabin allowed him to keep his eye on her, and he grabbed a candelabra off the bookcase and set it on the table then lit the candles. She leaned back on the couch and closed her eyes, folding her hands under her cheek. She rested a few minutes, and he retrieved the honey from the pantry. When he returned, she was sitting up.

"Powell?" Her voice rang out, clear and firm.

"Yeah? What is it?" He grabbed the loaf of bread and pulled the peanut butter from the cabinet.

"When we're eating, I want to talk." She twisted the edge of the blanket with her fingertips, worrying the edges.

He swallowed and pulled out two plates from the cabinets beside the sink. "Of course. Why wouldn't we talk?"

"About the kiss."

He paused. "Okay." He opened the silverware drawer and took out a knife, swallowing down the fear rising in his throat. "Whatever you want to talk about."

A woman who'd turned down Alfred wasn't going to let Powell get away with an unexplained kiss. He couldn't blame her. If only he knew more about the mating of bears and wolves, he might understand what was going on, because he definitely felt a strong sense of protectiveness when he was around her. He couldn't fully explain it, but it was something he'd never felt before.

A need to be near her. An urge to shelter her from anything that might hurt her.

A desire so white hot and pure, it could consume him if he let it.

Powell watched Olivia take a bite of the sandwich and set it back on the plate in front of her. He'd helped her to the table, letting her lean on him as she limped across the wooden floor. It'd taken every bit of willpower he had not to pick her up and carry her, though she was getting around better than a human would be so soon after an ankle injury. The last thing he needed to do was force her or overpower her. Make her feel weak around him.

He needed her to trust him. No, more than that, he *wanted* her to trust him.

The fire had heated the cabin, but a chill still filled the corners and dark areas, so he had retrieved one of his sweatshirts for Olivia. The gray shirt dwarfed her but provided some warmth, he hoped. She pushed her hair behind her shoulders.

"It's good," she said, mouth full. "I didn't realize how hungry I was."

He pulled the strips of crust off his sandwich. "Me either, though I'd rather be having a juicy steak than a peanut butter and honey sandwich." He laughed.

She sipped her water then set the glass down, smiling. "Me too."

He ate in silence, waiting on her to start the conversation he dreaded. The fire popped across the room, and occasionally, the wind whistled through small cracks around the windowpanes. Olivia was quiet, eating and seemingly lost in thought. Though blind, it didn't take her any time to figure out and remember where her food and drink were on the table.

He wiped his mouth and set his napkin down, his sandwich gone. After a long yawn, he drank another gulp of water. Things had been too exciting for winter. His body was tired, and he was used to napping much of the winter away. Lying awake the night before hadn't helped. Exhaustion crept through his muscles and he stifled a yawn.

If he had to stay awake, he would. For Olivia, anything.

"You kissed me." She pushed her empty plate away. "Why?"

He opened his mouth then closed it. Her straightforwardness both shocked and pleased him. Never a fan of games or passive aggressiveness, he was still a bit taken aback. He cleared his throat. "I wanted to."

"I see." She seemed to think about his answer for a minute.

He stood. "I'm going to put our dishes in the kitchen."

"Okay. But we aren't done talking." She drank the last of her water. "Aren't you afraid of Alfred? I mean, that you kissed me. He'd kill you for kissing me."

"No, I'm not afraid of Alfred. Are you?" He gathered their plates and set them on the kitchen counter. "Besides, I thought you didn't want to be with him."

"I don't, and I won't. But I'm still afraid of him. He's…mean."

"I can handle him. You don't need to worry. We're safe here."

"I wouldn't want something to happen to you." She shivered and rubbed her arms.

"I can take care of Alfred if I need to. You don't need to worry. Let's go back in the living room by the fire where it's warm."

"Yes. Please."

He took her by the arm, and she leaned on him as she limped. He breathed her in, trying not to be too obvious. If she'd allow, he'd take her in his arms and kiss her again. But he didn't get a read on whether she'd liked the kiss or was upset by it. He couldn't risk another one.

Not yet.

She sat on the couch.

"I'll be right back. I need to grab something from the bedroom." He glanced at the fire to make sure the wood situation was okay. The fire blazed, the wood filling the fireplace.

"I'll be here." She yawned. "Not like I can go anywhere. But you know that."

"Yeah, we're stuck. Give me a minute."

He headed to his room and grabbed his hairbrush off the dresser then returned to the living room. She had her head leaned back on the edge of the couch, her eyes closed, her neck bare. His pulse quickened at the sight of her exposed neckline, pale and long. He reached out to run his fingertips along the skin, but pulled away.

Did this mate thing always make bears crazy? It seemed like he was barely in control of his actions. Olivia was like a strong magnet—stronger than any he'd ever been around. And he was pure metal.

He moved to sit beside her and she turned to face him. "You're back."

"Yes. I'd like to brush your hair." He used his low and calm voice. "If you'll let me."

She raised her head. "Is it that bad?"

He smiled. "It's a bit of a tangle. I thought we could talk while I do it."

"Okay. That'd be nice. Thank you. What do you want to talk about?"

"Turn to the side." He helped her move. "I don't know. What do you want to talk about?"

"Not snow or winter or injured ankles or Alfred."

He brushed her hair in long strokes from scalp to end. The pale strands glistened in the firelight as they fell from his fingertips. Maybe she'd relax. His father used to brush his mother's hair, and Powell saw how much she'd loved it. He never thought that one day he'd use the same technique to try to relax his mate. He took a deep breath and steeled himself against a possible pushback.

"Let's talk about your shifting ability. I'm curious to learn more about it." He stopped to pick at a tangle.

"You mean my inability to shift." She winced. "Ouch."

"Sorry. That was a pretty tight tangle." He continued. "So you've *never* been able to shift? Not once? Not even when you were a child?" Shifting had come so easily for him, he couldn't imagine not being able to change into his bear. In fact, he couldn't remember a time when he had to think about the process. It was always accessible. A part of who he was. His bear was right there, waiting to come to the surface and take charge. He'd assumed that was true for all shifters.

"Never. And I've tried. Really hard. I simply don't have the ability." Her shoulders slumped. "I'm simply not meant to shift."

How to respond to her? He brushed another section, detangling the knots and straightening the length. Never shifting? He couldn't deal with that. Being a bear was such an integral part of who he was—to not be able to shift? He'd want to die.

"Are there other wolves that can't shift?" He tried to keep his tone light, but she was bound to feel lonely. Being among shifters and not sharing the ability was a fate he wouldn't want to suffer. Maybe he shouldn't push it, but he wanted to know what was going on.

"Not that I've ever known or heard of. I'm the only lucky one." She turned her face toward him, smirking. "And bonus! I'm blind too. Don't you think I'm incredibly lucky?"

A burst of wind rattled the windowpanes, and she turned her head toward the sound. He sensed her fear rising.

"It's the wind. Nothing more." He paused his brushing.

"I guess I'm a bit jumpy."

"Understandable." He ran his fingers through her hair. "You've had a lot of things going on. And Alfred isn't someone to mess with. You're right, he's dangerous."

"If I could shift, I would be able to fight him on my own. Or escape without falling down an embankment."

"To be honest, I think you can shift. I think you have the ability inside you, somewhere. You're a wolf, and wolves are strong creatures. Majestic. Maybe you haven't found your magic yet. But I'll bet it's there."

"I don't think so. Otherwise, I would've found it by now. It's not like I haven't tried."

"Maybe you haven't been looking in the right place."

"Maybe. But maybe my being blind keeps me from seeing what I need to see to be able to shift."

He placed his hand over her heart. "I think you can see everything you need to see right here."

She touched his hand for a moment, her hand trembling. "I don't know, Powell. I've tried everything. Maybe it's time to accept that I'm damaged and I'm simply not like the other wolves. It happens, right?"

"You're definitely not like any wolf I know. You're better." He took a deep breath. "If only you could see what I see in you."

She moved her hand and ducked her head. "You're as blind as I am. Maybe more so."

He started brushing again, and she closed her eyes as he twisted the silken strands gently. Anguish nearly consumed him. He hurt for her. Yet she was kind and empathetic. She hadn't turned out bitter and hardened as some people would. She accepted things and made the best of them, and when things happened to her that she didn't like, she made an effort to change them. Running from Alfred had taken more courage than most people could imagine, much less muster.

He ran the brush through her hair, teasing out each tangle. Every brush stroke sent an electric impulse skittering up his arm. It was as if her wolf called to him.

Her heart beat a rhythm composed especially for him. His bear paced, growling for release.

And Powell wanted to answer that call.

He did think she knew how to shift, somewhere deep inside. She needed help. A clue where to begin. How could he help her? There had to be a way.

The sudden realization made his mouth go dry, and he set the brush in his lap.

"What about Shoshannah? Maybe she could help you." Excitement coursed through him. The ancestral spirit might actually be able to help Olivia shift. Healing her would be exactly the type of thing Shoshannah would do. She might cure her blindness, though that was less likely.

Olivia's shoulders drooped. "The cave spirit? I thought she was merely a legend until Alfred said she helped Claude when he was shot. But I didn't realize she helped anyone. Especially someone like me."

"She helps shifters. Not everyone, but some. She also offers advice, kind of like an oracle of sorts. You should talk to her. She might help."

Olivia tensed. "And she truly heals people? Alfred wasn't lying about Claude?"

"She does. She takes care of all the shifters of Deep Creek. Sure, she mainly helps the shifters who guard the cave, but yes, she did help Claude. No one knows how she picks and chooses."

"It's hard to believe."

"Yes, I know. But it's true. I've seen her."

"What does she look like?" Olivia cocked her head. "I've heard she's very beautiful and pure. Of course, I'll never see her."

He paused. "When I've seen her, mostly she's been a large white bear, sometimes made of smoke or light or rain. White, like the brightest light. She often speaks aloud and occasionally in a person's head. Sometimes, a shifter might go and meditate all day and she won't appear. She's not a simple creature, but she knows when and who she wants to help."

"Hmm. Definitely sounds magical. I wonder if she would speak to me."

"I don't know. If she could help you, that would be great. We should go to her and find out." He moved the brush onto the pillow beside him. "It wouldn't hurt to ask her, anyway. If you want to, that is."

He waited for her response, hoping she would agree though he could tell she wasn't fully buying the idea of a cave spirit. He couldn't blame her.

Nar leapt onto the couch. "Meow."

He reached for Nar, but the cat hopped down.

"When can we go?" Olivia's voice betrayed her excitement. "If she can help me see, or shift, I don't want to waste any more time. I want to talk to her. As soon as possible."

"Maybe tomorrow if it stops snowing. We can take the snowmobile and be at the cave in no time. If Shoshannah can help, it could be the miracle you need to free you from Alfred's grip."

"Do you think she can? I'm afraid to get my hopes up."

"It's worth a shot. What have you got to lose?"

Olivia nodded. "Yes, I want to go. I hope the snow stops soon."

"Me too."

Chapter Seven

Olivia turned over in the bed and pulled the ancient quilt up to her chin. The fabric, softened by years of use, had thinned, but the batting was compressed and warm and the flannel back smooth against her cheek. Powell had to retrieve another one from his cedar chest since she'd dragged the one he'd had on his bed through the snow.

The air in the room stilled with the chill, the heat from the fire barely radiating to the far corners of the cabin. Still, she'd insisted on sleeping in the bedroom, and they'd propped the door so the warmth could trickle into the room. The couch wasn't comfortable or large enough for the two of them to rest comfortably, and she didn't want to be alone.

Powell snored beside her, his breath rattling in his chest. She'd asked him to lie down with her, both to share warmth and because she was frightened. Though used to the dark, something about having no electricity made the world seem darker and scarier. She worried that Alfred was waiting outside to pounce on them at any moment, though that made no logical sense.

They hadn't heard any howls at all, only the gusty

wind as it beat against the little cabin and the distant crackling of the fire that warmed the space enough to keep them from freezing to death. Nar lay between her and Powell, curled up in a perfect circle of fuzzy warmth. Olivia stroked him and he purred louder.

She wiggled her toes and moved her ankle. It felt so much better than when she'd taken off hiking. Such a stupid idea. She'd known she wouldn't make it to Oakwood, but she'd thought she was protecting Powell from Alfred and the other wolves.

The bear changed things when he was around. Her dark world seemed to light with color.

Since he'd first wrapped her ankle she'd known he was different. Initially, she thought it was because he was a bear. Slowly, she'd realized it was more than that. With each gesture to make her comfortable, to help her, or simply listen to what she had to say, she became more aware that the growing spark in her gut was something special.

And now she was more certain of it. She'd wondered what it was about Powell that made her stomach turn flips when he was around. The feelings were so trite to describe and yet so wonderful to experience. She'd never thought she would have them, being an outcast in her pack. But obviously she'd been wrong because it had happened. Faster than she'd thought possible too.

Mate.

It had become very clear when he kissed her but she didn't say anything or admit the realization to herself, it'd been so unexpected. She'd barely had time to let the possibility form in her mind before he'd pulled away and acted like he'd kissed a frog.

Why did bears act like wolves had leprosy?

Had he felt anything when he kissed her? He hadn't acted like it. Nothing beyond lust, anyway—certainly not that she was his fated mate. Her questioning him hadn't revealed anything either.

Surely he'd have said something if he felt they were mates, wouldn't he? Men were so confusing.

Not lust, though.

Lust was a feeling she understood a lot more since Alfred was always sniffing around her. Thank goodness he'd been holding off till marriage to claim her. She shuddered.

She could never go back to Alfred, that was for sure. Especially since men like Powell existed. Even if he didn't realize they were mates, the gentleness with which he treated her was enough for her to realize she did deserve more than Alfred.

She tugged the quilt higher.

Odd that her mate would show up when she needed a rescuer, but she'd heard the knight-in-shining-armor story a million times.

He'd agreed to take her out in the deep snow, through Deep Creek, to the ancestral spirit's cave. She could ask for healing. Olivia tucked her hands under her cheek on the pillow.

What would she say to Shoshannah? She didn't feel worthy to speak to something so special. What if the spirit took one look at her and offered her a place in hell, instead? A shifter who couldn't shift?

Defective.

Why would anyone offer to help when there were many who were more worthy?

That wasn't supposed to be Shoshannah's style, but she also wasn't known as a spirit to simply hand out healing. She might pity Olivia or she might tell her to live with the blindness because wolves were considered evil. No way to know how she would respond or if she'd appear to them at all.

Anxiety gripped her and burned in her gut. The sooner the sun came up, the better. She'd barely dozed all night, and it was bound to be morning soon.

Olivia reached for Powell, putting her hand on his side and feeling the rise and fall of his breathing. He seemed to have not a care in the world, and she had the weight of everything on her shoulders. She took a deep breath and began to count backward from one hundred.

"Liv?" Powell's sleepy voice broke the silence. "You awake?"

"Meow." Nar rubbed against Olivia's knees.

"Yeah, I'm awake." She pulled her hand away.

He coughed and the bed shook as he moved to turn. Nar meowed then hopped down. "Looks like we made it through the night, but the power isn't back on yet." He got out of bed and she heard the curtains rustling. "The snow's stopped."

"Is there a lot?"

"Oh yeah. It's beautiful. The woods are white and pristine and pure."

"And cold." She giggled and burrowed into the quilt.

"Yes, very cold. Glad you're inside." He yawned. "I'm going to go toss more wood on the fire. Be right back."

"Okay." She listened to his footsteps. Bare feet on the wooden floor. He had to be chilly.

She lay still, waiting on Powell to return, hoping they'd be able to go see Shoshannah after breakfast. Hoping she'd be able to heal her. Olivia held more hope than she'd had in a long time.

And it was all because of Powell.

"That should heat us right up." Powell walked into the room and sat on the bed. "How's your ankle feeling?"

"Much better today." She lifted her foot under the cover. "I think I might be able to walk."

"That's great news. You are a shifter, after all."

She felt the tone of happiness. Yes, things were looking up. "Are we going to go see Shoshannah today?"

"I think we can make it to the cave, yes. The snow has stopped, and it won't take long to get there on the snowmobile. If you're up to it."

She sat up. "Oh, yes. I can't wait to hear what she has to say. I hope she can help me."

His voice lowered. "I hope so too."

Olivia licked her lips. Though the power was off in the cabin, there was electricity in the air. Charged with emotion, she wanted to act on her desire. Touch Powell. Have him touch her back. But what if he refused her?

Nothing would be more humiliating.

She sighed.

"What is it?" He scooted closer on the bed. "Are you nervous about meeting Shoshannah?"

"Sure I am. But that's not what I'm thinking about." She rubbed her face.

"Well, spill it. What are you thinking about?"

"The kiss—"

"Not that again." His voice held a level of exasperation she'd not heard from him. "I'm sorry I kissed you, Olivia. Can you drop it? I didn't mean to upset you."

"It's not that. I—I *wanted* you to kiss me." Her heart nearly pounded loose from her chest.

For a moment, he didn't speak. "You did? I couldn't tell."

He didn't believe her. Did that mean…he had wanted her? For real? "Lean this way." Surprised at the strength in her voice she reached her hands toward him. "I want to touch you."

The bed rocked as he moved close, his knees touching her thigh. She put her hands in the air and felt for his face, and he guided her hands to his cheeks. "Right here," he said.

She cupped his cheeks, warm with exertion or embarrassment or merely life, the scruff of a day or two's beard. Mouth parted, she ran her index finger around the curve of his jawline. Strong and angular, he must be very attractive. His lips were smooth and soft, but she knew that from the kiss. When she ran her finger down the bridge of his nose, he shivered, and she lightened her touch, feeling one eyebrow, the other, then feathering each row of lashes.

"Mmmm." He let out a groan. "That feels good. Like your touch is healing or stress-relieving."

She didn't answer but continued to trace his features in the darkness of her mind. She splayed her fingers in his hair, then moved on to his neck and his broad shoulders, massaging and feeling the strong muscles. No wonder he'd been able to carry her so easily. Her breath quickened.

"Powell?"

"Hmmm?"

"Kiss me?"

He leaned in, his lips meeting hers, and she arched against him, opening her mouth to let him explore and to revisit the magical sensations his kiss had brought to life the day before. She wouldn't stop and she hoped he felt the same. He growled and pushed her back onto the bed, lying alongside her, his hand in the small of her back and keeping her pressed against him.

She kissed him back and tugged at his shirt, trying to pull it off and feel him at the same time. He pulled away, and for a brief moment she worried he didn't want her—then he came back, his mouth crushing hers. She wrapped her arms around him, and her hands found bare skin, hot to the touch. Muscles flexing and moving as he kissed her jawline and down her neck.

He pulled back again, his breathing ragged. "Are you sure you want this, Olivia? I don't want to take advantage of you. I couldn't bear to hurt you."

"Yes!" She tried to tug him toward her. "Please. I need you."

"Shit."

"What is it?" A lump lodged in her throat. Did he not want her?

"I don't have any condoms."

She smiled. "Wolves know when their fertile times are, and this is not my time. And you know shifters don't carry human disease. We don't need a condom." She tugged at her shirt hem. "I want the warmth of your skin on mine. I want to see you with our touch."

"I've no argument with that." He slipped off her shirt and bra, giving a quick kiss to each nipple before pushing her back on the bed and sliding her pants and underwear off. She'd have had to be deaf to not hear his intake of breath. Was he pleased?

What she wouldn't give to see him.

He stood and she heard clothing hit the floor, one piece after another. A louder thump.

His pants.

Her legs quivered from excitement, a little fear, and the chill in the room. She held her arms out to him. "Hurry. I need to feel you."

"Honey, you're going to feel me, all right. And you're going to love it." He clambered back onto the bed, and it shook under him.

She giggled. "Is that so?"

"Have I ever lied to you?" He placed his hands on either side of her hips and slid her toward him.

"Well, not that I know of."

He pinched her thigh gently. "I don't lie. If I promise you something, I mean it."

"Then make me love it." She let her legs fall open.

"Not so fast. I need you to be ready."

"I am ready." She tried to sit up but he pushed her down.

No sooner than her head hit the quilt, his fingers traced her inner thighs and streaks of pleasure raced up to her core. Feather-light touches followed, growing ever closer to her sex, and she panted in anticipation.

"I want you to enjoy this." He stroked the fine hair on her mound, dipping inside little by little.

"I am." She breathed, her hips automatically responding to his touch and pushing forward, seeking more.

"That's it. Relax."

Eyes closed, she watched the colors of pleasure swirl in her darkness. When he slid one finger inside her, she cried out and bucked her hips forward. This was what being with one's mate felt like? Nothing else would ever come close.

She was sure he was smiling, so she lay still except for her body's growing need to push against him. He had two fingers inside now, or maybe three, and his thumb pressed rhythmically on her clitoris. She strained to capture the pleasure, pushing against him. Slowly, the snow disappeared then the cabin, the room, the bed…and all that was left was Powell and his fingers.

The orgasm hit her hard and fast, and she cried out without shame as waves of sensation pulsed through her. Powell wasted no time. As soon as she relaxed he moved between her legs and positioned his cock against her then pushed.

She breathed in as he entered her. She'd not ever seen stars except in her dreams, but she saw them behind the window shades of her eyes now as he thrust into her again and again. His weight on top of her didn't give her much room to move, but she tried to meet every thrust with a counter of her own, taking him as deeply as she could, savoring the long strokes as he made love to her.

How long had they been together? She couldn't tell. Maybe it was nightfall or a week later. Powell's lovemaking had made her lose all sense of time.

He sped, the thrusts shorter and faster. Warmth spread through her, like a puddle of sunshine, and she tipped her head back to savor the sensation. He kissed her throat and nipped at her collarbone and she giggled. With another push, long and strong, he paused and laid his head on her shoulder as he came undone with a long, low groan. She wrapped her arms around him and held him close.

Was it possible for a bear and a wolf to mate forever?

If anyone could, it had to be them. Powell felt so perfect. So right.

She'd ask Shoshannah.

But not yet. Now, she would enjoy Powell some more.

Chapter Eight

Powell zoomed through the woods, the snowmobile gliding easily over the fresh-fallen snow and Olivia clinging to his back. He smiled and took a deep breath of crisp air, scented with pine and ice. The rush of speed, coupled with the natural beauty of the forest, and the knowledge his mate was holding on tight, all came together into a happiness he'd not felt before.

Making love to Olivia had been better than he'd ever imagined it could be, with anyone. He was sure the stupid grin on his face was now a permanent fixture. He squeezed the gas and the snowmobile raced ahead over the path.

Fortunately, he had two helmets in the basement from riding around with Derek to check out the far reaches of the park when the snow was deep. And thank goodness she had healed enough to be able to walk again and wear her boots. He'd had the snowmobile out recently when he'd scoped out Deep Creek during ranger duties, so it was ready to go.

"Shit," he mumbled, his voice lost under the grumble of the engine. He'd not sent in his log or updates on his last check of the park. He'd meant to email before the power went out. Not a big deal, because the other rangers would understand and not worry. Still, Powell would've liked to report the brewing issues with the wolves.

He was sure the bears had heard the wild howls the last few nights and wondered what was up. The howls were definitely echoing each other and not the normal "howl at the moon" crazy shit the wolves usually did when they were bored.

Most of the bears were likely napping or gorging themselves while bingeing on TV cop shows anyway. With the gates now closed to the public and the one open road impassable because of the blizzard, Deep Creek would be quiet.

A wonderland.

He slowed the snowmobile to go over a mini hill between two large oaks that bowed over the path like a tunnel.

"Hold on tight," he hollered.

Olivia clutched him as they sailed over the hill, the snowmobile plunking into the snow on the other side of the hill with a spray of fine particles fanning into the air like sparkling rain. He felt Olivia laugh and he leaned back into her. She squeezed him tighter.

He held the moment in his mind, savoring it. True bliss—the purity of the snow settled over Deep Creek, the echo of Olivia's laugh, and the warmth of her body pressed against his.

He turned the curve on the path that led toward the cave. The woods grew denser and blocked more of the sunlight, but the sun that did get through laid down notched shadows across the crystalline ground—rows of shadow branches like a fractured landscape.

If he hadn't been out patrolling, he'd not have found Olivia down the embankment. With her injury and the amount of snow that had fallen, she'd have surely died of exposure. Not much chance the wolves would've found her.

Even if they had, it would've been bad for her. Amazing how things seemed to work out the way they were supposed to. Meant to.

Alfred wanted her as a toy, nothing more.

Anger pounded in Powell's temples and he throttled the snowmobile, edging the speed up. If he ever ran into that smarmy red wolf, he'd kill him. The thought that a wolf, anyone, believed he could prey on the disadvantaged for his own pleasure? It enraged him.

Olivia scooted closer, holding tightly, and he slowed down, willing himself to calm, and edged the snowmobile to turn eastward. They'd be at the cave in no time. He couldn't meet up with Shoshannah while angry with Alfred. He needed to focus on Olivia. He took a breath of cold air and let it out slowly. Then, he could focus on the mating bond.

He hoped Shoshannah would help her. If not, Olivia was perfect to him.

Slowing to cross the earthen bridge over a small stream, he gazed at clear water rushing through an ice dam of snow and leaves and sticks and slippery rocks, creating a cascade of cold beauty. If only Olivia could see it too. A pang of guilt pierced his heart and he hit the gas. He'd figure out how to share the beauty of Deep Creek with Olivia, one way or another.

She could hear the birdsong and the splash of water. She could touch velvety moss and rough bark and smell the natural composting of leaves. He'd help her feel the beauty in every way he could.

Maneuvering the snowmobile was more difficult as he eased through the dense copse of trees as he neared the cave entrance. Where were the Sentinels? Even in winter, bears guarded the cave entrance. Powell knew where they stood guard, but he didn't see them.

They'd be there somewhere though, hidden from plain sight. With the lions pawing around, the security threat was high.

He slowed more as they approached the cave, looking for a place to stop. He'd have to leave the snowmobile close but not by the entrance. Ah, there was a Sentinel in a tree stand. He nodded his head, hoping he'd be recognized under the helmet then realized they'd know his snowmobile.

He drove as near to the cave entrance as he could then killed the engine and unbuckled his helmet. They'd have to traipse through the drifting snow to get into the cave, but it wasn't far.

No one shoveled the path. In fact, the bears had covered part of the entrance during winter to keep snow from blowing into the cave, and the snow had piled several feet up the barrier.

Olivia struggled with her helmet, so he helped her pull it off. He set it on the seat of the snowmobile.

"We're here?" She took in a deep breath. "That wasn't a long ride."

"Not too far, but a long way to walk." He set his helmet beside hers. The freezing air bit at his throat. "It's always warmer in the cave, so let's go inside."

The cave, like most, stayed at a constant ambient temperature—not warm but not freezing, either. There were some areas deep in the tunnels where warm spring water increased the humidity and warmed the air more, but the main part of the cave where the lake was stayed at around fifty-five degrees Fahrenheit. Winter or summer, it was a tad cool but not cold.

His teeth chattered as he scanned the woods for signs of anyone besides the Sentinels. Always on the lookout for infringing lions or wolves, he relaxed at the virgin landscape. Apparently no one had ventured out in the snow—even the small animals that usually filled the trees and underbrush with scurrying and scampering seemed to be hunkered down in their dens. The woods lay pristine in their covering except for the snowmobile tracks that led to the cave area.

"I'm all for warmer. Lead the way."

A bright pink flush settled over her pale cheeks from the snowmobile ride, and her hair, in a loose braid when they left, was now in a tangle from the helmet and the wind.

Goddess, she was beautiful.

She held out her arm, and he took it in his own and guided her through the deep snow. Knee-deep near the cave, the snowfall had varied from a foot to several feet throughout the park. As much as he loved the snow, his bear loved it more, and he wanted to shift and play. But now wasn't the time. He didn't want to make Olivia feel bad that she couldn't join him, either.

"I hope she'll appear." He guided Olivia into the

cave's entrance, helping her duck under the narrow part that wasn't blocked for winter. "We may have to wait a while."

"Me too. I'd heard talk of Shoshannah before, of course. The wolves never mentioned that she might help me." She'd lowered her voice to a whisper.

Powell grabbed a flashlight from the bears' stock in the anteroom to the lake and then lit a lantern as well, setting it on one of the tables. Though he'd been visiting the cave since he was a cub, he still didn't feel comfortable being inside in total darkness.

He'd never be able to handle the world Oliva lived in. She was stronger than he'd suspected.

"I don't know what she can or can't do, but we're going to find out. Sometimes it takes a bit for her to show up. I'm going to grab a couple of blankets."

"You bears are prepared."

He chuckled. Yes, that was one word for the bears. Prepared. Well, they tried to be. Speaking for himself, he surely hadn't been prepared to stumble on his mate in a snowbank on a cold day when he felt like napping.

He grabbed two dark wool blankets from the chest then closed it, setting the blankets on top.

"I'm going to need a little help carrying this." He pushed the flashlight into Olivia's hand. "Hold this for me and hang on to me. My arms are going to be full."

"Okay." She took him by the waist and turned her face up to him, eyes closed.

He kissed her on the forehead then hugged her. "Whatever happens in here, don't forget that you'll always have me. No matter what. It doesn't matter to me if Shoshannah helps you. I mean, I hope she will, but if she doesn't, it does not change the way I feel."

"Always?" She laid her head on his chest. "Do you mean that?"

"Always. That's what mate means, isn't it?" He stroked her hair. He'd said it aloud. *Mate*. A thrilling sensation raced through him and he wanted to shout. *Mate!*

"You feel it too?" Her voice cracked. "Really?"

He brushed her hair back and planted kisses on her forehead, cheeks, chin, and finally her mouth. "I felt it the first time I held you in my arms."

"I wasn't sure bears—"

"Oh, yes. I knew you were my fated mate, even though you're a wolf. I wasn't sure wolves knew if their mates were bears."

She laughed. "Yeah, but I was afraid to believe it. I mean, of course we know when our fated mates are wolves. But there aren't many instances of fated mates being other shifter species. We're in new territory."

Her voice echoed in the chamber like a thousand tiny bells, sending shivers up his spine. He'd seen Griff completely smitten by Amy and thought it was all hogwash. Now, he was starting to understand. He was sure Griff and Derek would rag him about it. But he didn't care as long as he had Olivia in his life.

The other rangers could tease him all they wanted. He'd still be the winner.

With a single finger, he traced the sides of her face. "Believe it, Olivia. Since meeting you, I can't imagine life without you. I can't explain why things have changed, only that they have. And I don't know all the details about how we'll deal with our den and pack, but we will. Whatever it takes to be together."

Her smile was so big, he thought he might burst open with happiness. He traced her eyebrows. "I know you can shift. I feel your wolf so close to the surface. She wants to be set free."

"I hope you're right."

"Let's go talk to Shoshannah."

"I'm ready."

Powell stretched, his back aching from sitting on the ground for so long, his muscles stiff from the penetrating cold. Why hadn't Shoshannah appeared? He looked to Olivia. Her shoulders slumped and her head down, she looked like someone who'd lost a loved one.

Defeated.

He'd made a mistake bringing her to the cave. Getting her hopes up. For some reason he'd thought Shoshannah would help. Now what?

"How much longer should we wait?" Olivia's voice turned down in despair. "I don't think she's coming."

He sighed. "I don't know. I had hoped she'd show up."

"I told you I wasn't worth it."

"You are worth it! We never know why Shoshannah chooses to do what she does or show up when she does. I'm sure it isn't you. I know plenty of bears who've sat here for days at a time with no response."

"I wish I could believe that." She propped her arms on her knees and laid her head down. "Tell me what the cave looks like, Powell. Every detail. I want to know."

He scooted close to her and put his arm around her

back, tugging her close in an embrace. "Okay. Let's see, where to start. The area we're in is the largest, I guess you'd call it a room. The cave is open here and in front of us is the lake I told you about. It spans most of this area, though we're on an elevated part that is somewhat like an entryway."

"Okay. Are the walls all stone?"

"Yes." He glanced up. "I can't see very far with only the light of one lantern, but the ceiling and walls were hollowed out a long time ago by the river that ran under the mountain. Water still drips through from above sometimes, especially after a heavy rain and when the snows melts in spring. The rocks are slick with moisture, almost always, and we keep a few boats by the lake in case we want to cross the water or go out to one of the small rocky outcroppings in the center." He paused. What point of reference did she have for all the information he gave her?

"Go on. Please. Tell me more." She turned her face upward, as if she was gazing at the stone ceiling.

He kissed her on the forehead. "Okay, well... There are a few tunnels in the cave that spoke out from this main room. A few of them are waterlogged and some are on higher ground and dry. We store things deep in select caverns and crannies, and we bury our dead in an area that we use for catacombs. There are many shifters buried there. Bears, wolves, lions, and more."

She nodded and laid her head on his shoulder. "When's the last time you saw Shoshannah?"

He started to speak but, just as he did, a white light filled the cavern, rippling off the surface of the water and casting bright wavy reflections on the walls.

"What's that?" Olivia clasped his arm. "I feel something. Is it Alfred? Did he find us?"

"No, it's Shoshannah," he whispered. "She's here." He squeezed her tightly.

"Oh goddess, I don't know what to say. Is she wolf or bear?" She sat up, her voice quivering and her eyes wide.

"I don't see her yet, only her light." He stood. "But she's coming." His heart raced. Thank the gods, Shoshannah was coming. If only she would help Olivia. Dare he hope? He couldn't stand the thought of Olivia being let down again. If he could offer his own ability to shift to her, he would.

A voice called out through the light. "Powell, go."

"Don't leave me." Olivia scrambled to her feet. "I'm scared."

"I need to speak to Olivia alone." Shoshannah's voice came from everywhere and nowhere at once.

He took a deep breath. Shoshannah would not harm Olivia. She would help her or give her guidance. He needed to convince Olivia that everything would be okay.

"We need to do as she asks." Powell took Olivia in his arms. "She won't hurt you. But she won't help you if I stay. I'll wait right outside with the snowmobile."

"But—"

"I won't leave you, I promise. This is a chance that might not ever repeat itself so we need to do as she says."

"Go." Shoshannah's voice grew louder.

"I need to go. Will you be okay?" He leaned close. "I will be right outside."

"Okay. I can do this." Olivia trembled.

"Yes, you can. You are the bravest person I know."

"Thank you. I don't feel very brave."

He kissed her quickly on the lips and when he opened his eyes, a twinkling of white lights had locked together to form the shape of a wolf. Larger than life, the creature stared at him, teeth bared. Shoshannah meant business.

"She's a wolf, sweetheart." He kissed Olivia on the head again. "Call to me when you are done, and I'll come back for you. Don't try to leave on your own or you may end up in the lake."

She smirked. "I won't fall in the lake. I'm not so blind I can't sense things other ways."

He smiled. She'd be okay. One more quick kiss, and he headed toward the cave exit and the snowmobile.

As he made his way outside, he prayed to the gods and goddesses that Shoshannah would help Olivia.

Chapter Nine

Olivia couldn't stop the tremor in her body. She shouldn't be scared. Powell said Shoshannah was a good creature, and that there was no reason to be afraid. Still, the unknown of the situation made her doubt her reasons for being there. What if the ancestral spirit was mad?

"Shoshannah, are you there?" Olivia called. Powell had said she was in wolf form. That had to be a good thing. Right?

"I'm here, child."

A cool breeze washed over Olivia's face, scented with lavender and roses. She breathed it in and felt her body relaxing.

"Why have you summoned me?"

Shoshannah's voice seemed to come from inside Olivia's head and from loudspeakers in the cave too. Olivia crossed her arms and took a deep breath. Where to begin?

"I hoped you would help me," she began.

"If your need is true, I might." The spirit wolf's voice was hypnotic, low and soft. Loving yet authoritative. Familiar.

"I'm blind." Anxiety almost caused her not to try, but the thought of Powell waiting outside in the cold pushed her onward. "I hoped that you could make me see. I also cannot shift, but I don't know why. I know it is a great thing to ask, but I feel like my life would be so much more fulfilling if I could be more independent."

"These problems are connected." The voice floated on the scented air.

"Yes. I'm supposed to be able to shift, but I can't. I think it's because I'm blind." Olivia took a deep breath and waited. "Will you help?"

Shoshannah paused before replying. "You are partially correct, my child. You cannot shift because your heart is blind, not because of your eyes. Once you remove the blindness you have placed there, you will be able to shift."

"What does that mean?"

"It means I cannot help you. You must help yourself."

"What about my eyesight? I can't fix blindness. It would take a miracle." Hot tears formed and dripped down her cheeks. Shoshannah wasn't going to help. The whole day had been a waste and Powell would be so disappointed.

"I cannot help with that either. Your problem is not so simple, but it can be solved. You must find a way to remove the blindness from your heart, and then you will run as wolf. That's all I can tell you. I give you the guidance of the gods, and they are never wrong. Trust yourself. You will find your answers."

"I don't know what to do!"

"Peace be with you, child. If your obstacles cleared

easily, you wouldn't appreciate the gifts you have. Trust yourself." Shoshannah's voice trailed off and the scent of lavender and roses dissipated.

Olivia strained to hear an answer, but the only sound in the cave was the dripping of a fountain or something nearby.

"Please, won't you help me?"

No reply came. Shoshannah was gone.

Tears streamed down her face unabated. Shoshannah had not helped her. If anything, she'd confused things with her riddles. If the spirit knew her, she'd know how hard Olivia had tried to shift. So many nights, as a cub, she'd stayed up and tried, hiding so that no one would make fun of her. What would she do now?

Well, time to call Powell. Tell him the bad news. Would he stand by her, knowing she couldn't shift and would never see? She wiped her tears away. In all the sadness and disappointment, he was the one thing that had been solid, unwavering.

She had to trust her mate.

"Powell?" Her voice rang through the cave, echoing off the walls. She waited but he didn't come. Could he not hear her from outside? They'd come through a couple of rooms on the way in. She called to him again but no response.

Despite what he'd said, she'd have to go outside herself. She could find her way. He misjudged her ability to navigate. Well, barring snowstorms.

She felt along the cold stone wall of the anteroom and made her way toward the cave opening, following the rush of frigid air to its source. Had Powell left the lantern and taken the flashlight? It didn't matter. Tears continued to flow, and she laid her head against the damp cave wall and sobbed.

She didn't want Powell to see her crying.

Broken.

Unfixable.

Blind and unable to shift, why would Powell want her as his mate? He'd said those things when he thought Shoshannah was going to fix her. He wouldn't have been so emphatic if he knew she'd never be able to shift.

Trust your mate. Shoshannah's voice sounded in her head.

What if their pups were also blind and unable to shift? How tragic a life to lead. Shifter babies almost always took on the species of the mother. What would Powell and the bears do with a bunch of blind babies who couldn't shift and learn all the things that shifters did?

Would she want to condemn offspring to her fate? Would Powell?

Trust him!

She wiped her eyes. She'd surely been a disappointment to her own parents. No one wanted a child as damaged as she was. She should go back to Alfred while he would still take her.

Her brief moment of happiness with Powell would have to sustain her for her whole lifetime. A time spent in ignorance of the burden she'd become once they found out she wasn't ever going to be able to shift.

Somehow, the little bit of hope she'd felt at the possibility of Shoshannah helping her had made her situation stand out in stark contrast to normality. Being with a bear wasn't possible. She'd been kidding herself. The other bears would never accept a blind wolf into their den. They'd see her as baggage.

And she was.

She pushed aside Shoshannah's voice. This was reality, not some magical spirit wolf's life.

No, she was going right outside and telling Powell that she needed to go back to Alfred. He could take her on the snowmobile. They didn't have to tell Alfred anything about what had happened.

And she didn't have to tell Powell anything more than Shoshannah couldn't help her.

If she'd known the oracle was as crazy as the lady reading tarot cards at the street fair in Oakwood in the summer, she'd have not bothered. That lady spoke in riddles too. Alfred had stopped by with a group of wolves, and Olivia had listened to the reading. She couldn't make heads or tails out of it, and the wolves had laughed it all off as nonsense.

She knew how they felt. Laughing would be as effective as crying, and neither was going to change the circumstance.

"Hey, you! I saw you come in with Powell." A voice sounded to her right. A voice she didn't recognize. "You need to go! Quickly, before they come back."

She turned toward the voice. "What's wrong? Who's there?" She felt her way closer to the cave entrance.

"The wolves. They took him. Attacked me too. I've radioed for help but I need to get to the lake."

"Where's Powell?" Was that her voice screaming?

She didn't recognize herself. Oh gods, what had happened? Alfred had taken Powell?

"I told you, the wolves attacked. A tall red one and some smaller greys. I know you're a wolf, but you're in danger. I assume they're after you—they kept asking for a she-wolf."

"Yes, they're after me. Is Powell okay?"

"I tried to help him, but they injured me badly. I'm losing blood." The voice headed away from her. "They hurt him, too. He didn't have time to shift, either. They attacked him beside the snowmobile. There's blood everywhere. You've got to escape now before they come back."

"Where are you going?" Her heart thumped in her throat, and her tears dried on her cheeks. She had to get to her mate! Alfred had attacked and taken Powell. Back to the Green Glen den, no doubt. They'd torture and kill him if he didn't tell them where she was.

"I've got to get these injuries into the lake to heal." The man paused. "I've radioed that we have a man down and that I'm injured. With the snow, it'll take a while for anyone to get here. I doubt he has a chance unless those wolves need him for something. The big red one was asking for Olivia, but he wouldn't tell them anything. I assume you're her. If you can help save him, you'd better do it. Otherwise, he's a goner."

"But, I can't help him!" She pleaded, "You have to get the bears to come. They can rescue him from the den."

"Listen, lady, I don't know what your issue is that you can't tell I'm barely standing myself. I'd help him if I could. You'll have to excuse me though. I need to get to the lake."

"I'm sorry I'm not more help. I'm blind." She chewed her bottom lip. "I'll be okay till reinforcements get here. You go take care of your injuries."

She paced a moment, her heart in her throat. If anything happened to Powell, it was her fault. He'd brought her to the cave. He'd waited outside while she made her plea to Shoshannah. Now, her mate was in peril. And it was entirely her doing.

My mate.

Though she was prepared to let him go, and defer to Alfred's wishes, she couldn't let Powell suffer because of her. She had to save him.

But how?

Energy flowed through her, like a shot of stamina, and she stood a little taller. What was it Shoshannah said?

Remove the blindness from your heart, and then you will run as wolf...

What did she mean? And she'd said *trust yourself.* What did she have to lose? With Powell's life in the balance, there was no time like the present to give it all or nothing. Failure wasn't an option, nor was not trying.

She began stripping. Could it be as easy and clear as it seemed? One way to find out. Push all her energy into the manifestation. This wasn't for her. It was for her mate.

She focused inward, reaching back to the warm feeling she had when Powell carried her out of the woods with an injured ankle, the comfort when he dragged her back to the cabin after she crept out his window.

Then, she savored the taste of the peanut butter and honey sandwich he'd made her, and Nar's soft fur and the scent of burning pine logs, ripe with sap and spitting and popping in the fire.

Socks and pants came off, then shirt. She dropped them where they fell, trusting that she was doing what Shoshannah guided her to do. What she had to do.

She could almost sense the touch of Powell's fingertips along her spine, across her cheek, along the side of her breast...and feel the wetness of his mouth, his tongue hot against hers, their climax as they moved together. Chills raced through her, but not from the cold.

The mating bond was strong. Unlike anything she'd ever felt.

Her body hummed and she fell into the sensation, lost on the ride of emotion she could only term as love. Love for her mate, who needed her now. Love for the man who'd saved her not once but multiple times, with very little complaint—and all of it in the best interest of her well-being.

It was happening! Her body moved under the thoughts of love and self-sacrifice for her mate.

Her legs and arms stretched and changed, and her face changed like warm clay sliding down a windowpane, realigning into something new. Olivia fell inside her psyche, over and over, her body struggling not to panic as it moved in ways it was meant to but never had. Shifting didn't hurt, but the buzz and burn was something new. Strength filled her bones as they lengthened and hardened into wolf bones.

She sensed paws at the end of strong legs and a long bushy tail.

She opened her eyes.

Her vision was so radiant and bright she had to squint. This was the white of snow that Powell had mentioned. She'd never imagined that a color could be so pure and bright. She placed a paw over her nose and eyes then peeked again.

By the gods, she'd not only shifted, but she could see!

The world, bright and new, held so much color, she could barely take it in all at once, though she didn't know all the color names. Pine trees were green, she knew that. But so many shades. Were they all green?

She shook her head. No time for enjoyment. Her heart thumped wildly, and she breathed faster as her blood pumped through wolf veins. She had to get to her mate. Save him. She sniffed the air, his blood rode the currents like a beacon.

Injured.

Alive.

Running would be the fastest way to reach him. She couldn't wait around for more bears to show up to help. Her clothes lay in a pile at the cave entrance, and deep snow greeted her feet as she dashed out into the light. Leaping into the air, she stared at the blue sky. All her life wolves had mentioned the blues of the sky. Such a color! With what must be clouds floating across the sunlit sky, the sight was more beautiful than she could've dreamed.

She never would've imagined such glorious beauty in Deep Creek. Thank the goddesses that she was gifted the power to save her mate. And thanks to Shoshannah. The sun shining through the trees like bright strips of warmth would lead her west to where the wolves lived. She knew exactly where to go.

Where she would find her injured mate and save him from the wolves that would surely kill him once they were done questioning him.

She turned her nose to the air and howled, the sound echoing through her chest and throughout her spirit.

She was wolf.

Chapter Ten

Powell winced. The salty, metallic taste of blood filled his mouth. Ties bound his wrists, and he sat in a chair in the center of a room in the Green Glen wolves' pack compound. If only he'd had time to shift when they'd attacked, he might not be in this predicament. Shifting now would be difficult, if not impossible. If he could get the bindings off, he'd have a better chance. But as soon as they saw him shift, they'd likely kill him rather than face an angry bear. If only shifting were instantaneous.

Several pack members stood around, half-interested, half-afraid of Alfred. None spoke up against him. A scraggily bunch, they looked like the scavengers they were. Powell scanned them, looking for weaknesses. He'd figure out how to escape. Thank the gods, they hadn't captured Olivia. The Sentinels would've called for the bears to come, and if he held out long enough, they might make it in time to save him.

A slap brought him out of his reverie. Alfred stared at him, hand back, ready to strike again.

"There's more of that, if you need it. Or if I decide you need it." Alfred snarled.

Powell didn't answer, realizing that the wolf was posturing in front of his pack and nothing he said would help his predicament. He hoped Olivia understood that he hadn't left her.

"I'm going to ask you one more time." Alfred circled the chair. "Where is she? I know she was with you. I scented her."

"I don't know who you're talking about." Powell stared Alfred eye-to-eye.

If Alfred killed him, he hoped that Olivia had learned enough to fend for herself and not come back to the lunatic. And perhaps Shoshannah had helped her. He could only hope at this point that she was safe.

The punch came swiftly, and his cheek numbed under the blow as his head snapped back.

"I know you had her at your cabin. I scented her there too." Alfred bent and inched closer to Powell's face. "She's mine. And I want her back."

No way was he giving Olivia back to this monster. Hell, Alfred's own pack was afraid of him. What kind of leader ruled by fear?

A bad one.

He spat in Alfred's face. The wolf staggered backward, and a collective gasp rose in the room. The pheromones of anger wafted through the air. Tension grew, and Powell knew the wolves wouldn't bother keeping him around much longer.

Alfred wiped his face and howled a ragged, enraged human howl. Powell laughed.

"You'll pay for that!" the wolf screamed, crouching and prepared to lunge. "You bastard! No one gets away with disrespecting me."

Powell closed his eyes and waited for the blow to come. He'd gotten in a jab of sorts. And Olivia was safe.

The door burst open and a blast of icy air rushed in, sending chills over him. He looked, and silhouetted in the doorway was the most beautiful she-wolf he'd ever seen in his life. His heart swelled and his mouth fell open.

White, with guard hairs tipped in silver sparkles, the wolf practically shimmered like a frozen mirage in front of him. She bared her teeth, fangs long and sharp, her guttural growl setting everyone in the room back a step. She walked into the room, and Alfred remained crouched, ready for combat, though his human form wouldn't have much of a chance against the she-wolf. She'd tear him to shreds.

He wouldn't have time to shift before she attacked.

Talk about karma.

She leapt. Powell watched her powerful legs propel her through the air and into Alfred, knocking him onto his back, his head hitting the floor with a pleasing thump and groan. Alfred pushed back against her with his hands, but her bites came fast and strong, and spatters of red dotted her white coat.

"You bitch!" Alfred screeched.

Powell couldn't take his eyes off the gorgeous white wolf and the way she took charge and dominated Alfred. Her strength seemed magical, super powered.

She tore into his throat, blood gushing from the wound, and a frothy blood-tinged spittle poured from his mouth. She shook him until the life had left his body and he lay limp on the floor. The other wolves stood back, and she panned her head from one to the next, daring any to move.

None did.

"Untie me," Powell called to the wolves, and one young man rushed over and worked at releasing his bindings. Powell pulled free, rubbing his wrists. "Anyone else want to fight? Or are we going to call this a day?"

Another man lunged toward Powell, and the white wolf snarled, standing between Powell and the others, crouched and ready to leap. After taking a look at Alfred, the man stepped back.

"Anyone?" Powell repeated.

The wolves looked down, none making eye contact. Clearly they were a bunch of scaredy-cats who followed whatever leader they had, without thought or regard to what was going on. Disgust filled Powell and he shook his head.

No matter, this fight was over.

Powell knelt. "Olivia? Is that you?"

The white wolf turned to him, her bright and clear blue eyes like lakes or patches of summer sky. His heart warmed and he hugged her neck.

Epilogue

Olivia panted, her paws still tender from being some-what new to shifting. She dashed around a thick, heavily scented flower bush and stopped to wait on Powell. He was so slow. Moonlight lit the path almost as well as midday sun, and she glanced up to look at the pocked orb that shone, bright and ever-changing.

She never tired of seeing the stars and moon sitting in the sky like bright pinpoints of hope on a background of darkness. Ever since her victory over Alfred, she'd felt more alive and more independent. It wasn't her shifting powers or her newfound love for her fated mate that had opened her eyes to life, though those things helped. No, the catalyst for her metamorphosis was overcoming her fear and finding that she was stronger than she could've ever imagined.

Nothing could stop her now.

Powell loped up behind her, his bear large and not as graceful as her wolf. She smiled a wolf smile, her tongue lolling.

A nightly run had become part of her and Powell's bedtime ritual. The snowfall had melted and the forest had greened under spring's warmer temperatures and sunshine, and every night, her wolf and his bear ran through the forest together, scenting new things and exploring Deep Creek's grandeur. She imagined that any park visitor would think the sight of a bear and a wolf running together odd, but she didn't care.

He was her bear.

Her mate, forever.

She raced ahead, stopping on a large boulder and turning to wait. The scent of night jasmine filled the air, and a lone call of a hoot owl sounded from somewhere deep in the glen. The forest, alive with spring's rush, sang to her in new ways. Though she was only able to see when in wolf form, it was the most wonderful blessing and she was grateful for every moment of vision in the miraculous world of Deep Creek.

Powell caught up to her and leaned against her, panting.

I'm tired. His thoughts were clear to her, though he swore he didn't hear any of hers. He nuzzled her ear.

She licked his cheek and nodded her head in the direction of the cabin. Tonight, they'd cut the run short. Soon, she'd need to scale back on the running anyway, and she needed to tell him why.

Two new little heartbeats thumped their own cadences inside her. Baby girl cubs due by the second full moon. She lifted her snout and howled with gratitude. A long bay of respect for nature, Deep Creek, and the shifter bond.

Shoshannah had been right.

Love had broken the barrier that had kept her heart blind to her own power, and now that it was unleashed, nothing could stop her and her mate.

* * * * *

To purchase and read more books by Kerry Adrienne, please visit Kerry's website at kerryadrienne.com.

Acknowledgments

Many thanks to my editor, Anne Scott. She's exactly the right amount of patient for neurotic authors and her red pen is on point. I appreciate her professionalism and command of language and her author-whispering skills. I've been so fortunate at Carina Press. I'd also like to thank my agent, Marisa Corvisiero of Corvisiero Literary Agency. She's always working hard to keep me working. Aside from that, I'm thrilled to call her friend. Also, many thanks to all my Facebook author friends who kick me off Facebook when I have a deadline, sprint with me when I need it, give me pep talks when I'm sure that my story is the worst and listen to me complain about whatever is bothering me. I only hope that I provide half the support they give to me. Lastly, thanks to my husband, who has been to every take-out place in Raleigh to pick up dinner and who hasn't complained (much) about picking up Japanese food at least once a week.

About the Author

USA TODAY bestselling author Kerry Adrienne loves history, science, music and art. She's a mom to three daughters, many cats and various other small animals, and spends a lot of time feeding everyone. She loves live music and traveling almost anywhere. Music and travel feed her muse like nothing else. She loves driving her Mini Cooper convertible on long, winding roads with loud music playing and no one else around.

In addition to being an author, she's a college instructor, artist, costumer, bad guitar player and editor.

You can connect with Kerry on her website:

Facebook.com/AuthorKerryAdrienne
Twitter.com/KerryAdrienne
KerryAdrienne.com

For information on upcoming releases, great contests, free books, cat pics and no spam, please sign up for her monthly newsletter here: eepurl.com/1T6PX.